The Woman

Leah Konen is the author of the thrillers *One White Lie*, *The Perfect Escape*, *You Should Have Told Me* and *Keep Your Friends Close*, along with several young adult novels, including *Love and Other Train Wrecks* and *The Romantics*. Her books have been published in nearly a dozen countries, and her essays and articles have appeared in *Marie Claire*, *Vogue* and more.

She lives in Brooklyn and Saugerties, New York, with her husband, their daughters, Eleanore and Mary Joyce, and their dog, Farley.

Also by Leah Konen

Keep Your Friends Close
You Should Have Told Me
The Perfect Escape
All the Broken People

The Woman in Room 13

LEAH KONEN

PENGUIN BOOKS

PENGUIN BOOKS

UK | USA | Canada | Ireland | Australia
India | New Zealand | South Africa

Penguin Books is part of the Penguin Random House group of companies
whose addresses can be found at global.penguinrandomhouse.com

Penguin Random House UK,
One Embassy Gardens, 8 Viaduct Gardens, London SW11 7BW

penguin.co.uk

First published in the United States of America by G. P. Putnam's Sons,
an imprint of Penguin Random House LLC 2025
First published in Great Britain by Penguin Books 2025

001

Set in 12.5 / 14.75 pt Garamond MT Std
Typeset by Jouve (UK), Milton Keynes
Printed and bound in Great Britain by Clays Ltd, Elcograf S.p.A.

The authorized representative in the EEA is Penguin Random House Ireland,
Morrison Chambers, 32 Nassau Street, Dublin D02 YH68

A CIP catalogue record for this book is available from the British Library

ISBN: 978-1-405-96289-6

Penguin Random House is committed to a sustainable future
for our business, our readers and our planet. This book is made from
Forest Stewardship Council® certified paper.

For Mary Joyce

February 1, 2023
4:43 p.m.

It hit me hard as the motel came into view through snow-flakes thick and white: This was my last chance.

Carefully, I pulled off the highway and into a gravel parking lot mostly coated in snow, completely empty, not a car in sight. I turned at the front office, following the line of rooms until I found the last one on the left, then put the car into park and leaned forward, taking in the motel through my windshield, wipers going double time, the sun already setting, sky quickly losing light.

The place was a retro-modern Instagram dream. I'd seen plenty of photos, of course, had trolled through the Twilite Motel's carefully curated grid, dreaming of cozy, tucked-away spaces that would revive my floundering writing practice, but even those hadn't done it justice. Atop a snow-covered roof was a bold red sign, lined with neon lights, that proudly proclaimed MOTEL in letters that had to be several feet tall. The place was painted pink, with baby blue doors and yellow chairs stacked in the corner of each patio—a color scheme that would have had Siobhan, much more visually minded than me, sali-vating. Pretty, most definitely, but for me, the lure was the history—the stories that had to be contained within, inspiration practically bursting through the seams. I dutifully pulled out my phone and took a quick snap through the snow-dusted windshield, knowing I couldn't upload anything without service but imagining the future social media post already: *This is where I finished the book that changed my life.*

The owner, Maisy, a self-styled "patron of the arts," was far from a trailblazer. Lots of revitalized motels had been popping up in recent years, luring not budget travelers on road trips but people with Tribeca lofts and cash to burn. My husband, Frank, and I kept noticing them, after reading an article in *The New York Times* about places just like this. Roadside motels that had gained new life for the Instagram set. Throwbacks updated with modern conveniences. Sixties stopovers meet Sub-Zero appliances.

I shut off the car, then checked the backpack next to me for all my supplies. The sandwich I'd grabbed on my way out of the city, plus nuts, chocolate, granola bars, and the full guide to caring for the Twilite Motel, all fifty pages of it printed and bound and sent to me by Maisy, since she didn't pay for Wi-Fi in the winter months and cell data was spotty at best. Maisy had even warned me that most mobile hot spots didn't work well, had mentioned the "lack of digital amenities" three times before I'd signed the contract for the month. Little did she know, the absence of internet was among this job's largest selling points. It prevented me from obsessively poring over everyone else's feeds, watching as both babies and books were birthed into the world. From googling things like "fertility at 39," "divorce lawyer cost," and "can a publisher force you to declare bankruptcy?" From sharing carefully staged updates on my writing process (MacBook open in front of a window; sharpened pencils against fresh notebooks), knowing full well I wasn't getting any writing done at all.

A gust of wind smacked me across the face as I got out of the car, reminding me what I'd signed myself up for. It was no wonder the place shut down in January and February. Who in their right mind would want to come here in the deep of winter, with the more touristy Catskills towns forty-five minutes northwest and the ski resorts even farther still?

And yet for me, it was perfect, my own little Overlook Hotel, where I could finish my book (minus the ghosts, psychotic break, and homicide, of course). And *unlike* Jack Torrance, I didn't even *have* a family to terrorize and I wasn't going to be drinking a single drop. All work and no play was finally going to make Kerry a truly successful girl.

See, where Jack had gone wrong was bringing the people he loved *with* him. I, on the other hand, had solved that problem. Frank, my other half for the past ten years, had gone to his brother Danny's in Jersey for Christmas and not returned, sending Danny and his girlfriend over to pick up his things. And my best friend, Siobhan? Well, I hadn't spoken to her in two months. She was blocked, in fact, on all social media. Couldn't even get in touch with me if she wanted to.

I was alone now, completely so, and that meant things had to change. No more missed deadlines. No more excuses. No more booze.

Because if I didn't have *something* to show my publisher by the end of the month, my agent had warned me that the whole project could be cancelled—and even worse, the publisher could demand repayment of the money I'd already received. Money that had long ago been spent. Fruitlessly, of course, but spent nonetheless.

I walked up to Room Thirteen, where Maisy had told me to stay. Her instructions had said that the prior caretaker would leave a large ring of keys in a flowerpot beneath the room's window. I quickly spotted a substantial clay receptacle, filled up with large rocks, and knelt to retrieve the keys.

I pulled out one rock and then another, but the bottom of the pot was empty. Fingers freezing, I stood, wondering if there'd been some miscommunication, if the keys had been left in the room instead.

The doorknob turned easily, and relief flooded my veins. I pushed open the door to the sound of jangling and quickly stepped inside, out of the biting wind, the bitter cold.

I looked down. The noise had been from the ring of keys, left, inexplicably, right behind the door. I grabbed them, stood up, and it hit me fully then: Everything was wrong.

The kitchen stood out the most. The countertop was littered with paraphernalia, like someone had had a full-on rager. I stepped forward, the smell of wine and whiskey hitting me from a collection of mismatched, half-drunk glasses, crusted with lipstick and dregs from the drinks, bottles, some more than half full, open beside them, empty ones standing proud like the rocks of Stonehenge.

I felt it instantly, that tickle of desire, of anticipation, my mouth nearly watering, just looking at it all laid out.

How easy it would be to grab a fresh glass, pour a drink, take some of the edge off, from the storm, from the drive. From the fact that things weren't starting out at all the way I'd planned. Then my eyes caught the rest of it: the glass pipe, the burned remnants of weed on the counter, the half-empty pack of Parliament cigarettes, a light dusting of white across the marble countertop. The thought of partying like that again, of giving up all concerns but the *now*, but the *moment*, but the *more more more*, it was—no pun intended—intoxicating. Why could some people do it without losing everything, that was the real question. People like Frank, people like Siobhan, people who could let loose for a night and in the morning, nothing about their world had changed, apart from a massive headache and maybe a serotonin crash. People who could get an everything bagel, turn on some reality TV, and lose little more than a day of their lives. Probably the same sorts of people who could get a book deal as massive as mine and finish the godforsaken book.

I turned away from the kitchen, forcing myself back to the issue at hand. The bed was made but rumpled, as if someone or some*ones* had sat on it, passed around a glass pipe, and clinked highballs of whiskey. Next to the bed, a navy, hard-shell suitcase, half open; and next to that, another suitcase, brown—this one shut and standing— almost like the occupant had been in the middle of packing and then all of a sudden stopped. On the wall opposite the bed, a cast-iron woodstove crackled, coals still within it, radiating heat. What was going on?

"Hello?" I asked. "Is anyone here?"

No answer.

Had I somehow gotten this wrong? Mixed up the dates, walking into the aftermath of someone's rager a day too early? It wasn't possible. There wasn't even another car in the lot.

I flipped through Maisy's instructions again, read the words three times over. Arrive any time after four on Saturday, February 1. I grabbed my phone, checked the date, but it was indeed the first. And it was nearly five o'clock. I was *supposed* to be here. *Only* I was supposed to be here.

I opened my email, wondering if there'd been a change in plans, something I'd missed. It wouldn't load, of course. No data up here. Barely a single bar, my phone already proclaiming it was now "roaming."

My eyes caught a rotary phone mounted to the wall—retro avocado green. Maisy had mentioned each room had a landline, but I hadn't expected to find one so . . . old.

Sure enough, a tone.

It took forever to dial, the curl of the numbers interminable—motions I hadn't made since I was maybe seven or eight years old. It rang four times, and I got a cheerful voicemail. I left a rambling message, hung up. Tried sending a text instead, but it wouldn't go through.

My heart began to race as the cold bit against my cheeks. It was already twilight. Twilight at the Twilite Motel. It would be fully dark in a matter of minutes, and through the window, I could see that the snow was coming down even harder now, the wind making the trees across the road dance.

What was I supposed to do, get in the car and drive nearly three hours back to the city? A family from Europe

6

was arriving at my apartment today, the place booked up for the whole month. I couldn't very well get a hotel. I had no money for one. Besides, why should I leave? I hadn't done anything wrong.

"Hello," I called again as I walked past the kitchen and to a door open on the right—the bathroom. "Hello, is anyone here?"

I flicked on the light and quickly jerked at the shower curtain over the claw-footed tub, then sighed with a bit of relief. No one hiding with a knife in the shower, waiting to make me the next Marion Crane. Still, there was a mess of toiletries, what looked like a woman's things: press-on nails and bright red polish spread out on the counter, lipsticks uncapped, standing upright and eerie.

My bladder full from the long drive, I used the toilet, then got up, washed my hands, and returned to the main room.

My mind ran through possible explanations. There had been a party of some sort, that much was clear. Maybe the woman, whoever she was, had gone home with some guy, was currently sleeping off a hangover? That would explain the lack of a car in the lot, wouldn't it? Maybe she'd gone somewhere, to get more coke, maybe, and was in the midst of a bender. Maybe she was a fuckup, just like me—maybe she'd been so drunk and high her whole time here she didn't even realize what day it was.

My eyes caught the ring of keys, which I'd set on the table by the door. Why had she left these behind?

Drinking would explain that, too, I supposed. More than once I'd buzzed Frank because I'd left my keys in a bar or in my drunken state I hadn't had the wherewithal to check every pocket of my bag.

At some point, this woman would surely resurface: face red, mouth full of apologies.

The issue was what I was supposed to do in the meantime.

My eyes returned to the keys. Not just to this room but to the front office, the outbuildings, and all the other rooms as well. I was the caretaker, of course. I had access to it all.

I stepped back into the cold, pulled the door shut behind me, leaving it unlocked should this mysterious woman come back.

Room Twelve, right next door, seemed as good a place as any, and I slipped that key into the lock, opened the door to reveal a new room, same style and layout as the one I'd just been in but clean and made up. Only one thing was off: an open wine bottle on the nightstand, a corkscrew sitting next to it.

I grabbed the bottle and took it over to the sink, pouring it down the drain before I could lose my nerve. Then I found a thermostat, set to fifty-five degrees. I shot it up to seventy.

I slipped off my snow boots, pulled on an extra pair of wool socks and a heavier sweater, unwrapped the sandwich I'd brought with me, and grabbed my laptop, intent on completing Day One with at least a few hundred words written.

I stared at the blank screen while I housed my sandwich, suddenly ravenous, and soon it was gone, the trash was in the bin, and then the blinking cursor was flashing at me, metronomic. A reminder that I was so very much behind. Like a clock. *Tick-tock, tick-tock.* Book finished or bankruptcy. Your choice, Kerry. Your choice.

Without thinking, I found myself reaching for my phone, hungry for my onetime vices: Bitching about publishing with fellow authors on Twitter; drooling over the gorgeous covers of books that were already coming out on Instagram. Texting Siobhan—before we stopped talking, at least—silly GIFs because I didn't have it in me to write. Googling, for the umpteenth time, the type of research questions I'd already covered over and over.

Instagram was fully open before it hit me that I didn't have service. The speed with which I'd gotten there when my brain knew full well my phone wouldn't work scared me a bit. I set it down and returned to my screen.

Forced myself to type.

She never wanted it to turn out this way.

I read the sentence before it, realizing this new one made no sense in context.

So I deleted it, watched the cursor once again as the weight set in, pressing against my chest, as if all the books in the world, all the books I'd ever read, all the books I would ever read, all the books that *anyone* would ever read, ones that were being published, left and right, up and down, when mine almost certainly never would be, were balancing atop my breastbone, pressing and pressing and pressing, ready to crush my heart.

My pulse quickened, my breathing sped up, and I grabbed my water, guzzling it down, and for a moment,

I could have sworn I was standing in the wilderness, facing down a ferocious beast, fangs exposed, ready to tear my body to shreds, instead of sitting on a comfy bed in a renovated motel, trying to type out a novel that had sold for a healthy six figures on a rose gold MacBook. How could I be panicking like this? How could I not see that none of this was really life and death? That all I had to do was imagine words and then type them?

And yet, my breaths came fast, and I could smell the wine still in the sink, and it reminded me of darker vices. Of the warmth on my tongue, the fire in my belly, the way it could make everything else around it just disappear.

I pushed myself away, slammed my laptop shut. I walked to the window, pulled back the drapes, and considered going out for some air, but even though it was only just past seven o'clock, it was dark as anything, the dead of night, only the light of the moon illuminating the falling snowflakes. No way.

Back at my desk, I took five deep breaths, counted backward from one hundred, then opened my laptop once again.

Only as soon as I did, there was my heart, my breath, and suddenly I couldn't catch myself, I was gasping for air, and I was out here in the middle of nowhere and there was a snowstorm and what was I going to do? What was I going to do on my own?

My chest tightened, like someone was sitting on top of it, and knowing I couldn't go any longer, I rushed to my bag, pulled out my toiletries kit, found my pillbox, plucked one of the new antianxiety meds my doctor had prescribed for this very occasion, reminding me that they did not mix with alcohol and he could only continue to prescribe them if I gave up drinking, a lesson I'd learned firsthand a few weeks ago.

Now, I swallowed one back quick, then sat on the bed, trying to force myself to breathe.

Pillbox still in my hand, I spotted the other pills, the Ambiens I'd found in the back of the medicine cabinet, the ones Frank used only for flying.

I hesitated. I didn't know how the two would mix. Not to mention, popping pills that weren't prescribed to me wasn't exactly the definition of sobriety.

Still, I'd had quite the start here. I could barely even catch my breath, much less write. And all I wanted in the world was to numb out. I couldn't do that with wine. I couldn't do it with social media, with the endless *scroll scroll scroll*. So I would do it with the last refuge—sleep.

I pulled back the duvet cover, nuzzled in, and popped the pill into my mouth, swallowed it back before I could change my mind, and then I flicked out the lights and nestled in between the covers, even though it was still so early.

This is all going to be okay, I told myself as I counted back from one hundred. It will all feel better in the morning.

2

I woke with a start, bright sunlight streaming through a gap at the edge of the curtains. My head was aching, and my brain felt beyond fuzzy.

My phone was next to me in bed, and I tapped it to life, found my Photos app open, stuck on a photo of Siobhan; her boyfriend, Charlie; and Frank, laughing around the tiny table in our even tinier kitchen, a nerdy board game that Charlie and Frank had become obsessed with splayed across it. Siobhan and I had met in a screenwriting class in the city; she, a videographer trying to brush up her writing chops, me, a writer dabbling in the visual medium. Quickly we'd become close as anything, between near-weekly coffee dates where we'd talk about our projects and long walks around Prospect Park where we'd talk about everything else. And then, once the boys met, bonding over their passion for Frank Lloyd Wright and hatred of sports, we started having semiregular game nights that left us all cackling.

We were a perfect foursome—until we weren't, the cracks in our friendships, our relationships, turning so quickly to chasms.

What would Siobhan think, I wondered, if she knew

I was here? That I'd only found out about the opportunity from her old college roommate's newsletter? Allison Romy's "Creative Journey" Substack, a far-reaching publication that detailed the woman's journey as a working actress, as well as updates from her fabulous friends and creative opportunities she'd heard about, had landed in my inbox right after Frank decided to leave, advertising "monthlong winter caretaker positions available at a stunning Catskills motel," and it had felt too fated to pass up.

Siobhan didn't know, thankfully, since she was blocked everywhere. No access to me, or me to her.

I rubbed my fingers along my temples and forced myself out of bed. After all, I'd slept for more than twelve hours.

There was a coffee machine on the counter, and I fumbled around until I found some grounds, hit brew. No milk in the fridge, but I could go without for now.

My laptop was still open on the counter, my Word document glaring at me, the title of the document in all caps like a dare: THE HOUSE OF HER DREAMS— A NOVEL. Yes, I had taken a screenshot of all this and blasted it out to my feeds. I'd felt bold then, before everything had exploded, after success had come raining down on me like a typhoon. It was a reminder, then, little more than eighteen months ago, that this was no longer a pipe dream, a story that lived in a digital file and nowhere else. This was real. This would be a thing out in the world. A *novel*. A novel by Kerry Walsh.

I looked at the cursor, still blinking.

The success had been such a surprise, after two (badly written) novels that had never been published, when I'd all but given up on my dream of becoming a novelist and was content to charge a decent day rate to write advertising and marketing copy. And then, this idea had come, so complete, so fun. A woman leaves Brooklyn in the height of the pandemic and pours her and her husband's life savings into a run-down Victorian home in upstate New York, one she's intent on renovating. She falls in love with the house—it seems to bring her inexplicable joy, a balm for all the ways the world has hurt her—until she begins to believe that the very house she loves is somehow destroying her from the inside, shooting mold and rot from the depths of its walls into her own organs, her veins.

It was always meant to be a novel, but, sure it would never actually be published, I'd started with a short story, one in which the woman discovers termites eating the wood of her beloved house and wakes up that night to indescribable itching, then rushes to the bathroom and spits up a cluster of gelatinous termite eggs. I sent the story around to all the usual suspects, all the publications whose rejection letters could paper every inch of our Brooklyn apartment, and then—miraculously—an email from an editor at *The New Yorker*: They were going to publish my story.

And then it had come out, and somehow it had completely taken off. The editors said there hadn't been such a response to a piece of fiction since "Cat Person" had swept the internet. Siobhan talked about it all the time in her Reels on Instagram, saying, in her earnest way, "Everyone *needs* to read this! They just do!" Frank insisted on taking me out for oysters and champagne, which we, naturally, had snapped and shared, both a celebration of the story and a recognition that if luck continued to favor us, I'd soon be coming up on nine months of abstaining from both.

Yet it was the strangers who really touched me, the people I didn't know who were saying all sorts of things—that it was a metaphor for the way the world doesn't believe women, for our lack of bodily autonomy; that it also showed the dichotomy between the way our world looks from the outside and from the inside—these people were picking up all the things I was putting down, emailing me through the contact form on my website, telling me how much they loved the piece. And then, suddenly, the agent who'd all but forgotten about me was calling, was asking how many pages of the novel I did have done, and even though I had little more than fifty, she was going out to publishers with it. *The House of Her Dreams* was getting me the book deal of *my* dreams.

Then the next week, as if things couldn't get any better, there he was, a major director on the phone, wanting to turn my little book—once I finished it, of course—into his next masterpiece.

The New York Times feature had been glowing: "An Author Toiled Away for Years. Then She Got a Call from One of Hollywood's Biggest Directors."

Yet, here I was, a year and a half later, with so little to show for it. I'd added pages, sure, but I had no clue where the story was going. I sold everyone on a big idea, one I couldn't figure out how to pull off—and I was running out of time.

I shut my laptop, forcing myself not to dwell. The panic attack, rushing for my pills, that was just a reaction to the strangeness of my arrival. Once things were settled, I would be in the right headspace to write. I headed for the bathroom, where I brushed my teeth and splashed some water on my face. Then I returned to the main room, put on clothes for the day, and poured a cup of coffee.

My plan for that morning had been to explore the grounds, situate myself with the whole property, and check off the caretaking duties from Maisy's list, but I didn't want to go exploring until I at least figured out what was going on with the room next door.

Maybe whoever it was left already, I thought hopefully. Maybe she'd come to her post-party senses and returned, gotten her things, and gone back to her life, to where she belonged.

I walked to the front of the room and pulled back the curtains. Snowdrifts covered half the windows, and all I could see were blankets of white, my Honda nearly fully submerged. Damn.

My heart sped up, and before I could lose my nerve, I pulled on my puffy coat, gloves, a knit hat, and a scarf. Then I grabbed the snow boots that had seen me through many a slushy winter in the city and laced them up tight. I twisted the dead bolt, then turned the door handle.

About three feet of white stared back at me, drifted up against where the door had been closed. Holy shit. I stepped forward, the powder soft, and kicked away as much of it as I could, then shut the door behind me and locked it. The snow was still coming down—and hard. Flakes swirled around me, wind cold and whipping, as I shuffled through the snow and to the next door.

Please let this woman be gone. Please let me put all this weirdness behind me.

Her door was unlocked, as I'd left it the night before, should the woman have come back. I pushed the door open to see the very same picture as I had the day before.

"Hello?" I called again, before walking through the room, carefully cataloging it all against what I remembered from yesterday. Didn't look like a single thing had changed.

Remembering Maisy's list of duties, I headed for the thermostat first—might as well check off my responsibilities while I was in the room. The temperature was set to seventy-two, and I kicked it down to fifty-five, as directed. Then I walked to the kitchen sink, the smell of wine and whiskey and who knew what else still pungent. God, how I wanted to just have a little sip, numb the hard edges of this unexplainable situation.

The water in the kitchen sink ran fine, so I turned it back off before walking through the main room and into the bathroom, looking for any signs of anything—water in the shower, different toiletries around the sink.

It was all just as before. The uncapped lipsticks. The nail polish, bright red, OPI printed on the side of it, next to a set of blank press-on nails. I lifted the bottle up, looked at the bottom. *Big Apple Red.* My favorite color. I set it back down. Where could this woman be if not here? It was a winter wasteland outside.

I turned on the water, my eyes finding the window that looked out onto a back patio, one that had been too dark to see through properly the night before. So much snow. Snow everywhere, and what was I supposed to do now?

I couldn't very well drive in this. And what if Maisy never called me back?

I flicked off the water and was about to turn back, return to Room Twelve, when something caught my eye through the window, which looked out on the lawn behind the rooms and the pool and outbuildings beyond that.

About ten or fifteen feet back, there were a couple of blue Adirondack chairs, mostly covered in snow. There was supposed to be a fire pit, too, but I couldn't see it—it must be fully submerged.

And just in front of the chairs, something else.

A flash of red.

My eyes struggled to focus, and I gasped as the picture became clearer, as the horror hit me full-on. I grabbed the sink to steady myself, sending the lipsticks and nail polishes clattering to the tile floor with an awful sound.

I looked back up to the window, half doubting myself, half thinking I'd imagined it all.

As my heart raced and I held back a scream, it was clear—beyond clear—that I hadn't.

There, poking out of the snowdrift, five little dots of red.

Red that belonged to nails.

Nails that belonged to fingers.

Fingers frozen in the cold, reaching out through the blanket of snow like vines popping out of the ground.

Fingers that had to belong to a body, covered up by the drift.

A body that had to belong to a human.

Someone *was* here with me.

Buried beneath a mountain of snow.

3

February 2, 2023
9:22 a.m.

I rushed from the bathroom and pulled the door closed, quick as I could, as if I could keep what I'd just seen inside—those awful frozen fingers—like a kid asking Mom and Dad to shut their closet door all the way. And yet, the view before me wasn't any better, was it?

All these things—the empty glasses and bottles, the suitcase not fully packed next to the bed—they weren't paraphernalia anymore, remnants of a party never cleaned up. Now they were the remains of a woman who *had* to be dead. Someone frozen to the bone only steps from where I stood.

Or was there any way . . . could she possibly survive out there? Could she still be alive?

A retch began to climb up my throat, but I swallowed quickly, holding it back.

Help, I had to call for help. I dug for my phone in my pocket and keyed in 911, but the call wouldn't go through, and why would it, anyway? The whole point of coming here was to be removed from it all.

I found the rotary phone and lifted it to my ear, but there was no dial tone this time. Damn it. I depressed the hook a couple of times, but I still couldn't get it to work, so I slammed the phone back on the cradle.

My heart beat fast, and my breathing started once again to come in gasps.

I had to check on her. I had to at least *make sure*.

Wind slapped me in the face as I rushed out the front door. I ran around the edge of the motel, beelining for the Adirondack chairs, then stopped maybe ten feet short of the scene.

There she was. Even with the snow coming down still, with the wind turning the flakes into flurries, the vision before me was beyond clear. A hand. A person's hand. Another human's painted nails. I took a few steps forward, needing to be sure it wasn't some prank, some severed plastic arm from a Halloween shop . . .

Then I was there, only a couple of feet away. Again, I counted her fingers—one, two, three, four, five. The exposed skin was an icy blue, like blood had abandoned her body, but the polish remained bright red, the nails round and coffin-shaped, definitely those press-ons I'd seen in the bathroom. The drift was at least two feet tall, the snow nearly up to my knees, and the scene surrounding her hand was unblemished, like all of it had fallen around her.

She had been here overnight, at the very least. Maybe even longer.

Still, I had to check, didn't I?

Terrified, I closed my eyes, reached out my gloved hand, like Adam's finger approaching god, moving slowly forward until I felt a jolt through my entire body as my hand connected with an object hard as stone.

I stepped back, quick as I could, turned away from her

hand, felt a retch again, and I bent at the waist, spat into the snow, then coughed and coughed and coughed, even though nothing more would come up, coughed until tears hit my eyes.

Any lingering doubts were gone.

This woman, whoever she was, was dead.

Back in Room Twelve, I grabbed another of the anti-anxiety pills, swallowing it dry, then looked around the room. My eyes caught on the rotary phone, and I lifted it again, depressing the hook like I was playing the drums. Still nothing.

On autopilot, I reached for my own phone then, so used to service, so used to turning to it anytime I wanted to escape, that it was like second nature, but naturally, there was still no signal. I put it back in my pocket, focusing on my breathing, knowing that the pill would work very, very soon.

Utter, terrifying loneliness crept through me. Yes, I'd been on my own since Frank had left at Christmas, Siobhan out of my life only a month before that, but this was different. No bustling city full of apartment neighbors and deli owners and *people, people, people* all around me. Alone in New York City wasn't really alone at all. Nothing like this.

Again, my hand went to my pocket.

Stop it, I thought. The phone isn't any use right now.

I counted to five, trying to still my breaths.

Sitting here with a dead body out in the yard was beyond the question. I had to get some help.

I'd passed a police station on the way here, maybe five

miles off. I could drive there, tell them about this woman. They would know what to do. And if I couldn't make it all that way, there'd been another house—an old Victorian—maybe a mile back. At least I could tell *someone*.

I retightened the Velcro of my gloves, grabbed the car keys. I hadn't equipped the Honda with snow chains, something ever-practical Frank certainly would have thought of, but I'd figured I wasn't going *that* far from civilization. I thought I'd be fine if a storm hit for a few days.

Back out front, the wind was still strong, but it had calmed just a bit.

Snow crunched beneath my boots as I stepped off the patio and into the drifts. I approached the car, clicked to unlock, heard the *beep-beep-beep* that felt almost reassuring, after nothing but the sound of the wind and the falling snow and my own beating heart.

I unlocked the trunk as well, trudged around to the back, dug out the snowbrush-slash-ice-scraper that of course had been bought by Frank when we first got the car. Even though it had been in the summer, the man had thought to equip the trunk with everything we might need, from winter tools to a first aid kit.

Brushing the snow from the roof, I walked around the car, sending a flurry of flakes around me, dusting off the front and back windshields, the snow heavier than I'd ever really given it credit for, using two arms to get it all.

Then I tossed the scraper back into the trunk and got inside. I took a deep breath, then put the key in the ignition. It turned over a couple of times before the engine started, but then it did.

Good.

Good good good.

I took another deep breath and shifted into reverse.

Please work, Honda. Please just *work*.

I lifted my foot from the brake, pressed it to the gas, gave it a little, but nothing. I pressed a little harder, felt the car shift.

Thank god.

It moved a couple of inches back, and I pressed the gas harder, but then all I heard was a *crunch crunch crunch*. I jammed my foot down, really giving it my all, and the car lurched back easily a couple of feet, but immediately I felt the wheels spinning beneath me, the car twisting around, all that gas wanting to push it ... somewhere. The car begin to spin, and I lifted my foot from the gas and slammed it on the brake instead. The car spun the other way, overcorrecting, and I lifted my foot from the brake, too, prayed it would stop, and, then, finally it did.

Moisture built in my eyes, and my breaths came short again. What had I been thinking? I couldn't drive in this. Couldn't get more than a couple of feet, much less the five miles to the police station.

Tears fell on my cheeks, but I brushed them away. I put the car into park, secured the emergency brake, stepped out, and struggled to catch my breath. All I'd done was make circles in the snow, as if the Honda had drunkenly attempted a snow angel.

Again, I reached for my phone, hoping that out here, where it was wide and open, there'd be better reception. There wasn't a single bar, but I keyed in 911 anyway. Nothing.

Back in Room Twelve, I paced, trying to slow my

breaths. I couldn't stay here, not with that woman outside. That Victorian house, it wasn't more than a mile back—I knew because Maisy had mentioned clocking the distance on the odometer so as not to miss the turnoff for the motel. You could walk a mile in twenty minutes—at least in the city you could. Even with the snow, it couldn't take more than double that, could it?

It didn't matter. I had to try.

I grabbed my backpack, emptied it of everything I didn't need—Maisy's large packet, a book, lipsticks, and the folder full of ideas for my book. Then I grabbed my large water bottle, filled it from the tap. Put it into my pack. I still had the granola bars. I added an extra pair of socks and gloves, put on another sweatshirt and a pair of leggings underneath my jeans. Then I tossed in the bottle of antianxiety pills, too. I was nearly ready when there was a flicker of lights—the power went out.

Christ.

The sun was still bright, but that meant my hours were numbered. I had to figure out all of this before the totality of darkness took over around five o'clock.

Fifty-two percent left on my phone—I should have charged it the night before instead of drowning my anxiety with a cocktail of pills and a trip down memory lane via my camera roll. I set it to airplane mode so the battery would drain slower.

I shut the door behind me, locking and twisting it twice to check, and turned to face the world before me. The elements, smarter and craftier than I was. I had never been an outdoorsy person. The snow was still steadily coming down, but the wind had calmed a tiny bit.

Sucking in fresh air, I pulled out my backpack, shoved the keys inside. I looped the pack across my shoulders, looked again at the motel. At protection from the storm, if nothing else.

Then I turned away from it, trudging into the sea of white.

4

February 2, 2023
10:33 a.m.

Despite every layer—gloves and sweaters, warm wool socks—I was getting colder with every step, the bone-chilling kind that not even the day's bright sun could alleviate. It was the damn wind, calmer than earlier this morning but still the kind that seems to whip through you, to seep in through every seam, every gap. Not to mention the snow, coming down even harder now, refusing to let up, blanketing everything in yet another sheet of white.

Errant hairs blew against my face, and I brushed them aside, pulled the hood of my coat tighter over my head and clenched and unclenched my hands in an attempt to get the blood flowing. Then I did the same with my toes, which felt icy, despite my waterproof boots.

I paused and surveyed my surroundings. I was still on the road that led to the motel, and I hadn't seen so much as a single car or—hell—a snowplow. Just me out here, entirely alone. It was a bad one, this storm. And I was foolish to be out in it.

The long line of my footprints were already nearly filled up with new snow, the path behind me empty and stark. The road had curved a couple of times now, so I couldn't see the motel, only tall trees on either side, weighed down with flakes, some of whose branches had fallen, scattered across the road.

I turned to keep walking, but as I did, my foot caught something, and suddenly, my hands, my face, my body, were prone in the snow, cold touching my every inch. I scrambled up, my pulse pounding, snowflakes on my lips. An ache shot through my wrist as I brushed off the snow. The speed with which I'd fallen was staggering, the sheer isolation of being out here terrifying. If I had really gotten hurt, what would I have done? Who would even pass by and find me?

It was beyond clear: I should never have come out here. Because surely I should have gotten to the old house by now. Soon *I* would be stranded in the snow, trapped in my own nightmare—someone finding *my* cold dead hand reaching out of the drift tomorrow . . .

Slow down, Kerry, I could practically hear Frank saying. *You've got this, if you can keep your cool.*

It was always so easy for him to stay calm, I thought. So impossible for me.

Still, I retrieved my phone, checked, once again, for a signal—none—then opened the Health app, which automatically tracked my steps. Nearly two thousand, which was a mile, if I remembered correctly. Frank had gotten super into fitness tracking one year. Sure, at least a few hundred of those steps were from walking around the motel this morning, but I had to be making progress, I had to. I slipped my phone back into my pocket and faced once again the direction I'd been going, the unblemished falling snow. There was another curve in the road, maybe a hundred feet ahead.

The house is probably right around the bend; that's what Frank would say if he were here. *There isn't any reason to panic. You're almost there.*

Just one step in front of the other, I told myself as I pushed forward, ignoring the cold, the fact that my toes were tingling already with numbness, which I knew couldn't be a good thing.

Then, finally, I was rounding the curve, and when the trees opened up, I nearly cried with relief.

The Victorian house.

I was here. I had made it. Imaginary Frank had been right.

The front steps creaked beneath my weight as I trudged across them. The porch held a series of planters, domed with snow but getting ready for spring, plus a porch swing that was full of powder. I lifted my hand to the door, taking in the lightly peeling lavender paint, fresher on one side than the other, as if whoever lived here was improving the place, little by little, slat by slat. A pickup truck sat in front. On the drive in, not even twenty-four hours before, I'd marveled at how even the waypoints to the motel were charming, almost felt curated, and now, the idea felt absurd. People out here—they had to deal with *this*—batten down against winter storms. Against women lying dead out in the snow. It wasn't for show, for likes. It was real.

Heart thumping, I delivered a quick knock. It was difficult not to imagine the worst: Big, angry men, guns in hand, ready to tell me to get the hell off their property. Locals furious at people like me coming up and changing everything with my sheer presence.

No sound, no shuffle of footsteps. I forced back the fear and knocked again, louder this time. *Rap rap rap.*

Again, I turned back, stared at the road, empty apart from my footsteps in the snow. I couldn't go back to a dead body and just *wait*. I felt tears in my eyes as my pulse pounded even faster—I was supposed to be getting everything together. It was never supposed to be—

"Can I help you?"

I jumped, practically leaping out of my skin. In my panic, I hadn't even heard someone approaching, or maybe they'd just been quiet. I brushed away my tears, the material of the gloves scratchy against my face, and turned to see a woman.

Thank god, I thought. A woman.

I opened my mouth to speak, then found myself not even knowing where to start. "Something's happened," I blubbered. "Something—" More tears spilled, but the woman only looked at me, impatient. She had gray hair clipped short at the sides, wrinkles at the edges of her mouth, and her lips were set into what looked almost like a permanent frown. She had a gruff, no-nonsense way about her, and here I was, on her doorstep, spouting little more than nonsense. "I'm sorry," I went on. "I walked here, from the old motel, about a mile up the road. I . . . I need *help*."

The woman stared at me a moment, then opened the door a bit wider.

"You shouldn't be out in this weather," she said, a touch of reprimand in her voice as she reached out, hand on my elbow, ushering me in. Instantly, I was hit by the warmth of fire, roaring in an enormous cast-iron woodstove, a pipe reaching up through the ceiling. She led me to a sofa, indicated that I should sit.

I took off my gloves and hat, left the coat on—still way too cold—then sunk back into the well-loved cushions. The woman took the seat opposite me. She adjusted a pillow behind her back, then set her palms on the knees of a well-worn pair of jeans. In her own surroundings, obviously chosen and cared for with love, she looked less gruff—more like someone who was used to working hard day in and day out. A glance at her hands—cracked, chapped, and red—seemed to confirm it.

"It's just you?" she asked.

For a moment, her words were like a vortex, sucking me into the past.

To a few years before, when Frank and I were watching some easily forgettable TV show, and there was an especially cute kid on it, and he turned to me and said, his round face almost bashful, his slightly thinning brown hair mussed up like it always was: "I think it's time, don't you?"

Or to years before that, standing on the waterfront at Brooklyn Bridge Park, Frank's adorable Italian family in from New Jersey, my friends and family up from North Carolina, us making promises to each other while the officiant made a joke about starting a family and turning our parents into grandparents, both of us blushing with anticipation, with joy.

Or before that, even, to that day I walked into the ad agency where I was freelancing for a couple of weeks and met the nerdy marketing director with nineties-era frameless glasses, a scraggly beard, and an "Architecture is so punk rock" sticker pasted across his laptop. He caught me eyeing it, said, "But it really is, though," and I laughed so hard, and he started laughing, too, and then there we were, two strangers cackling in the middle of an office before I'd even filled out my paperwork.

To the moment I knew my world was going to be different with him in it. Even then, it felt like we would one day be a family.

It was never supposed to be *just me*. But three years of trying and two failed rounds of IVF had changed all that, of course. It had stolen our love, the stability of our marriage, our money.

Or maybe I was lying to myself. Maybe it was only me: my drinking, my failures, my "inhospitable" womb, my inability to finish a damn book.

"At the motel, I mean," the woman clarified, bringing me back to the present.

"Yes," I said. "Just me. Well, I guess that isn't true. There is someone else, the other caretaker. She was supposed to have already left, but her room was a mess. Stuff everywhere, like there'd been a party. And then this morning, I saw her, outside . . . buried in the snow. She's . . . she's dead." The words brought more tears to my eyes, from the release of finally saying it out loud, if nothing else.

"Dead?" she asked, rearing back. "You sure?"

"Her fingers were blue," I said, as I used my own to wipe away the tears. "I touched her. I tried to call the police, but my phone doesn't have any service. And the land lines at the motel aren't working. Also, I lost power before I headed out."

The woman nodded, gesturing around. "Same thing here. Obviously."

"Right," I said. "Do you know how long it takes for everything to get fixed?"

The woman laughed heartily, almost a cackle. "This isn't Manhattan," she said. "Could be a few hours, could be a few days."

She must have seen the worry in my eyes because her own widened kindly. "It's okay," she said. "I can help you. My brother, Billy, is a cop. He doesn't live too far from here. Radio's working. Let me get you something warm to drink, try to call him. I'll be right back."

Without the hum of power, of plugged-in TVs, computers, refrigerators, the sounds that were left stood out: the crackle of the logs in the woodstove, the *tick-tock, tick-tock* of an antique grandfather clock in the corner, the banging of cups and running water coming behind me from the kitchen. I pressed my palms into the scratchy floral print of the sofa. It reminded me of the set my mother had gotten in the nineties, covered in blooms in different shades of mauve. My mother, who budgeted through our family's health scares and job losses on a handful of rotating credit cards, had always maintained that you had to invest in your space, that looking at something beautiful was worth loosening the purse strings. My mom had been so happy when the book and movie deals had come through. When I'd dared to share numbers that made her and my dad's heads spin, not to mention my little brother, Nick, who was a teacher, along with his wife, in North Carolina, their dual incomes barely enough to support their twin girls, I could just hear the pride in her voice. "A real writer," my mother had said. "I always knew it, you know. You were always telling your stories. And you never stopped trying. And now you won't have to worry about money anymore. This is *it*, Kerry. Your *big break*. I'm so happy for you."

The woman returned then, a chipped mug in one hand, the radio in the other. "It's just hot water and honey. Drink it slow. You're red as anything. You need to warm up."

"Thank you," I said. The water scalded my tongue, and I blew on the cup, then nodded to the radio still clasped in her hand. "Were you able to get in touch with your brother?"

"No," she said. "But don't worry. I'll try him again in a few minutes. Or he'll try me. He's always looking out for us, my brother." She retook her place on the sofa. "Now, do you have any idea what might have happened? So we can tell him, when he calls?"

"No," I said. "I don't know if she wandered out there or if there was some sort of accident. But her car isn't even in the lot. It doesn't make any sense."

"Oh," the woman said. "Well, I can explain that. I had it towed."

"Wait," I said, doing a double take. *"What?"*

"She kept parking on my property, even when I told her not to. She didn't move the car, so I called it in."

"I don't understand. Wouldn't she park at the motel?"

The woman rolled her eyes. "She parked to the side of the dumpster, for reasons that were beyond me, but the dumpster is on *my* property. I've asked Maisy to move it, but she won't—we're battling it out right now—but that girl, she wouldn't listen. Even when I warned her. Never had that problem when the Rivers family owned the place. They were good folks, you know. Shouldn't have sold, you ask me."

The mug shook in my hand as the woman's words—*I warned her*—rang in my mind. I lowered it to my lap, hoping she wouldn't see the quivering. "Sorry," I said. "I didn't realize you knew her."

"I didn't *know* her." She tapped her foot on the knit rug beneath her. "But I'm only a mile away, on the road, that is, and our properties touch. I see everyone who goes in and out of that motel. She was there a month, you know. Impossible *not* to see her, really. And like I said, it's awful she's dead, but I can't say it exactly surprises me. The way she was carrying on."

"Carrying on?"

"People in and out. Partying and drinking. Like she was just asking for trouble."

My eyes widened, and I shifted in my seat. I set down my mug on the scuffed-up wooden coffee table, then eyed the radio. It hadn't made a single beep, and I realized I hadn't heard anything when she was in the kitchen, either, not over the sound of water running and the whistle of the kettle. My hands felt suddenly clammy, a cold sweat taking them over. Was the radio even working? It seemed a bit convenient that every phone line was down and there was no power to be found, but she happened to have a personal device that went straight to the police.

The grandfather clock began to sing its hourly refrain, the tune feeling suddenly interminable, the *ding-dong-ding-dong* ringing in my ears as my heart pounded twice as fast as the rhythm of the swinging brass pendulum caught behind glass.

And as the song moved into the *ring-ring-ring* to denote the hour, crawling, too slowly, toward its eleven chimes for eleven o'clock, I felt trapped, too. The snow, the weather, was brutal, but how did I know here was any better? What if I had walked straight out of the frying pan and into the fire?

The chiming stopped, and my ears rang as soon as it did, as if trying to fill the emptiness with something else, and my chin trembled as I stared at the door, at the dead bolt, which I only now realized the woman had turned, and wasn't that strange? Wasn't it odd to lock a door in the middle of nowhere and in the middle of this weather?

The chiming stopped, but the ticking remained—*tick-tock, tick-tock*—and it felt like my own time, my own security, my own *safety*, was slipping away with each new pendulum swing.

I stood, because all I wanted in that moment was to be out of here, to be far away from this woman, from her hot water and honey, from a radio I wasn't even sure was real.

"You okay?" the woman asked.

I took a step toward the door. I didn't care how cold it was outside; it wasn't worth feeling like this.

"Maybe I should—"

Before I could get out the rest of the words, the radio beeped.

"Denise. Denise. This is Billy. Come in, Denise."

She jumped at the radio, pressing a button and holding it close to her face. "Billy, thank god! Young woman walked over here, says she came upon another woman, dead, right outside one of the rooms at the old motel. We need your help."

Another beep and then: "Dead? I hear you right?"

The fear inside me deflated, and I sighed, then retook my seat.

The woman nodded vigorously, then pushed the button again. "Yes, Billy. *Dead.*"

An agonizing pause stretched between us. Then another beep.

"Aw, shit," he said. "I'm out on a call, but let me wrap this up, and then I'll be right there. Tell her to meet me at the motel." Another pause. "You can have Tyler drive her over."

5

February 2, 2023
11:08 a.m.

The dead bolt turned, and the door burst open, slamming against the wall and ushering in a gust of pure cold, and a boy walked through—well, a man who still looked like a boy. He was bundled up in an enormous winter coat and rugged tan work boots that he stomped against the mat. In each hand, he held a canvas carrier packed with chopped wood.

"You didn't have to lock the door," he said. "I told you I was coming right back."

"Too many new people out here these days," Denise said, practically leaping from the couch. "But forget about that. I'm glad you're back."

His cheeks were red from the cold, and a pimple sat atop his nose, but his chocolate brown eyes were wide and round as a doe's, and his long lashes were dusted with snowflakes. He'd probably made his high school classmates swoon. "I was just getting more wood," he said. "What's going on?"

"Someone's *dead*," Denise said.

One of the canvas carriers began to slip from his hand, but he adjusted it quickly. "Wait, *what*?"

"This woman—"

"Kerry," I said. "I—"

"Kerry *found her*," Denise practically crowed. "Buried in the snow."

He set down the bundles of wood, even though he was still a few feet from the fireplace. "Let Kerry talk, Mom."

Mom. I nearly did a double take, because the two couldn't have looked less like relations if they tried, but then the woman's eyes widened a touch, and I could see the beauty in them, frayed at the edges from years of hard work—maybe a hard life—but it was clear that he'd gotten those eyes from her. "She says there was some kind of party," Denise said.

"I *think* there was some sort of party," I said. "I wasn't actually there. I only got here last night. The woman who was staying there before me, she was supposed to have checked out, but her things are everywhere."

"And no one else was there?" he asked.

I shook my head.

He took the logs over to the fireplace, knelt down, and stacked them neatly in a wrought iron holder. Then he pushed himself up and turned back to me. He looked almost scared, and even younger, like these kinds of things didn't happen in towns like his. "That's horrible."

Denise turned back to her son. "Billy wants her to meet him at the motel. You'll drive her?"

Tyler hesitated only a moment, then locked his gaze on mine. "Of course I will."

The drive was fast with the utility vehicle, and Tyler was quiet, his eyes focused on the road, handling every curve, every bump, with the grace of someone who'd done stuff like this a million times before. Still, I was freezing by the time we were back in front of the motel, the snow still coming down, the wind icy, and my head was aching with what I assumed was a combination of adrenaline, dehydration, and the aftereffects of the antianxiety pills.

Tyler turned, and before he took the last curve, he pumped the brakes, sighed. "I might as well tell you, because I'm about to tell Billy: I wasn't totally up front with my mom."

My breath caught, and I felt the familiar panic beginning to build.

"It's okay," he said, instantly picking up on it. "It's nothing big; it's just that you probably saw all that stuff in the room because there *was* a party—two nights ago—at the motel. Bunch of city people. I left early; it was getting a little wild. Drugs aren't my thing."

"Wait," I said. "You were *there*?"

"I know, I know," he said. "I'm twenty-three years old, too old to be lying to my mom about partying, but—it's not just the party, it's the way she is about people from the city. She's nuts about them. She doesn't want me having anything to do with them. Thinks it's bad enough I do odd jobs for Maisy. And if she knew that I'm actually saving up to move downstate one day, it would break her heart."

"Okay," I said. My eyes locked on his, as my own breathing calmed a bit. I could see it so clearly, boyish shame. That primal desire to not upset your mother. "But you're going to be honest with the police, though?"

He nodded eagerly. "Of course."

A pause, only the sound of tires against snow. "Do you

43

know anything about the woman, then? Since you were at the party?"

"Not a whole lot," Tyler said as he maneuvered across a drift. "Just that she was up from the city and she was driving my mom crazy—some argument about the dumpster." He added a little gas, getting us over the hump. "My mom is tied up in a property-line dispute. She thinks everyone is hell-bent on ruining the land, the community—exploiting us so they can look cool for their city friends, that kind of thing. But, like I said, I do odd jobs for Maisy, and so I got invited, and I stopped by. When I left, everyone was fine."

He revved the engine, zipping diagonally across the lot and right in front of the motel's office to a pair of utility vehicles with the Ulster County Sheriff's Office logo printed across each side. In front of them stood two officers, decked to the nines in snow gear and winter caps, badges on the sleeves of their coats. One man, one woman, snowflakes swirling around them.

"Hi, Billy," Tyler said. "Jeanine."

Tyler shut off the vehicle, stepped down, and I followed him.

"I'm Officer Rice," the man said. He was gray at the temples like his sister, face clean-shaven and hair cut neatly in what looked like a military style. A hint of the family resemblance in his eyes, which were a touch bloodshot. He nodded to his partner. "This is Officer Madison."

She had red hair that was curly as anything, spilling from beneath her cap, and her face was tight, betraying nothing. The kind of woman who looked like she took no shit. I imagined she probably had to work twice as hard as her partner to be treated with respect.

"And you are, miss . . . ?" she prompted.

"Kerry," I said. "Kerry Walsh."

Officer Madison cleared her throat, crossed her arms so her winter coat crinkled. "Denise Rice says you found something out here?"

They all looked at me.

"Yes," I said. "A body." I pointed. "Back there." I turned to Tyler. "Tell them what you know."

His eyes locked straight on his uncle's. "There was a party here two nights ago—lot of drinking, some drugs. I didn't mention it to my mom—you know how she is with city people—but I was there, for an hour or so."

"And when was that?" Officer Madison asked.

"Got there around nine," Tyler said. "Left little after ten."

Both officers nodded, then exchanged a quick glance.

"Do I need to stay?" Tyler asked. "Mom still needs me, especially with the power down and all. And there's a neighbor who hasn't got any wood. We need to head over there, check on her. Mrs. Singer, you know."

"I think we're good, Tyler," Officer Madison said. "If anything changes, we'll swing by Denise's place."

"Mrs. Singer's," Tyler clarified. "Might be there all afternoon."

"Wait," I said. "Doesn't he need to, I don't know, identify her or something?"

"We're good," Officer Madison said again, winter-chapped lips pressed into a thin line. "And if that changes, we'll come by Mrs. Singer's."

Within moments, Tyler had nodded and driven off, leaving just me and the cops.

"Well," Officer Madison said, arms still crossed, a touch

of impatience in her voice. "Why don't you take us over to what you think you found."

I stared at her for a moment, trying to figure out why her words were so clipped, then took a breath, steeling myself. "All right," I said. "Follow me."

I turned to the left, walking briskly through the snow-covered parking lot, my car still askew from where I'd tried to drive earlier.

The motel was an L-shape, Rooms One through Five shooting from the main office toward the back, Six through Thirteen forming the bottom of the L along the parking lot and the road. We walked down the line until eventually we passed Room Twelve, then Room Thirteen. I curved around the edge of the motel, noticing what I hadn't in my panic before: the woodshed along the side of the property, the gravel drive that led to a dumpster, the pool and outbuildings just past the back lawn.

I made another left, seeking out the Adirondack chairs, then quickly realized that everything looked wrong.

The chairs were turned over, for one, when they'd been right-side up before, and the snow had covered them in ripples and drifts, as if sculpted by the wind, an ocean's waves frozen in time. Surrounding the whole thing, a pair of utility vehicle tracks—had the officers already been over the property before I even got here?

As my brain struggled to process the scene, I realized just what else was wrong.

The body. The hand. The red nails.

They were gone.

I turned back to see both officers staring at me, and it suddenly made sense.

The crossed arms. The brisk attitudes. The quick dismissal of Tyler. The implications—

What you think you found.

—they already knew there was nothing here. They knew, and they were waiting for me to show them.

"She was right here," I said, snowflakes swirling in my vision. "Right where I'm standing. I *swear* to you."

The woman crossed her arms and sighed. "Look. We've both circled the motel and the outbuildings, and there's nothing here. Nothing but snow."

Had the woman been fully covered, submerged in the drift?

Frantically, I began to kick up the powder, sure she was right here—that she *had* to be right here—expanding my radius toward the Adirondack chairs. Finally, my toe caught something hard, and I sunk to my knees, sure of it, and I scooped aside what felt like buckets of snow, until I hit—

Stones and rocks. I kept scooping the snow away. It was the fire pit, the one Maisy had mentioned.

I turned away from it, using my arms to scoop more and more snow, practically diving, sweeping back and forth.

Nothing. Nothing but piles and piles of fresh snowflakes.

"I don't understand," I said. I was still on my knees, surrounded by the tipped-over Adirondack chairs, the officers looking down on me, pity on their faces.

I realized, then, how wild I must have looked, what they must have been thinking.

"You don't get it," I said. "She was *right* here."

Both of them stared, and for a moment, I wondered: Had she really been dead at all? Had she—somehow—gotten up, of her own accord, and just . . . left?

But no, I'd felt her. She had been right here, right where I was kneeling, unless . . .

A chill crawled up my spine, and it hit me for the first time how many assumptions I'd made. The booze, the drugs, the cold. I'd just concluded she was a mess like me, that she'd gotten tanked, wandered out into the snow, maybe hit her head. It was a rock bottom I could totally imagine for myself.

What if that hadn't been the case at all? What if . . .

"Someone could have moved her," I said.

The woman's eyebrows shot up. "In all this snow? In this weather?"

"The chairs," I said. "They've been turned. And the tracks from the vehicles. We wouldn't know if they did."

The officers exchanged yet another look.

"Listen," the woman said, "I get it. It's scary out here on your own. No power, no service, nothing. It can be scary for us, and—hell—we're used to it. But we're not seeing anything close to what you called about, and right now we're using valuable resources when people are having emergencies, people who need our help."

"No," I said. I pushed myself up, brushing the snow from my hands, shaking my head almost viciously. "You can't go. I swear to you. She was *here*. She was—" Already I could see them starting to move, to walk away. "Wait. Just follow me. *Please*."

I retraced my steps, rushing around the side of the motel, the cops behind me, then kicked aside the drifted snow and pushed open the door to Room Thirteen. "In here," I said. "Come in here."

Reluctantly, they followed me inside, and I gestured around. The clothes tossed every which way, the suitcase next to the bed, the paraphernalia on the kitchen counter.

"Don't you see?" I said. "She came here, but she never checked out." Absurdly, the lyrics to "Hotel California" began to play through my head. *You can never leave.* "There was a party—we know that for sure from Tyler—and now where is she, this missing woman? This woman who I *know* is dead, whose—whose hand was out there in the snow?" I found my voice cracking, wavering, and then something occurred to me, something horrible, vicious.

I ran past the bed and into the tiled bathroom, the woman's toiletries still scattered about. Heart racing, I reached up to the curtain that cordoned off the clawfooted tub. I put one hand on it, my pulse a metronome.

I jerked it back, almost sure she'd be there, lying face down in the tub, waiting for us to find her, like something out of a horrible movie.

All I could see was the clean white porcelain. No body. No woman. Nothing.

"Ma'am."

I jolted, turned to see the officers behind me, staring at me like I'd completely lost my mind.

I pushed past them, stalking out of the bathroom and back into the main room, then gesturing wildly around. "Where did she go, then?"

"There are a million places she could have gone," the

woman said. "If you'd like to report a missing person, well, I suppose we can do that."

"But I don't know *who* she was. You'd have to talk to Maisy, the owner. Or Tyler. I don't know anything."

"Ma'am," the man said. "Ma'am, listen. You *are* from the city, right?"

"And why does that matter?"

"It's just, like my partner said, you probably haven't been in a situation like this before. All on your own, far from others; it can be scary. Especially with a nor'easter like this. It's a lot. And"—he gestured toward the kitchen—"drinking, drugs, I mean. It can affect you."

"They're not even mine," I said. "This isn't even my room. It's hers. It was from the party, a party that happened before I even got here. I'm sober," I said. "I don't even drink."

Officer Madison tossed up her hands. "Regardless, there *was* a party, there was obvious drug use. You know how many calls we get, saying a young man or woman didn't come home, and then it turns out they were on a little bender? If I had to guess, this woman probably left to get more drugs and now is stuck because of all the snow. I'm sure if we give it a day or so, it'll clear itself up." They both turned, walked out the door, headed to their respective vehicles.

"No," I said, frantic now. "You can't just leave. I don't have power. I don't have a phone. And if there's a murderer out there, I—"

"No one's got power," Officer Rice said. "Or phone lines. I assure you the county is working on it. I saw a woodstove in there. That's all any of us have right now.

50

Get a fire started; keep it burning. It will give you all the heat you need. Then you'll have to wait out the rest of it like everybody else."

"But—" I said.

Already, the utility vehicles were turning on, engines rumbling.

"Please," I said. "You can't just go."

Officer Madison seemed to hesitate, then got out of her vehicle, pulled off a glove impatiently, and dug around in a pocket. Finally, she retrieved a business card, held it out to me—*Officer Jeanine Madison*—the end of her name already smudging from the wet. I shoved it in my own pocket, protecting it from the snow.

"We really have got to go, ma'am," she said. "But phone lines should hopefully be up soon. Or the cell service restored at the very least. And if you see anything else suspicious, you call me, okay? That's my direct number."

She turned, gestured toward my car, then back to me. "And don't you dare try to drive again in this—or go out on any more walks, either. You're lucky you didn't get hurt. Just stay here until the roads are plowed and the power's back. Keep your fire burning, and try to remain calm."

She didn't wait for me to answer.

Together, they drove off, away from the motel, from the crime scene.

Leaving me entirely alone.

Alone with a dead woman.

A dead woman who had somehow disappeared into thin air.

6

February 2, 2023
11:58 a.m.

I built my fire, just like the cops had told me to.

As I struck a match and tossed it in the woodstove, setting the kindling, the newspaper, ablaze, I wondered if there was any way I really could have imagined it all.

What I didn't tell the cops—what I *couldn't* tell the cops—was that this had happened to me once before. My doctor had told me not to mix the new medication with alcohol, but I'd figured that they always said that. I told myself it was fine, that maybe I'd get a little drowsy, maybe the alcohol would hit me a bit stronger. And what did it matter if I got a little drunker, anyway? It was early January, and at that point, I hadn't spoken to Siobhan in over a month; Frank had left for his brother's a couple of weeks before, and he and I were only texting about logistics. I hadn't even had the guts to tell my parents and my brother that my marriage was falling apart. The Twilite position had been secured for February 1, and I told myself that that was when I was going to get my life together. In the meantime, I had my little rules: No drinking before noon. No hard liquor. No going out to bars. No drunk-dialing. If I wanted to get a little (or a lot) tipsy in the privacy of my own crumbling world, who was even around to see it? And so the pills had been taken, the bottle and a half of wine consumed, and I was in the middle of an alcohol-fueled cleaning rampage when I'd come across a box of pregnancy tests and decided to take one on a whim. And there they'd been, those two pink lines, and quickly I'd done the math, remembered the heartbreaking sex Frank and I had had the night before he left for good, realized that this could be it.

It was funny, but I had almost wanted to call Siobhan first. She didn't want kids, and for some reason that had made it easy for me to open up about my fertility struggles with her. When the IVF didn't work, she, always intent on looking on the bright side, had been full of stories of coworkers who'd gotten accidentally pregnant at forty-one, of an old college pal of hers and Allison's who had done three rounds of IVF before having regular old sex with her husband and getting twins. "It could happen when you least expect it," Siobhan was always saying, and I had never believed her. The temptation to text her a photo—*you were right; it did happen!*—was so strong, but that hadn't been an option by then. Besides, the news wouldn't change her life; it would change Frank's. So, breaking my own rule, but for a very good reason, I'd picked up the phone, and I'd called him blubbering, sure that this would solve it all, finally heal us.

It was only as I heard the genuine joy in his voice, heard the tears over the phone, even if all the joy had to be complicated, that I looked down, and there was the test.

One line. Negative.

"Hang on," I'd said to Frank. "Just hang on."

"What is it?" he asked. "Kerry, what do you mean, hang on?"

"The test, it's not . . ." I scrambled to find the right words as, in the background, I heard Frank's little nephew calling for him. *Uncle Frank! Uncle Frank!* "It must have—"

It had to be wrong; it *had* to be, and so, still drunk, I ripped open another package, took the test again, the phone sitting on the counter as I did.

It was only when the full three minutes had passed that I lifted the phone back to my ear.

"Kerry?" Frank was saying. "Jesus, Kerry, you scared me. Is everything—"

"It's negative," I managed. "I'm sorry."

"What? What do you mean? You just said—"

"It was a mistake," I said. "I—I read it wrong."

Silence across the line, and I could hear only my husband's breathing—my soon-to-be-ex-husband's breathing—and I could practically see him biting his lip, adjusting his nerdy-and-not-even-in-a-cool-way glasses, like he always did when he was struggling to control well-deserved anger, the kind that surfaced when I'd disappointed him yet again.

"You're serious?" he asked. *"Really?"*

"Yes," I said. "I'm serious."

Another pause, and then tears, but not tears of joy this time. Tears of desperation. Tears of heartbreak.

"Get some help, Kerry, please," he said. "And don't call me again."

I hadn't had a drink since.

Now, I tossed another log in the fire, watched it begin to blaze.

This was different, wasn't it? I *wasn't* drinking. I'd mixed the pills with the Ambien, sure, but I had seen her hand. I'd *touched* it. Hadn't I?

My eyes had been closed when I reached out. Was it possible that I'd touched one of the stones of the fire pit, felt the hardness, and assumed it was a dead body?

No, I thought. It wasn't. There was no way.

The fire blazed bright, but I pushed myself up, backing away. I had to look around the other rooms. I had caretaking duties to do anyway, which I didn't want to skimp on, especially with the power out. Maisy's instructions had made it clear that if there was an outage, that meant the boiler wouldn't run and the pipes would be in danger of freezing. I had to run the water at a trickle in every room to try to prevent that. It was something to do, if nothing else. And maybe I would find something—anything— that could explain what had happened.

My own room taken care of, I made my way through the others, tromping through snow and wrenching each door open, then checking for signs of this mystery woman as I ran each faucet, checked the traps for mice.

I was exhausted by the time I got to Room Six and cold cold cold, with no heat in the other rooms, the realities of being upstate and alone in a winter storm so different than the way this place had appeared on Instagram. I still had one room to go on this side and another five on the other, and the prospect of all of it felt suddenly maddening, as anxiety-inducing as opening up a blank Word document and watching the curser blink.

I slipped the key into the lock, opened the door.

At once, I could tell the smell wasn't at all right. It was

ashy and tinged with char, like a kiss after smoking. There was something else, too. A languid, roasted scent, something almost . . . fleshy.

Carefully, I approached the fireplace, knelt down to look. There were ashes everywhere, a veritable pile of them, and sooty footprints on the hearth.

It wasn't possible, was it? That someone could have burned a body in the time I was gone? Chopped up that poor woman, fed each bit of her into the flames before letting them burn burn burn, down to nothing more than ashes and soot?

Hairs stood up on the back of my neck, and I held back a retch.

No way. There simply hadn't been enough time. And a fire hot enough to incinerate a body, it wasn't possible . . .

Still I backed away, out of the room, locking the door tight behind me.

Screw my caretaking duties. Screw the goddamn pipes. Screw the rest of the rooms.

I rushed down the path and back to Room Twelve, careful not to slip, then shut the door, bolting the chain.

Carefully, I built my fire even higher. I checked my cell service over and over and over again, flicking back and forth between airplane mode to conserve battery. I placed calls to 911 that wouldn't go through, only managed to run down my battery, kept trying the landline over and over, even though I never got a dial tone. I paced back and forth, wondering what I was supposed to do. Wanting numbness, release, a break from the endless train of thoughts running through my head, from the panic building in my chest.

I tried opening my computer, pulling up my Word document, a distraction, if nothing else. Buck up, Kerry, I told myself. Just write your damn book. Forget about that hand, those fingers. Forget about it all.

The panic came back even stronger, and I slammed the laptop shut, popped another antianxiety pill, paced the room as I waited for it to kick in.

You can handle this, Kerry, Frank was crowing, straight into my brain. *You don't need pills or booze or your phone to numb yourself. You're strong.*

And what if I'm not? I thought. I'd been white-knuckling it without drink for the last three weeks, and what had it gotten me? I was up here alone, potentially imagining bodies. I only wanted something—just a little something—to take the edge off, to soften the frantic corners of my mind. To warm my insides, prepare for a night with no power, no phones, nothing to do but fear the worst.

Something that had always worked to calm me down before.

You don't have to do this, Kerry. You don't have to throw it all away. Stay away from it. It's never done you a bit of good.

In seconds, I was in my snow boots again. I told myself that I only wanted to check her room one more time, just to make sure nothing had changed. I told myself that there might be a clue in there, something that could explain what had happened, who had hurt her. I told myself that I was *not* going into the room for precisely the reason I knew I was going.

But soon, the door to Room Thirteen was open, and

there was the same vision, only the floor was wet where the cops and I had tracked in all that snow.

Look for your clues, then, Frank chimed in my brain. *If that's really why you're here, do it. Because you don't have to do the other thing. You haven't fallen off the wagon yet. You haven't crossed any lines. You're still in control, Kerry. You're always in control, if you'd only let yourself believe it.*

The thing about it was, I wasn't looking for clues. Imaginary Frank knew it. *I* knew it.

There was so much wine. Bottles and bottles of it, many of them still unopened. A corkscrew sitting there, shining in its chrome glory, like a gift from above, waiting for me.

I needed a drink, damn it. I *deserved* a drink.

Before I could stop myself, I grabbed a bottle and the corkscrew, too. Then I turned around, leaving the room— the crime scene—behind me.

Back in Room Twelve, I locked back up, not even bothering to barricade the door—it was just another thing that stood between me and this drink. I beelined toward the kitchen, opening and shutting cabinets until I found a suitable glass. There was a light sheen of dust at the bottom, and I rinsed it quickly, not bothering with dish soap. I stabbed the corkscrew in, twisting it hard and fast, suddenly desperate.

It's not even how much you drink, Frank was always saying. *It's the urgency with which you do it. All you have to do is slow down. Slow down and remember that you can take that control back.*

The cork popped with a satisfying *thwap!*, and it was scary how much I loved that sound, how much I'd missed it. The sound of promise, of possibility. Of knowing that for the next however many hours, life was going to be so much more fun. Shimmering and joyful. With soft, fluffy edges. With laughter and friendship and love love love. Like layering a pretty filter over the whole damn thing.

For me, drinking wasn't only for escape. Sometimes I drank to make it all mean more, to give everything more life, to make the narrative of my real life feel as good and full as the curated one I posted on the screen. To take the pressure off the metronomic blinking cursor, sitting in the middle of an empty page. To be more creative, more bohemian, to do what I wanted and not give a damn. Only problem was, like everything—the googling, the obses- sive scrolling, the walking so close to the line that you might finally toe it, might trip right across—I never knew when to stop.

Now, I tilted the bottle, letting the dark liquid slosh out, not caring that some of it splashed against the gray coun- tertops, my eyes flitting to the clock on my phone: 12:05. Hell, at least it wasn't before noon—it wasn't hard liquor, either, and I wasn't at a bar, and drunk-dialing remained an impossibility. My old rules remained intact.

I lifted the glass to my lips, took a sip—no, a gulp—and savored the taste, the feeling, the warmth of it, already infusing my skin, my cells, my *soul* with that kind of joy that only came from this source, really.

God, it felt good. Like coming home.

Hunger. I was two glasses in when the rumbling hit me, deep in my bones. I stood from where I'd been warming myself by the fire, and I nearly lost my balance, the world spinning a bit around me. Turns out my tolerance had taken quite a dip these past few weeks.

Or maybe it was the pills that my doctor had warned me against mixing with booze—*ha!*

Well, I mixed them, Doc, and—imagined positive pregnancy tests aside, potentially imagined dead bodies aside—I haven't keeled over yet, have I?

My stomach rumbled again, and I grabbed my backpack, knowing a little grub would even me out, ground me so I could manage one more glass before going completely off the rails.

The granola bars had crumbled in their packaging, tiny little maracas in the bottom of my bag.

The pantry, I thought. Of course. It was one of the outbuildings on the property that had been listed in Maisy's guide. Quickly, I found the right page: *There are three small structures to the right of the pool: the pantry, the laundry room, and the boiler room. Help yourself to any food in the pantry, including perishables stored in the freezer, and there's a closet in the laundry room with extra linens and supplies. Don't enter the boiler room except to let in a contractor.*

It was after one o'clock already, which meant I had four hours, five tops, before I wouldn't have light. I should go now, shouldn't I? Not just for the food, but for supplies, too? My phone was hovering at thirty percent. I'd need a real flashlight, and there might be one in the laundry room. I slipped on my snow boots, lacing them tight, added my layers, grabbed the ring of keys, and headed out.

The snow was thick as ever, and I trudged through it, hugging the side of the motel, the lawn with the Adirondack chairs and fire pit on my left, the outbuildings straight back. There were three of them, arranged in a line and connected at the sides, made of windowless cinderblock and sharing a flat roof, but with three individual doors—and individual keys—Maisy had made it clear that I couldn't access one from another.

That old game show popped into my head, the seventies one where all the audience members dressed up and people would accidentally trade a brand-new car for a scruffy goat: *Let's Make a Deal.* I'll take Door Number Two, I thought, approaching the middle one first, opening it to see a laundry room packed with machines. I stepped in, flicked on my phone's flashlight, finding my way to a large closet in a corner. I opened it, scanned shelves filled with detergent and cleaning products, a vacuum and an industrial-size mop, and—bingo—right there on top, three substantial flashlights, each about the size of a pint glass. I checked that each worked, then turned off the one on my phone to save its charge and loaded the extras into my backpack, as well as a pack of D batteries.

My stomach made its hunger known again, growling, and I still felt fairly woozy. New flashlight in hand, I left the laundry room, locking it behind me, and moved on to Door Number One: the pantry.

This one was unlocked—didn't even require a key. Maybe the previous caretaker had left it like that, just like she'd left her own room? I pushed open the door, walked in, and shut it behind me, using the flashlight to peek around. There were shelves upon shelves of packaged food—but all things you had to cook. Then I saw exactly what my drunken heart desired: bags and bags of pita chips, all unopened. I set my flashlight on the shelf, grabbed one, and ripped it open, ravenous now.

The taste of salt was exquisite, practically dancing on my tongue, and I downed the first handful fast, then grabbed another bunch, stuffing them into my mouth, savoring the crunch. Again, I pictured Frank or Siobhan, watching me somewhere, seeing me like this, drunk on two glasses of wine in the afternoon, pills popping in my bloodstream, shoveling chips into my mouth. I imagined all my followers, the ones who thought I was a smart, creative, put-together author. But who cared, anyway? None of them were here now. It was only me me me. No one really knew what any of us were like behind our screens, did they?

When I'd finally had my fill, I folded over the bag, stuffing it into my backpack. I needed something else, too, for later. Some kind of real sustenance.

My eyes caught the freezer: Could there be something in there that could be warmed or cooked over a fire— sausages, maybe? Anything?

I set down the flashlight so it pointed right toward the long freezer, then ran both hands along the edge of the lid, ready to heave it open. I pulled hard, but it didn't budge. I looked along the bottom, to see if there was a lock, but there wasn't one. Must have been a heavy door.

I took a deep breath, realizing how knocked out the wine had already made me, and then I bent my knees, secured both hands beneath, and lifted up. *Push!*

It opened, and at first I didn't even notice it.

Then the light, hazy and eerie but there all the same, made it all too clear.

I screamed, whipped my hands away. I screamed again. No food. No sustenance.

Only hair, so much hair. And clothing, frozen stiff.

She was lying face down in the freezer, as if she'd been tossed aside like a piece of trash.

The woman I'd been looking for, the woman the police hadn't even believed I'd seen.

I screamed again, then stepped forward slightly, my thigh brushing the edge.

The lid slammed shut.

I didn't have to open it again to know.

I wasn't imagining things. I wasn't hallucinating.

The woman was dead.

And that could only mean one thing: Someone had moved her.

Someone hadn't wanted her to be found.

Someone who could still be out there now.

7

February 2, 2023
1:17 p.m.

My boots sunk into the snow as I rushed out of the pantry, the bright light blinding. Another few steps, and my ankle twisted, my center of gravity shifting, my body unable to stop it.

The fall was soft, against all the snow, like when you're careening down in a dream before crashing into the comfort of your bed, but the cold was sharp, the snow on my cheeks and sneaking into the gaps between my gloves and coat, like ice that somehow could burn.

To my right, only a few feet off, was the fire pit, the Adirondack chairs. The walk from there to the pantry couldn't have been more than twenty feet.

Snow was still coming down, covering up evidence of what had happened, and I realized something: This changed things, irrevocably so. All the other explanations for what had happened to this woman—a drunken fall, even an overdose on drugs—none of them could explain why someone had moved her, had hidden her away, had tossed her in that freezer.

Why *would* someone move her unless they had *killed* her, unless they were trying to cover it up?

A shiver shot through my spine, and I pushed myself

up all the way, coming slowly to my feet. Could I go back to that Victorian, to Denise? Have her call her brother again, beg him to return? No. She and her son had said they would be at the neighbor's.

Could I go somewhere else? The wind whipped against my face—brutal—and my toes, deep in their boots, were still sore, prickly from the cold from the last time I'd gone out. The cops had said it was dangerous to go out in the storm like this—and wouldn't they know? It had been hard enough before, and my belly hadn't been full of wine then, my pulse hadn't been throbbing with alcohol and fear.

Feeling like I had no other choice, I curved back around the motel, heading for Room Thirteen. It suddenly seemed like the safest place. Why would the killer return to this room, to this . . . *crime scene*? Not to mention all that still awaited me in that room . . .

In seconds, I'd stepped across the threshold, shut the door behind me, and locked it. With a heave, I pulled the side table in front of the door to create a barricade, the lurch sending a pair of wineglasses, tucked away on the bottom shelf, onto the floor, rolling across the hardwoods, crusted dregs and prints of lipstick kaleidoscopic.

Slow down, Kerry. Just breathe.

Right. I checked that the door was tight, closed the curtains, and headed for the landline on the wall in the kitchen. I lifted to check, listening for even the faintest dial tone. Nothing.

I set the phone down gingerly on its cradle, turned to the counter. Pushed aside ashes from weed, another cigarette butt, hesitated only a moment.

Screw it, I thought, reaching for another bottle. This time, I glugged it straight from the neck—no glass required. Bottle still clutched in my hand, I glanced around, checking my theory that the killer wouldn't come back to this room. Taking in the paraphernalia on the table, the items spilling out of the suitcase, the rumpled bed, I lifted the bottle to my lips yet again, slurping. Nothing looked particularly different from when I'd seen it before.

For a moment, I was thrown back to that night in November, Siobhan and I out on our own, without the boys. We'd gone to that nice Italian restaurant at the top of the park, halfway between her apartment and mine. A bottle of Chianti to share, and maybe I had been drinking a bit faster than she had, but I'd been careful not to go too wild. And then it had been empty, and the waiter had taken it away, asked if we wanted another. My heart had flickered at the prospect, but Siobhan was already shaking her head. Before the waiter walked away, I reached out, grabbing him by the elbow. "Maybe just one glass for me, then. The pinot noir."

"Five-ounce or ten-ounce pour?" he asked.

"Ten, I guess." As if I hadn't even considered it, as if I hadn't taken in all the options on the menu when we'd ordered the bottle. As if I didn't *always* take in all the options on the menu, all the ways that could lead me to *more more more* without letting anyone know just how much, how often.

Siobhan was staring at me, her eyebrows narrowed. She tugged at the ends of her brown hair, twirling it around her pointer finger, a tic of hers when something was bothering her, then looked down at the table, a few spatters of tomato sauce all that remained.

"Oh, I'll do the whole tip to make up for the extra glass," I said. "Don't worry about it."

She adjusted the sleeves of her stretchy black dress. "It's not about the *cost*, Kerry."

My stomach turned. I felt I'd been so careful to not show my hunger, my thirst. I'd tried to play it all so casual, and yet she'd seen right through it.

The waiter returned with my mammoth pour, and I grabbed it, thanking him, tipped a bit back. I needed it for whatever was about to come out of Siobhan's mouth.

"I've told you about Charlie," she said, voice kind, slightly upbeat, like it so often was. "And I know I told you I don't think his drinking is really a *problem* problem"—Siobhan was always, always looking on the bright side, sometimes to the point of being willfully obtuse—"but I mean, it's starting to feel like *all* the people in my life, all the people who are important to me, at least, all they care about is drinking. Well, not everyone, I guess, but, you know, Charlie and . . ."

And *me*.

She didn't have to say it. I didn't have to hear it.

"It's just," I said. "Since the last round failed . . . IVF takes its toll, you know. I'm letting loose a little. That's all."

Siobhan forced a smile. To my surprise, she reached across the table and grabbed my hand. "I really care about you, you know. You're important to me, and I want you to be okay."

"I *am* okay," I lied.

"You promise?" Siobhan asked.

68

I nodded. "I promise."

Little did she know—hell, little did *I* know—that she and I would see each other only a couple more times before all of it blew up, our friendship shot to smithereens.

Now I looked around, the empty bottles staring at me. Who *was* this woman? Had she had her own Siobhan in her life, braving a topic that had to be hard to bring up? Had she lied to her friends, too, pretended things were okay when they weren't? Had she, like me, been wanting so badly to turn things around only to have her life cut short—stolen from her—before she'd even had the chance?

Does it matter? Imaginary Frank asked, reminding me what was at stake as I approached the suitcases by the bed. *You might have lost everything, Kerry, but the world still needs you. Don't mess around with your safety—with your life—right now.*

It *does* matter, I thought, because I'd seen her. Her crusted, frozen hair. Her bloodless hand.

Kneeling in front of the suitcase, I glugged back more wine. Her clothes were simple, clean-lined, but smart, stylish. Size 6 or 8, which fit with the woman I'd seen. And nearly all black, apt for someone from the city. *Time to trade your all-black summer clothes for your all-black winter clothes,* Frank used to say to me, poking fun. He was the sort who thought a bright shirt could do wonders for your mood, who'd made the four of us—him and me, Charlie and Siobhan—cheesy matching T-shirts that proudly proclaimed DON'T MESS WITH GAME NIGHT. I took another sip and continued to dig. Lacy underthings. Faded jeans. Mismatched socks. Nothing to identify this woman, but then, at the bottom of the suitcase, some-thing hard.

A leather-bound sketchpad, baby blue, a ribbon mark-ing a page. I opened it to see a pencil drawing. The motel, its enormous letters, sketched across the page. I flipped another, found the interior of the room I was in, only per-fectly clean, like someone had come in and sat down, captured every detail, memorializing each piece of furni-ture, each rustic touch and bit of subway tile before messing it all up.

Another page. This drawing was through the window, curtains drawn, looking out on a gorgeous clouded sky.

Flipped again. Now I saw a swath of woods, trees fill-ing a horizon line, undisturbed but for a shadow in the corner, not fully made out, but it looked like a figure, like a man . . . watching. A chill crawled up my spine, tickling me, vertebrae by vertebrae, and I gulped more wine, as if doing so would push it down, bury it in my gut.

The next drawing was of the ground, footprints on the edge.

Another page, and this time I gasped, struggling to understand what I was looking at, to take it all in.

There, huge and spread across two pages this time, was the pantry I'd just been in, and right in the middle, about eight inches across, that enormous, god-awful freezer, only half-propped open . . .

Five fingers desperately reaching out.

"Goddamn it," I said as I dropped the sketchpad—and the bottle in my hand, too. Wine cascaded over the draw-ings, over the woman's things, eking across the paper, the spread of that horrific freezer, like blood from a gunshot wound. I righted the bottle, grabbed a black tank top to sop up the wine, and stared again at the notebook.

Had she somehow—inexplicably—known what was about to happen to her? I flicked back a page, to the shadow of the man in the woods, watching. And another page, and then another, seeing, suddenly, what I hadn't before.

There was a shadow, too, in the drawing of the window, of the view from within the room.

And another shadow, there in the reflection of the motel sign's enormous letters. Every drawing was in one way or another of a person being watched.

Every one until the last one, when the point of view was suddenly the watcher's, gazing at the violence instead.

Then another thought hit me, careening through my sloshy mind: What if this journal didn't belong to the woman at all? What if these weren't the drawings of a nervous woman, hairs standing up along her arms as she somehow sensed what was going to happen to her?

What if this was the sketchbook that belonged to the *actual* killer?

Fingers shaking, I flipped back farther, suddenly hungry for information.

Who did this belong to? And what did it mean? I went back a few pages, found, amid all the sketches, loopy handwriting, a collection of notes.

Three to six scenes
Ten to fifteen minutes tops
Editor, mixer, graphics
Deadline: March 15

Flipping back more pages, I found more and more drawings, and then I got to one that made me stop, my breath catching.

It took a moment for it to fully hit me. Like one of those Magic Eye puzzles that required time to compute.

It was a close-up of the front of the motel, of a window looking into one of the rooms.

There was a woman looking out, a look of concern on her face.

She had curly hair, wide-set eyes, and there, unmistakable, a mole at the edge of her lip . . .

I lifted my finger to my own lip, tracing my skin until I could feel the mole. It had first started to bother me in middle school, and no amount of pep talks from my mother, telling me just to embrace it, that it made me look like Cindy Crawford, ever made me feel better.

The reality before me was suddenly impossible to ignore, as real as the mole on my face.

This was a picture of me.

Beads of sweat, on my lips, on my forehead. I struggled to catch my breath.

What was going on here?

I reached for the wine, needing it more than ever.

Easy, Kerry.

Shut up, Frank. Why was my likeness in a murdered woman's—or a killer's—sketchbook?

Another glug, my hand grasping the bottle, shaking.

Had someone planned this, brought me here to . . . to what? To torture me, or that woman, whoever she was?

I set down the wine bottle, grabbed the sketchbook in both hands.

What in the world had I gotten myself into? What had been in the works, long before I'd even arrived? Before Maisy sent me that packet? Before I'd even left Brooklyn?

Weeks before, maybe, before the power had gone out, before the snow had fallen, before all of it, someone had sat here, had sketched my likeness in pencil. Had added that mole so there was no way—none—that I could try to tell myself it wasn't me.

Someone had done this, and I had to know who.

My hands shaking harder now, I fumbled over the pages, flipping and flipping until I got to the first one.

I had to know, I had to, and at the beginning of notebooks like this, there were usually a few lines, a place to scrawl, to leave your mark, to claim it as yours.

And then, suddenly, I found it.

This book belongs to . . .

A scream as the book dropped from my quivering hands.

My eyes widened. My pulse pounded. My brain ached, like the wine had swollen it up like a bug bite, was making it press against my skull.

No, I thought. No no no.

This can't be, this can't—

And then, I looked behind me. At the suitcase on the ground.

The chic black clothing. Size 6.

The OPI nail polish. My favorite, but also hers.

The brown hair, falling just past the shoulders.

I looked back to the book, my mind struggling to make sense of it all.

No no no, I thought. But as my brain raced, it was impossible to deny.

The drawings, the notes. She was making a movie—that was it, wasn't it? She was finally, after all this time, making a movie.

I stared at the name in the book, my stomach bottoming out, the fear pulsing through me morphing into sorrow, to pain, to an impossible truth that was staring up at me, daring me to believe it.

This book belongs to Siobhan Jones.

Siobhan, my friend. My friend who hadn't been my friend anymore.

My heart ached with knowing, with grief, with bone-shaking fear.

Siobhan was the caretaker before me.

Siobhan was the woman in that freezer.

Siobhan was dead.

One Month Earlier

8

Siobhan

January 1, 2023
4:02 p.m.

Drive all the way down until you find the last room on the left.

Even Maisy's directions were perfect. Something straight out of a Wes Craven movie.

And this place. I mean, hot *damn.*

I hopped out of the car, camera in hand. "And here we are—M-O-T-E-L," I announced to no one in particular as I panned across the cherry red, larger-than-life letters. This place was a visual dream, like rainbow sherbet turned into lodgings. Carnation-pink brick. Robin's-egg-blue doors. Taxicab-yellow Acapulco chairs. I might as well be flicking through Pantone chips.

"And here's my room," I said, homing in on the end unit. "The famed *Last Room on the Left*," I said, dipping into a deeper register. "The last place our victims were seen. Mwa-ha-ha-ha-ha."

Another quick pan. Then I forced myself to shut up, capturing the ambient noises. The call-and-response of the birds in the sky. The quiet shush of wind through trees. The click and whiz of whatever power source kept an old motel running. The far-off whir of traffic on a distant road.

Back to the car. Camera still running, I grabbed my

suitcase and a big ring of keys, which I used to unlock and dramatically fling open the door. Finally flicked the camera back to me. Raised an eyebrow mischievously. "Heeeeeeere's Siobhan!"

I turned it off, set it carefully on the nightstand, then tossed my bag on the bed, plopped my ass on it, too, bounced a couple of times to check for comfort. Very, *very* nice. Looked around the space. The baby pink Kilim rug. Exposed wooden beams the color of cold brew. Yes, perfect.

What first? Check the directions, of course. I dug in my bag for Maisy's packet and pulled it out, reading quickly over the responsibilities. Set heaters. Check mousetraps. Run the faucets. Et cetera, et cetera. The duties were perfunctory. I was here to focus, to make my movie. Make sure the place didn't burn down while I was at it.

My phone began to vibrate from its spot on the bed. For a moment, I thought—hoped?—it was Kerry, having emerged from whatever hole she'd fallen into. Because she had to be getting tired of rock bottom by now, right? And even if she'd checked into rehab or whatever, you got to make a phone call, didn't you?

But it wasn't Kerry—it was Allison, and I smiled genuinely as I tapped to answer.

"Hey hey," Allison said, her wide, toothy smile and hazel eyes filling my screen. "Tell me Bessie made it and got you there in one piece."

Allison had generously lent me Bessie, her beloved '04 Toyota Corolla, for the month, since she was traveling for the first few weeks of January and cars were a pain in the ass to park in Brooklyn. "Indeed," I said with a laugh.

"A little grumbling and getting her above sixty-five on the highway took Herculean effort, but the CD player worked, and I listened to my old Spice Girls album the entire way."

"Slam your body down and wind it all around," Allison said, deadpan.

"Exactly." I glanced around at a background of blue sky and willowy palm trees. "Where are you again? Bermuda?"

"Cayman Islands," she said. "And it's *work*, remember?"

"Sure it is. Looks absolutely *brutal*, too."

"The life of an ac*tor*," Allison said with flourish. "Really, though, it's so low-budget I had to buy my own plane ticket. Don't be too jealous."

"Still," I said. "Get some sun for me in any case."

"On it." She tossed a bit of hair behind her shoulders, and I glanced from her image on the screen to my thumbnail at the bottom. We were both Final Girls, through and through—basic, brunette white girls. The type who were always the last to die in slasher films—if we were mid-twenties instead of mid-thirties, that was. Still, I'd always been at least a little bit jealous of Allison's looks. Her high cheekbones where mine were round and soft, no matter how much I tried my hand at contouring. Her long-lashed eyes and delicate nose, so much more striking than my own prominent beak. I supposed it was why she'd always been more comfortable in front of the camera, me behind it. Which had worked for our friendship, so far.

"So is the place absolutely perfect?" Allison went on. "Tell me it's perfect."

"Adorable, right?" I stood and briefly zoomed the

camera around, catching every corner, before turning it back to me. "I think I'm going to really lean into it. You know, they design these places to appeal to a certain type of city person—but then it never goes how you planned it. A subtle commentary on Instagram culture, maybe? I'm still working it out. Obviously. But I'm not going to create aimlessly this time. I'm going to make a plan."

"You're going to do great," Allison said. "Now aren't you glad you open my newsletters?"

I smirked. "Yes, I am glad I open your newsletters."

Allison had started "The Creative Journey" weekly newsletter years before, and the thing had grown and grown, bringing her—kid you not—a healthy Substack income. She always listed opportunities in a paragraph at the bottom, and most of them didn't really apply to me—open auditions, elite artist retreats, the sort that occasionally hit me like a Mack Truck with the kind of jealousy none of my friends actually knew about—but for once, this one had. *Perfect Artist's Lodgings Two and a Half Hours from New York City!* After a quick Google search of the Twilite Motel, I'd called up Allison, asked her to put me in touch directly—and immediately. A place to live. A place to work. A place to prove to myself that I could do it. Now, here we were.

"And remember," Allison continued, "quality not quantity this time. Ryan is going to want a clean fifteen minutes."

"I know," I said, feeling myself blush. Creating—it had never been a problem for me. I always *always* had a camera in my hand, whether it was the first camcorder my mom had bought me from the Walmart electronics section or the short-lived Flip camera I used to carry everywhere or one of the myriad iPhones I'd gone through. I had stacks of external hard drives and SD cards, too many stories and Reels and Instagram posts to count, and in my work as an editor for soulless fashion brands, I'd made more sizzle videos than any one human probably should. It's what I'd never understood about Kerry and her constant battle to produce work. She'd done the hard part already— coming up with the idea, getting buy-in. Now she only had to write. Wasn't that supposedly what she liked to do so much?

"He's going to do everything in his capacity to push you through," Allison said. "He promised me a favor."

Of course he did, I thought. People were always doing favors for Allison, men especially, who fell fast— and hard—and who she always managed to keep as friends whether she dated, dumped, or fucked them. She was a charmer, the sort who seemed to know—and be known—by everyone. The Ryan in question was a filmmaker friend of hers who was on the board of a small festival that was quickly gaining clout. I'd dreamed of making a horror movie all my life, but since film school, since one tiny little documentary about a ghost that supposedly haunted my hometown in New Jersey, nada. I was tired of the question—at dinner parties, subway run-ins, everywhere—"Are you still doing your own stuff?"

I was always filming—sure—but I had nothing to show for it.

And now this connection—plus the *money*, of course— was making it all possible.

"I couldn't do it without you," I said. "Really."

"Isn't that the truth?" Allison said mischievously. "Oh, and the last thing: Ryan has some recs for good editors—he sent me an email with their rates. I'll forward it on—you can work it into your budget."

Budget, I thought. Right.

"Anyway," Allison said, looking around her fabulous locale. "I should go. I'm overdue to hair and makeup. But go shoot your dark, horror-loving heart out. And please don't just post a bunch of Reels. Once you get the lay of the land, put your camera down and figure out the plot."

"One step ahead of you," I said. "According to Maisy, the internet is only on through tomorrow. Then it's off for the whole month—she doesn't pay for it in the winter—and the service is apparently spotty."

"Perfection," Allison said. "But wait—how am I going to get in touch with you?"

"I'll go into town to check emails every few days," I said. "And I have a bar or two, so something might go through? But wait till you hear this: There's a *landline*. Let's make sure it works." I walked over to the old phone on the wall and lifted it up, listening to the tone before holding it to my cell, then putting it back on its hook. "Did you hear that? A real live dial tone. What a throwback."

Allison laughed. "Send me the number. And, Siobhan?"

"Yeah?"

"You *got* this. I know you do. And when you get stuck, just ask yourself: What are you going to do with your one wild and precious life?"

I smiled. Allison signed off all her "Creative Journey" newsletters by paraphrasing Mary Oliver. The sentiment was beautiful and simple, and she lived it, too. Better than the rest of us.

"Thank you," I said. "I love you."

"I love you, too," she said. "Now go get to work."

For a hot second, I was high on all of it—the promise, the hope, the possibility of actually. Finally. Making. Something.

I half wanted to skip the unpacking and wander the property, camera in hand, but a text popped up, buzzing against my palm. Flicking my heart into its familiar pitter-patter rhythm.

You can't do this to me, Siobhan.

A beat as he kept on typing.

I want my money back.

9

Siobhan

The pantry, what a gem.

What a perfect little gift from the horror gods.

I'd spent the day before going through every room, filming it all, from cedar closets to claw-footed tubs.

I'd ignored the texts, because of course I had. I'd spent the day exploring instead, sweeping the grounds like some kind of surveyor. But it had been near-dark by the time I'd gotten to the pantry, and I'd wanted to wait until morning so I'd get at least a little natural light.

Boy was I glad I did.

I ran my camera along the shelves, just a spot of daylight filtering in from the open door, making shadows on the reclaimed wood shelves, a raw, lovely contrast to the strength of the iron piping that hooked them to the wall. It was packed with fancy-people food. The kind of stuff I always saw stocked in Kerry's pantry when Charlie and I were over for game night. You know the type. Fair-trade Mexican coffee. Jams with combos that didn't quite make sense: plum and amaretto; kiwi and chia seed; watermelon and jalapeño. Honey made from hemp—who even knew that honey could be made from hemp?

Staples, too, of course, stuff that Charlie had been all

about during his short-lived vegan phase. Rainbow quinoa. Lentils, farro, and amaranth. Honestly, give me some plain rice over all that stuff any day. Couple of bucks for a couple of pounds of it.

I panned across another set of shelves—red potatoes, bronze-cut pasta, tins of stewed tomatoes, jars of pasta sauce, bags of pita chips—then across the door, which I'd left open, rain drizzling lightly outside. Closed-up spaces had made me anxious since my high school boyfriend had locked me in his family's storage shed as an ill-advised prank.

I kept panning, then zoomed in on a deep freezer in the corner, long as a coffin and tall enough to reach my hips. Holy. *Shit*.

The details became clear through the viewfinder of my camera, and I could hardly contain my excitement. The white exterior, yellowing with age, held together with rusted silver bolts and a lock in the middle. My fingers tickled with a mix of anticipation and fear—fear, because the very thought of it made me claustrophobic; anticipation, because it was the perfect device for my film. Little old me had read "pantry" on Maisy's packet and not even stopped to consider that the place could include a deep freezer, the sort that was practically designed to hold a dead body.

"What a thrill for the motel to be the setting for a film!" Maisy had said when we'd met for coffee at a pour-over place in North Brooklyn, before I signed the contract, which included—kid you not—a list of mandatory Instagram posts and essays to author about my "creative time" at the motel once I was back on the grid. Maisy looked a little older than me, maybe early- to mid-forties, her hair streaked with silver and bobbed at her shoulders, with chic angular bangs that had to take frequent trips to the salon to keep up. She wore expensive-looking clothes that skimmed a body I imagined was toned by regular Pilates Reformer classes, and she was the exact type of person who would use the word "film" instead of "movie." She told me that she and her husband "dabbled in real estate" but had done up the motel specifically to draw "artists and thinkers," and I'd done my best not to roll my eyes. What people with money never got was that the artist's life wasn't very glamorous at all. It was either a whole lotta sellout (cue the aforementioned ad agency videos), or it was a whole lotta overdrawn bank accounts. For me, it had, at times, been a mix of both.

Maisy didn't have to concern herself with problems like those. In that one meeting, it was clear to me that she'd begun her journey into adulthood with a trust fund. Hell, her trust funds probably had their *own* trust funds. Because that was how it always was, wasn't it? Pet projects like these?

Didn't matter. Maisy's airs—her single-origin espresso oat milk latte and the diamond bracelet on her wrist— they meant nothing. What mattered was that she was going to let me shoot at the motel for free. Last weekend in February. There'd be another caretaker up then, but she'd promised me they wouldn't be in the way. Which meant I could spend *this* month getting ideas, storyboarding, and writing the damn thing; cast and hire a skeleton crew in February; shoot end of the month; and have a couple of weeks for editing and sound before it was due to Ryan by March 15. It was tight, I knew that, but it was doable. So long as I kept that money.

If you'd told me a couple of years ago that I'd be trying for festivals—with a horror short, of all things—I never would have believed you, but the landscape had changed over the past few years. (Thanks, Jordan Peele et al.) Even though I'd been a fan since my sister and I had worked our way through all our local video store's slashers at the ripe ages of ten and twelve, I'd never thought horror was actually a legitimate path for me. My film program hadn't trended toward genre movies at all. And yet, here was Ryan, a real live filmmaker who regularly got hired on music videos, who attended parties with the Daniels of *Everything Everywhere All at Once* fame, and was currently at work on his first feature, telling me that horror, particularly if I could give it a feminist slant, was now quite a common way in, especially for someone who hadn't made anything in a while.

What's more, it was time. I was thirty-five. No kids. No partner anymore. Down a friend, too. I had to make *something*. I couldn't just keep doing the capitalist grind and pretending that was enough.

What are you going to do with your one wild and precious life?

Mary Oliver had been right. You *did* get only one. And what losing so much recently had taught me was that it really wasn't something to waste.

Camera in my left hand, I approached the freezer, tried opening it with my right. It stuck. Tried again. Wouldn't budge.

I checked for a lock I hadn't noticed, but there wasn't

88

one. So I set my camera on a shelf, pointing it just so, and I bent my legs, really got my weight under it, imagining all sorts of terrors inside. Severed heads. Dismembered arms. Fear and rot.

It took a couple of pulls, then the lid came loose all at once, slamming against the cinderblock wall behind it. For a moment, my heart raced, high, I supposed, on my own morbid imagination, but inside was exactly what you'd expect. Loaves of bread, bags of frozen veggies, and about a million different cuts of what I had to assume was locally sourced meat.

I surveyed it all, plotting. I guess I'd have to ask Maisy if it was okay to move the stuff to shoot. But surely she'd see just how perfect it was? See, my loose idea for the story was that four friends head out on a girls' weekend in the woods, only to realize a serial killer has fled a nearby prison and is at large. Of course, I'd put my own spin on it—mainly, I was thinking one of the girls would be responsible for the violence, not the serial killer at all. Turn the trope on its head, all that. Your friends can be more dangerous than strangers, that kind of a thing. Wherever I landed, the freezer would be the absolute perfect place for a first body to turn up . . .

Slam!

The room went dark, and my shoulders jolted as I whipped around, the hairs on the back of my neck standing straight up as I rushed toward the shut door.

My foot landed on something wet—probably rain I'd tracked in—and I slipped, falling straight on my ass. I scrambled up quickly, the smell of wood chips and propane and paint thinner in my nostrils. The way I'd clawed at the inside of that storage shed so fiercely I'd gotten splinters. The look on my boyfriend's face when he'd opened it twenty minutes later, cheeks red from laughing . . .

Don't be locked, don't be locked, don't be locked, I prayed as I felt for the doorknob.

Finally I found it, turned it, pushed with all my weight.

In an instant, I was out, back in the daylight, back on the grass, back in the lightly falling rain, looking at the lawn and the fire pit and the empty motel.

I sucked in air, steeling my breaths, trying to calm my quickly beating heart.

Slam!

I turned back, saw that the lid of the freezer had shut, too.

A gust of wind whipped across my face, and I felt instantly foolish, overdramatic. The wind, of course. The wind had blown the door shut. It was my own fault for not securing my only exit with a doorstop.

You are not fourteen. Your douchebag boyfriend is long gone, probably married with lots of kids, probably tortures a whole family with his stupid mind games. But you're okay. You're okay.

Another deep breath, and as I was about to turn back, I saw them.

There, beneath me, in the mud.

Footprints. Right outside the door.

Far too large to be mine.

10

Kerry

I hadn't seen Siobhan in sixty days, and I knew that for a fact, a number that ticked itself off each morning in my head, one I couldn't escape no matter how much I wanted to.

I stared at the book, scratching absently at my bottom lip. How could this be? How could it be *her*?

But the words were right there, of course, impossible to ignore:

This book belongs to Siobhan Jones.

This was real. That woman out there, it was *her*.

My face began to feel hot, and my chest ached, weighty. The world—my world—seemed to stand still on its axis, no longer spinning, and my vision began to blur, her name merging into alphabet soup behind my tears.

I tried to wipe them away, but a sob took me instead, and I found my shoulders hunching over the book, my body shaking.

No, I thought again. No, it can't be.

But it was. Christ almighty, it was.

And then, suddenly, the heat in my face was concentrating on my cheeks, burning with shame, with regret.

I pressed my hands against them, trying to cool them down, looked again at the name in the journal.

It'd been two months since Siobhan and I talked. Sixty days that I had no idea would be—that *shouldn't* have been—her last.

My chin dropped to my chest. How could things have gone differently if I'd never cut her out of my life?

Those days could have been spent going to get coffee or taking long walks around Prospect Park, dissecting our lives—the horrors of IVF and the strain it was putting on my relationship with Frank; the way she feared sometimes that Charlie would get tired of her, that his eye would wander to someone more classically beautiful, someone like Allison, whom Siobhan was always, always comparing herself to. Those days could have been—*should* have been—filled with the couples nights we used to have, Frank's nerdiness and Charlie's artiness a Venn diagram with artfully crafted indie board games in the middle.

If I hadn't cut her out, would she even have come here? Was it somehow all my fault?

Don't, Kerry, Imaginary Frank tried to comfort me. *You didn't kill her. Someone else did. It's not on you.*

But I pushed away the thought of Frank's kindness. I owed it to her to tell her what was going on. She deserved so much better than to be abandoned by me without any explanation. I had been so naive, so sure, somewhere in the back of my mind, that what had happened between us wouldn't be a permanent goodbye. That, in time, I would find a way to fix things with her . . . somehow . . . but I hadn't been ready. And now there was no time. There was no opportunity to text her, to apologize.

Now, she was gone, her life stolen from her, and here I was, surrounded by her things, holding her journal.

Her journal with a picture of me in it. Why had she drawn me, and sitting in the motel of all places? Had she known I was coming here? Had Allison found out from Maisy, passed it down the line like a game of telephone? I shook my head almost viciously, the thought too much— down, down, down it went—then I slammed the journal shut and tossed it onto the bed.

The shock, the shame, the *grief* were overwhelming, and part of me wanted to crawl into bed, shut out the world, and swim through the sadness, but I couldn't, could I? Someone had killed Siobhan; someone had *moved* Siobhan. There was no power, a snowstorm, the cops long gone, and I was stuck here. So I took deep breaths, trying, desperately, to focus, to process this new information, to figure out what it all meant. She was here to make her film—or, as she would say, movie; Siobhan was free of pretentions. That much was clear from the journal. And then it hit me head-on, so obvious, so clear—*she* was the one who would have been shooting up here the last weekend of February. We would have been forced to see each other once again. But now none of that was possible, was it?

Focus, Imaginary Frank was saying. *Stop shaming yourself and focus for a minute. Figure out what you have to do to keep yourself safe. I may not want anything to do with you right now, I may even hate you sometimes, but I don't want you to get hurt. I don't want to find you jammed in some freezer, too.*

Okay, I thought. Okay, Frank, okay.

And I'm sorry, Siobhan. I'm so very sorry. I'm so sorry that I wasn't there for you and this is what happened.

93

Another sob took me over, but I brushed away the tears, forcing myself to think straight. Something had happened to my friend, but when exactly? Between the last night she was here and when I'd arrived the next day. I knew it had to be then because there'd been that party; Tyler had confirmed it. And he'd said himself that the prior caretaker was there. Besides, her bags were packed like she'd been about to leave, but she hadn't. It must have happened that night, in fact, because if she'd woken up the next morning—alive and well—she surely would have started cleaning up, especially if she had to check out.

Only who would want to hurt Siobhan—and why? She was such a kind, such a positive, such a lovely, brilliant person. I'd never deserved her—and Charlie hadn't, either.

Charlie. His behavior had gotten more and more erratic as his drinking had increased. She'd told me as much. Was it possible that he'd been up here with her, that the party had led to some sort of argument?

That he'd . . .

No. I shook my head, my chest constricting, and pushed the thought away. Not Charlie. Not like that. No way. I turned back to the room, looking around. Shouldn't Siobhan's camera be somewhere? And maybe that footage would have some answers, would somehow tell me what to do next. Would help me figure out who had done this to her, so I could protect myself but for another reason, too—so I could make them pay.

Surveying the room now felt different. Checking the bathroom, knowing all the makeup, all the toiletries, were hers. Pawing through the other suitcase. Opening cabinets

94

and drawers, trying to find whatever my friend had left behind in her last moments on earth. I was beginning to think that whoever had hurt her had taken her camera, as well as any other identifying details, like her wallet and phone and ID, when I found myself on my knees against the patterned rug, looking beneath the white-pine bed frame, and there, atop a scattering of dust, was a camera. I reached for it, hungry for information, for answers, to see what was happening with Siobhan in the last days and weeks of her life. To see who had done this to her. Who had hurt her even more than I had.

Pulling it to me, I scrambled to find a power button, finally locating it at the top. I pushed it, again and again, but there was nothing more than the flicker of a dead-battery icon.

There were no answers here. No answers anywhere while the power remained out.

So what next?

What would Frank do? Practical Frank.

He would stop drinking, for one, but what about after that?

Frank would size up the situation, take an inventory of the tools at hand, like he always did.

Slow down, he was always saying. You don't have to be in such a rush. But that's the way I always was. Once I made the decision, I was full-in.

I hadn't wanted to do IVF and then once I'd come around, I'd obsessed about it with fervor.

I hadn't wanted to go back to drinking, but once the bottle was open, I practically fell right in.

I hadn't wanted to do a lot of things that I ended up doing.

There was a main office, and Maisy had mentioned in her packet that some extra phone cords and electronics chargers were kept there. Was it possible there were some sorts of backup power packs, ones I could use to charge my phone or this camera? If cell service returned before the power did, it wouldn't be any use if my phone was dead.

Another gulp of wine and a deep breath to follow; then I grabbed the journal and the camera, made for the door. I trudged through the snow, ears pricked for any kind of noise, until I got to the main office, situated right on the edge of the L's corner. I fumbled with the key ring, then checked the largest key first. It worked. I turned the knob and tried to push it open, but the door was stuck. Tossing the weight of my body against the door, I pushed again, but nothing. One more push, and it shoved open, about half a foot. I looked down, the obstruction instantly clear.

A manila envelope, wedged into the crack.

Siobhan Jones was printed across it, moisture from the snow making the S of her name bleed. I grabbed it, ran my nail under the flap, reached inside to find a stack of four or five papers, my eyes scanning quickly across a spate of legalese, the bottoms of the pages warping with water damage. I caught Siobhan's name once again, and then, the knowledge like a weight in my stomach, Charlie's. I kept reading, hungry for information, until my eyes locked on a number.

Twenty-five thousand dollars.

It took another minute for it to all fully connect.

Charles Mathis, the man Siobhan had been so worried about losing, who had been the topic of conversation on nearly every one of our walks and coffees and drinks nights and meetups. The man who'd schooled me in board games, who'd always been the one to order an extra round of drinks.

The man I knew wasn't good enough for her—a screwup, just like me.

Charlie was suing Siobhan for thousands upon thousands of dollars.

Money she probably didn't have.

I slipped the papers back into the envelope, then folded it in half, tucked it into the outer pocket of my coat, and approached the front desk.

There was mail there, too. A stack of bills and a couple of packages, all addressed to Maisy, and then, right on top, something that didn't fit with the rest.

Eight and a half by eleven, a sheet of computer paper, crumpled on the edges but clear as day—in bright red Sharpie, scrawled in capital letters across the page.

TAKE CARE OF YOUR MESS

My mind turned with possibilities as I tried to hold back more panic. Was this directed toward Siobhan, who had left the place in such disarray, or was it aimed at the killer, who'd first abandoned her body out there in the snow before moving her to the freezer? Either way, it was horrifying, wasn't it? Somehow more cutting, more creepy, than if it had been an outright violent threat.

Take care of your mess. It could mean so many things, couldn't it? A physical mess but a figurative one, too. Taking care of my mess was exactly what I'd been trying to do coming here, picking up the pieces of the chaos I'd made of my life.

And yet things had only gotten messier. Had the same been true for Siobhan? Would I know if I hadn't ghosted her, if I hadn't been so cruel?

I lifted the paper and flipped it over, checking to see if there was anything else, but was met only with blankness.

I turned it back around, my eyes returning to the message, angry and red—

TAKE CARE OF YOUR MESS

—my heart cinched up as I folded that paper as well, tucking it into my coat next to the lawsuit.

So much had happened in those sixty days, so much that had gone terribly, irrevocably wrong.

What mess were you in, Siobhan?

And why hadn't I been there to help?

11

Siobhan

January 3, 2023
7:27 a.m.

Clank, clank, clank! Clank, clank, clank!

My eyes burst open, and I fumbled for my phone. It wasn't even eight o'clock.

Clank, clank, clank! Clank, clank, clank!

What in the world was that god-awful sound? Wait until I told Allison that my country escape came with people banging about at ungodly hours of the morning. I could just picture her laughing.

I pushed back the covers and forced myself out of bed, struggling to adjust. I'd spent the night indulging in a meal of sourdough bread and a can of lobster bisque from the pantry—in addition to looking over the footage I'd shot so far while the soundtrack to *Twin Peaks* played in the background—delighting in the creepy vibes. In a place like this, even your own footprints could start to freak you out.

Because they *were* my own footprints, that's what I'd decided as I'd caught them close-up on my camera. Widened a bit by mud but otherwise mine. Had I wanted to call Allison—or Kerry, or, hell, even Charlie—to talk me down? Of course. But what I'd promised myself in coming up here, in addition to finally focusing on making this short, was that I would stop running away from my own company and get used to being alone.

As a thirty-five-year-old woman who'd been living in the city since twenty-two and had always been surrounded by a mashup of roommates, besties, and boyfriends, I'd never had to do that—to just be me.

But when you lose your boyfriend and one of your closest friends in a matter of weeks, well—you realize that maybe self-reliance is a good skill to have.

Clank, clank, clank!

"Christ," I said aloud, turning to a potted succulent on the window ledge, as there was no one else to turn to. "Can you believe this shit?"

Charlie used to laugh when he'd come across me narrating my own life, a habit picked up from always having a camera in my hand.

I stumbled out of bed, put on some clothes, and slipped my feet into Birkenstocks, then stole a quick glance at myself in the mirror—mussed-up hair, mascara smeared beneath my lids—lord knew why I was even applying the stuff when I was out here on my own, but old habits, et cetera.

Outside, I stepped across the grass, half green, half yellow, the blades tickling the back of my heels. It was supposed to be some sort of snowy escape up here in the winter, but I'd yet to see a single flake. I wasn't even wearing socks. The sound clanked on from my left, and I walked around the side of the motel and toward the east edge of the property, following the gravel path.

The racket was coming from the giant dumpster, lid tossed open, where a pickup sat, half parked on the gravel drive, half on the grass. For a moment, my horror mind imagined some monster in there, ready to eat me alive. *Be afraid, be very afraid.* But I stepped forward, and instead of an enormous mutant fly, a black trash bag came soaring out, landing just in front of my feet with a nauseating squish. A beat later, another bag flew, this one made of clear plastic, tied up and filled to the brim with bottles, which clattered against the gravel, the sound ringing in my ears.

A woman popped up then, hair fully gray and cut short above her ears. Her face was wrinkled and free of makeup, her eyes deep-set. She had to be at least fifty, but her body was lithe, her arms taut. She pressed herself up, hooked a leg over the rim, and tossed herself over.

"What do you think you're doing?" I asked. "This is private property. You can't just—"

"Ha!" she said. "Yes, it's private property. *My* private property. Which I've told Maisy over and over again," she said, a strong hand landing on her hip. Her voice was raspy and the kind of deep you only got from at least a decade of cigarettes. She punctuated her sentence with a cough.

"I don't get it," I said. "This is part of the motel property."

"No, it's not," the woman said. "See the end of those outbuildings?" She pointed about fifteen feet ahead. "That's where the motel land ends. This gravel. This area. It's all mine. And I'm not going to have trash just sitting on my property."

She grabbed the black trash bag then, spun around, and tossed it with all her might, as if she were an Olympian hurling a discus. The bag landed with a thud halfway between the drive and the outbuildings.

Then she grabbed the recycling and tossed it in her truck. "These I'll take. Valuable bottle deposits, wasted. Maisy makes a whole thing about having her guests recycle and never tells them that she puts it all in the same dumpster." She scoffed and then tugged at the bottom of a Grateful Dead T-shirt. Hell, maybe she smoked a bowl every day instead of a pack of Marlboros. "A lot of booze here for just a couple of days."

My baby hairs stood on end, and I stared at the woman, imagined her watching me arrive, step out of Allison's crappy little car, load my bags into my room. "It's not even mine," I said. "There were people here before me. I barely drink." It was true. Between Charlie and Kerry, I'd nearly lost my taste for the stuff. "And it's none of your business anyway."

The woman shut the tailgate of the pickup, then walked around, opening the driver's-side door before turning back to me. "Well, when Maisy starts respecting the property lines, then maybe it won't be. Until then, I'm forced to make it my business, especially with you people in a regular rotation."

"You *people*?" I asked, completely taken aback.

The woman's eyes scanned me, top to bottom, her disdain thinly veiled. "From the city. You *are* from the city, right? Maisy pretty much only brings in her sort."

"And what sort is that?"

The woman had one foot propped along the edge of the pickup now, ready to heave herself in, but she tilted her head, staring at me. "You know. Fancy. Creatives, that's the word she always uses." She coughed again. "Everyone who thinks they can come up here, come into our towns, our neighborhoods, buy up all the properties, not even get the goddamned lines right, and kick us out." She smirked. "But not all of us leave, of course. I certainly won't."

She tapped her foot against the side of her pickup, and that was when I noticed it, a beat-up pair of Timberland work boots, ones that would leave big prints, mud or no mud.

"Were you . . ." I hesitated. "Were you following me yesterday? Around the outbuildings?"

The woman crossed her arms. "Like I have nothing better to do than follow folks like a lost puppy. Watch as you all come up here, full of complaints. The water pressure's not good enough. The walls are too drafty. The pool isn't heated to a perfect seventy-eight degrees. You come up, thinking you're going to find yourself in a place like this—" She gestured around, at the land, the mountains, the trees, the sky. "But you don't belong here. We all know it."

Goosebumps rose on my skin, and I could practically feel the door shutting, locking me in. *Slam!*

"Wait," I said. "What am I supposed to do with this trash?"

The woman hopped into the cab then pulled the door shut, the window still cracked. "You're all the same, you know. You drink yourselves silly and leave the trash behind for the locals to take care of."

I walked up to her, fuming with anger and laced with fear. "I told you, it's not even mine. And you can't just throw trash onto the lawn."

The woman smirked, then turned the key, revving the engine. "I hope you find what you're looking for up here," she said, an eyebrow raised. "But I doubt you will."

She put the truck into reverse, tapped her foot to the gas. I leapt away, afraid she might hit me if I didn't.

"After all, you can get away from the city . . ." She paused, eyes piercing. "But you can't get away from yourself."

12

Siobhan

The next morning, I walked toward the outbuildings, bracing myself to see the trash again tossed out into the yard with the gusto of a woman who must be fully mad, but the lawn was empty.

I'd put the bag back into the dumpster as soon as she'd driven off, knowing if it got left it would be rifled through by animals, and promptly emailed the whole thing to Maisy, who had assured me that the neighbor, Denise Rice, was one hundred percent in the wrong about the lines and that I should continue to use the receptacle as instructed—and email again if I ran into any trouble.

No trouble so far, thank god. A small load of wash in my hands, mud from the day before on the ankles of my favorite jeans, I twisted the handle of the laundry room door, flicked on the light. Took in a small room painted bright white with a checkered linoleum floor, four washer-dryers stacked neatly on one side, shelves full of supplies, from detergent to flashlights, on the other.

A moment to imagine: The room in darkness, only the moodiest of lighting, the whites of eyes. Pure fear and a utilitarian feel, the sound of only a beating heart and then something falling, like that kitchen scene in *Jurassic Park*, the sound of metal on metal giving away a location, turning terrifying.

The *sound*.

I shook myself out of my imaginings, realized something was off.

A mechanical rumbling, a *whoosh whoosh whoosh*.

I approached the washer, stopped short. It was running. Six minutes left on the cycle. I pushed the power button, got an off-tone beep. Too far along to stop.

Outside, I paced back and forth.

"It's nothing," I said under my breath, trying to convince myself. "It's nothing."

But I found myself turning toward the gravel road. Toward the dumpster. If Denise had done that, she surely could have done this. But *why*?

Back inside, another minute left. I waited, watching, tearing at a bit of nail. Finally the click of the door unlocking. I turned the handle, pulled it back.

Towels and sheets. Looked like the same ones from the rooms. Why would someone break into the laundry room to do a load of the motel's own wash? Had Maisy—or a housekeeper—done it and forgotten it, and then the machine somehow tripped and restarted? Faulty wiring? Was that even a thing?

I tossed my own load into one of the other washers, added detergent, and got the hell out of there. Locked the door tight behind me. I was on my way back to my room when I heard the crunch of gravel in the lot.

"That *fucking* woman," I said, but as soon as I got out front, I saw it wasn't her at all.

A white SUV had pulled up to the front of the office.

One of those new all-electric trucks that Charlie had told me about. I took quick strides, waving as I walked.

The passenger window rolled down, and I saw a woman about my age who looked like she'd spent a lot of money to *not* look my age.

"Can I help you?"

Her eyes widened with what could only be described as *glee*. "We read about this place in *The New York Times*," she said, turning, briefly, to the man beside her, a clean-cut buttoned-up sort who looked far less excited than she was. "We called but couldn't get through, so we decided to just stop by. We're on our way to Mohonk for a babymoon."

She paused, and I realized that she was waiting for me to say something.

"Congratulations." I forced a smile.

"Thank you," she said. "Due in July! I'm hardly even showing, so you wouldn't know—plus I guess I'm in a car and all."

"Babe—" the man said. "I'm sure she doesn't need to hear about all that." *Definitely* not as excited as she was.

"Right," she said, turning back to me. "Can we book your nicest room? Just one night."

"Oh," I said. "No. Sorry."

Her face scrunched up. "But the place looks empty," she said.

"Yes," I said. "We're closed for the winter."

She stared at me. "So you're just up here—all on your own?"

I nodded.

"You're the owner?"

"The caretaker," I said.

"Oh." Her face fell. "And you're sure you can't make an exception?"

I shook my head.

She stared at me a moment longer, and I got the sense that she was used to the world bending to suit her. "Well, I guess we won't be staying, then."

"I guess you won't." It was out of my mouth before I even realized it.

The woman's eyes widened. "Well," she said with a huff. "It's too empty anyway." She raised an eyebrow. "Good luck. If it were me, I'd be scared as anything, out here all on my own."

She rolled up her window, and the car purred away, barely making a sound. I stared ahead until they were gone, then I went back to my room and grabbed the car keys, my skin already beginning to crawl.

The "town," if it could be called that, a full twenty minutes away, was little more than a liquor store, a small grocery, and a hardware shop that looked like it had seen better days.

Couple of months ago, I would have hit the liquor store first. Grabbed a few bottles of wine if nothing else. But drinking had lost its appeal, so I went straight into food shopping mode, heading into the store and filling a small cart with produce and eggs, cheeses and two large bottles of local kombucha that cost way too much and frankly looked a bit dusty, like they'd been stocked for city visitors during the high season and left to wait until more folks arrived in the spring.

The woman at the register put down a beat-up copy of

People magazine before silently scanning my items. In the corner, one of those convex mirrors looked down on me, turning the scene to a fish-eye. I realized it then, in a way that I hadn't been able to really vocalize before. The motel gave me the distinct feeling of being watched. And it wasn't just the intensity of the neighbor or the strangeness of the running washer.

It was the sounds, for one. A creaking up on the roof. A rustling from the back lawn. A shushing within the walls. I'd told myself there were explanations. The place had been built in 1956, which put it at nearly seventy years old. I figured, like most renovations up here, it was a largely superficial makeover, the Instagram special—designed to appeal to the couple who had pulled into the lot only an hour ago. There were a million and one reasons for an old place like this to creak—pipes; old lumber; a settling, or sinking, foundation. But I found myself not only talking to the succulents, one of which I'd lovingly named Spikey—she was an aloe plant, after all—but making sure music was always playing from my speaker, when I wasn't shooting, at least.

I was all paid up, shopping bags in each hand, when I saw him, crossing the parking lot in wide, confident strides.

"Charlie?" I said, my feet practically glued to the sidewalk, my hands clenched around the bags, the kombucha bottles clinking against each other like some sort of fucked-up wind chimes.

"Shiv," he said, his head tilted to the side. No one shortened my name, but he'd become obsessed with the diminutive after we'd binge-watched *Succession* together.

I'd once thought it was impossibly sweet. Sometimes I guessed I still did.

Charlie stepped onto the sidewalk, only a foot or two from me, and I was hit instantly with that feeling, right in the pit of my stomach. Butterflies. Followed by an awful bit of nausea.

"Fancy seeing you here," he said, a rakish glint in his eyes.

What you had to understand about Charlie was that he was incredibly good-looking, an actual verifiable ten. It wasn't any one feature either—sure, there were the big dark eyes, the thick, dirty-blond hair, the chiseled jaw that somehow always seemed to have just the right amount of stubble—but it was so much more than that. People used to come up to him, convinced they recognized him from one TV show or another. He had that kind of face you'd expect to see on a screen, playing an upstart lawyer fighting for justice—or a moody professor who can only be softened by the love of the right girl.

"I don't understand. I thought you were in Berlin?"

He raised an eyebrow. "I was, for a week or two. Saw the galleries, met a few artists. Got tired of the bitter cold. Came back."

"To upstate New York?" I asked. "I said I needed space. The plan—"

"I know," Charlie said. "Trust me, I know. I'm as surprised as you are. But I sure am glad to see you, in any case."

The earnestness in his voice caught me off guard. "So why did you come back, then? *Really?*"

Charlie pulled his bomber jacket tighter. "Look, it's freezing out here. If you really want to talk, can we go somewhere warm at least?" Charlie nodded to his BMW

SUV, parked two spaces over from Allison's old Toyota. "You can crank the heat on the leather seats, like you always liked to."

Charlie was already walking toward the car, the doors unlocking from his sheer proximity. He opened the passenger side for me, and reluctantly I got in, setting the bags on the floor of the car and sinking into the luxurious seat. He got in on the other side, pushed to start the engine. The sound of Dinah Washington filled the spaces between us.

"You still listen to her?" I asked.

Nearly three years before, tucked away over twenty-dollar cocktails in a cozy booth of a Brooklyn Heights bar, I'd adamantly argued that Dinah Washington, while never as famous as Etta James or Nina Simone, was just as good—if not better. Charlie had said he'd give her a listen, and he had. Now, the chorus of "Cry Me a River" filled the car, and it felt impossibly appropriate. Because my heart was still broken. Sometimes it felt irreparable.

"Of course I do," Charlie said. He turned down the volume slightly, then tapped a couple of buttons. I felt the seat begin to warm beneath my ass. "I always loved your taste in music," he said, his eyes practically boring into mine. "I loved your taste in everything, really."

I adjusted myself in the seat, and the bags clinked below. "It's kombucha," I said. "Not booze."

He rested his hands on the steering wheel. "I wouldn't care if it was."

Charlie could never see what I did, that he had a problem—a real one. If he could, then maybe I could forgive. But if not even this would change, how was I supposed to believe the rest of it would, too?

"Just tell me why you're here," I said.

"Storm King," he said.

"The outdoor museum?"

"Yes," he said. "They're thinking of partnering with the gallery. It could be big for us. The name recognition and the exposure. It could bring in a whole new set of clientele. I got word when I was in Berlin. I could have sent one of the junior gallerists to take the meeting, but I didn't want to. It's a huge opportunity." He shrugged. "So here I am. What about you?"

"I took a job up here. Caretaking. Allison set it up. So I could have time and space to write the movie. Storyboard it, figure it all out."

Silence between us a moment. Charlie looked down at his hands.

You can't do this to me, Siobhan. I want my money back.

"Why did you send me those texts?"

It took a second, but Charlie finally looked up. "I had a few in the airport on a layover on the way back, and I don't know, I was tired of the radio silence from you. I thought you'd at least respond. And then you didn't even argue with me. You didn't even write back."

I swallowed. "I didn't know what to say. You acted like I *stole* money from you."

Charlie just looked at me, not saying another word.

"Charlie," I said. "You gave it to me—freely. For exactly this purpose."

"I didn't give you that money as some sort of business patron—you know that as well as I do. I gave it to you as your boyfriend, your partner, because I loved you—because I *love* you—" he corrected himself. "You *know* that."

My face went hot, and my eyes found my hands, my nails, coated in my favorite shade of red, Big Apple. I stared at them, picking at a slight chip on the edge of my left thumb, for once silent.

"People move on from worse, Siobhan," Charlie said finally.

"Do they?" I asked, my eyes catching his. "Do people regularly pound booze and do coke and flirt with every woman within eyesight and carry on like they're twenty-five and single and not forty fucking years old with a live-in partner?"

Charlie winced, and I could see he was hurt, and I wanted to hurt him even more. Put it all out there. "Do people regularly fuck random women in bars?"

Karaoke for his fortieth birthday. His friends and mine. One of those private booths in Koreatown. Madonna, Jay-Z, Blondie, and Elvis crooned into microphones. A simple, festive night. But the booze had been strong, and my friends had already started to peel away. And then my own head had gone all swimmy, and it was barely past midnight, but I'd known it was time to go. I'd told Charlie I had to get home, and yes, I'd been disappointed that he hadn't wanted to come, that he wanted to stay and sing a few more, but it was his birthday, after all, and a big birthday, too, and he and his buddies had already loaded up NSYNC on the machine. So I'd told him to be careful, and then I'd put myself into a cab, chugged water when I'd gotten back to our apartment, passed out on top of the covers, clothes still on.

I hadn't heard Charlie come in, but I'd woken early, before him. I always had trouble sleeping after a night of heavy drinking. The bed was empty, and I'd rushed to the living room, wanting to make sure he'd gotten home safely. A bloom of relief in my chest when I spotted him, and I was already planning where we'd go to brunch that morning, overdue birthday sex that afternoon. Then I saw it, on the collar of his white undershirt, on the cleft of his chin. Red lipstick. I didn't wear red on my lips, only my nails. For a second, my mind had still made excuses. It was a birthday, after all, and we were all drunk. Maybe Allison, who did wear the color, had wrapped her arms around him and given him a playful celebratory kiss on the cheek between songs. But I knew nothing could have *actually* happened between them, because she'd left even before I did. Besides, it was *Allison*. She *wouldn't*. She could have any guy in the world. Why would she go after mine?

Then I'd seen his coat, tossed in front of the door, which he hadn't even locked behind him, he must have been so drunk. I reached into his pocket, like I had so many times, after so many nights. Always looking for proof, always happy I never found it.

Only this time, I did. A condom wrapper, open and empty, the kind they hand out for free in bar bathrooms. I'd immediately thrown up, immediately known that all my fears had been correct.

Now, Charlie looked at me, sadness in his eyes. "It was a mistake, Siobhan. A freak thing. A—"

"But it wasn't," I said. "Because I always worried that you weren't really mine. I told myself that you were just a charmer, maybe even a flirt. I told myself that you liked to party, have a good time. I told myself that lots of people in your world did the same. But I always wondered when you were going to slip up. I always *knew* you would. And you proved me right. And now you can't even admit you have a drinking problem. I mean, *Christ.*"

"Because I don't. Because it was a onetime occurrence. It was a—"

"No, Charlie," I said. "It was something that was building for a long, long time. And it will happen again if I let it."

I reached for the door.

"Wait," he said. His hand was on my elbow, the slightest bit of pressure there. He looked down, as if he hadn't even realized he'd done it, then let me go. "You can't just do this. You can't just—god—take my money and ignore me."

But I couldn't give it back. It was earmarked for the freelance editor. The sound guy. Without it, I couldn't make the movie. Without it, my one chance to finally create something would disappear. Poof.

"And what if I do?"

His eyes widened, and for a second, the mask of kindness, of love, it slipped, and I saw anger, hot and raw, instead. But then, just as quickly, it was gone. "Give us another chance, Shiv. *Please.*"

"I have to go," I said, grabbing the bags at my feet.

His hand was on my elbow again, squeezing just slightly. "Please. I love you."

I shook him off, opened the door, and got out.

"Wait," he said.

I turned back. "What?"

"You have to make a choice," he said, eyes serious now. "You take me back, or I take back the money."

I glared at him, and I felt anger flare within myself now, and I half wanted to drop the bags to the ground, fish out one of the dusty bottles of kombucha, and chuck it right at him, smash it into his perfect, beautiful head.

But I turned instead, stalking across the parking lot.

I didn't look back.

Not until I was back in Allison's car, revving the old engine, begging it to go faster, peeling away.

Back to the motel. Away from Charlie.

Away from the guy who had made me love him. Who had made me feel so lucky, so chosen.

But who'd broken my heart in the end.

Fuck you, Charlie, I thought as I pulled out of the lot.

Fuck you for hurting me.

Fuck you for being exactly who I feared you were.

I'm never giving you your damn money back.

13

Kerry

February 2, 2023
2:16 p.m.

In a drawer of the motel's front desk, I found a tangle of cords, messed up together like electronic spaghetti: iPhone chargers, micro USB, USB-C, all the sorts of connections that the modern world demands we have. I pushed the knot aside, looking for power packs or backup batteries, my fingers brushing against a file folder instead, *APPLICANTS* written in Sharpie across the front.

My eyebrows narrowed, and I pulled it out, setting it on the desk and opening it.

I found a printout of an Instagram profile, a man's handle and photo, a few lines about him—*IT guy working on my first screenplay in Queens*—and next to that his stats, following and followers, the latter number, a little more than a thousand, circled in red, a large X next to it.

There was a woman on the next page. Maybe early twenties. *Brooklyn-based YA fantasy writer. Equal parts sweet and sarcastic. #AmWriting she/her/hers.* Next to her numbers, a bit more substantial than the guy's, were handwritten notes in red: *Too young? Not yet published but has an agent. Very pretty.*

My stomach turned, and I flipped another page.

A picture of bright-orange dyed hair, the face mostly

obscured. Handle: *MissMaryMac06*. Name: *McKenzie Rivers*. About the same number of followers as the previous woman. Only next to hers, written in caps and underlined so hard it partially tore the paper: *NO*.

Flipped again, and there was Siobhan, her name and handle, her bio—*"Promising film student" turned Reel-maker extraordinaire. Jersey girl in Brooklyn. Will stop to pet dogs.*

Siobhan's healthy follower count was circled. Her Reels—mainly just her being Siobhan in the city, had always done well enough. She was so damn good at making them but had no interest in becoming an influencer. She just liked to capture what she saw. Hell, I was the one who had told her that her follower count had surpassed ten thousand. She hadn't even noticed. Beneath her stats, more handwritten notes, bulleted this time:

- *Great following and reach*
- *Allison Romy vouches*
- *Decently good-looking, potential brand ambassador?*
- *Hasn't made anything of note since college*

Again, my stomach soured, and another wave of grief—of guilt—took me over, bringing fresh tears to my eyes. It was awful to see Siobhan like this, reduced to what I assumed was Maisy's note-taking. Siobhan was dead now. Siobhan had come here to make something and been killed, and this was all she was to Maisy, the woman who'd triggered the first domino to put it all in motion? No more than numbers and avatars, quippy little words in a character-count-limited bio. It was sick. Twisted.

My vision blurred again, because I couldn't believe she was gone. I couldn't believe this was it for her.

I brushed my tears aside and continued flipping through a few more pages, a few more equally nauseating notes, and then there was mine.

The profile picture, one that Frank had captured candidly one morning, me looking over the top of my MacBook, coffee on one side, a notepad on the other. "This should be your author photo," he'd said a bit naively. "It's so *author-y*!" That was back before the big book deal. Back when Frank was my biggest—and only—fan. I remember thinking that if I ever got a deal, no way would that be my author photo—I'd get a professional one—but what I loved about that moment was the way Frank just treated it as a fait accompli. Next to that were the numbers that had exploded after *The New Yorker* story had taken off and beneath it all the grid of photos that made it seem like nothing about me was a lie.

My page was scrawled with notes.

- *Great following*
- *New Yorker and Vogue bylines*
- *Book deal/film deal*
- *Pretty/intellectual*
- *Definitely brand ambassador candidate*
- *February*

So here it was, not only Maisy's but in a way the world's assessment of me. It was wild, seeing it like this, because it had all seemed so important. My agent had gone on and on about how the numbers boded well for the book doing well, too (if I could ever finish it, that was), and yet now it all seemed so *frivolous*. It was a lie, through and through. Nothing about this was what my life felt like.

You only got one life, after all, and in the end, did any of this matter? Had any of this protected Siobhan? Saved her from a horrible fate that *no one* deserved, least of all her . . .

Crack!

I jolted at the sound, followed by a clear, thundering *thump* coming from outside. I looked up, through the wide picture window, saw a flood of white thudding against the patio, powdery flakes ballooning out, like a full bag of flour dropped on a bakery's floor. A mass of snow, right where the patio had only moments before been protected. Was the motel's roof caving in? Was this place going to fall apart around me, crumble under the weight of snow, yet another thing going wrong?

Another *crack*, and I rushed for the door, tugged it open, burst out onto the patio, looked up to see, just as I had suspected, the awning split like a seam of a too-tight pair of pants, buckling under the snow, shingles and wood and sheetrock buckling and breaking apart, falling to the ground like confetti, creating a clear chasm, one you could see right through up to the sky.

Not wanting to be crushed, I stepped away, out of the danger zone, but when I looked forward once again, there she was, staring at me.

She was only about ten feet away, and in the bright sunlight, the reflection of the blankets of white snow, I could see her so clearly.

A woman—no, a girl. Not even twenty, if I had to guess. With stick-straight icy-blond hair that hung limp across her shoulders. A faded and ragged red wool coat, the middle toggle buttons missing. Combat boots laced halfway up her calves. Piercing blue eyes trained unflinchingly on me.

"Who are you?" I asked, pressure building in my chest. "What are you doing here?"

My words seemed to break the spell, the trance she'd been in, because she turned, bolting across the snow, gait long, running as quickly as she could in her clunky boots.

"Wait," I said. On instinct, I chased her, needing to know who she was, why she'd been standing there, out in the parking lot, staring at me.

Almost like she'd been *waiting*.

The girl was too quick—so much younger than me, so much faster.

"Wait!" I said again, forcing myself forward, through the drifts, across the parking lot. She was heading toward the road, but what then? She couldn't possibly have a car—I would have seen it, wouldn't I? "Please just wait!"

The girl scrambled out into the road. I followed, lungs sucking in bitterly cold air, my chest already heaving. Snow, cold and icy against a bit of exposed skin on my legs.

What if she needed help? What if she was stuck out here, too? What if I had scared her off? What if we could somehow aid each other?

"Please just wait! I don't want to hurt you!"

At the road, she turned to the right, the opposite direction that I'd gone this morning, not toward Denise's house, not toward the track marks from the cops' utility vehicles. She jetted off even faster now that she was on flatter, more even ground, leaving huge footprints in the unblemished snow. I chased her as best I could, but it was no use. Hers was the run of someone desperate and young.

The run of someone guilty? Could this girl have had something to do with what happened to Siobhan? Was she even strong enough to drag a body into that horrible freezer?

"Hold on!" I called again, throwing myself into a run, pushing with all the energy I had left.

And then something in the road stopped me—an errant rock? refuse tossed out the window of a car?—and I tumbled face-first, my hands only barely reaching out in time to catch my fall. I wasn't even wearing gloves—those had been left somewhere back in the office—and the shock of the snow was hard and biting, followed by a searing chill on my face.

Pain and cold, all over my body. I tried to push myself up, struggled.

Move, Kerry, Imaginary Frank encouraged me. *You got this. Find the strength.*

The pain was in my wrists, my knees, and snow covered my eyes, blinding, but I managed to scramble up, push it all away, finally see clearly.

When I did, the girl was completely out of sight. I followed her tracks about a hundred more feet, to where they disappeared into the thick brush of the woods. I was about to turn back when I saw another driveway up ahead.

And at the top of the driveway, a mailbox.

A line of footprints caught my eye—they were different from the girl's, which headed into the woods before they reached the turnoff. No, these came from whatever house was back there, meandered down the curving driveway and up to the mailbox, as if someone had come out to check the mail before turning back around.

My heart leapt. If someone else was here—right here, all along—that meant help, potentially. Answers, even. To who that girl was and what she was doing. About Denise and whether I could trust her. Maybe even about Siobhan and what had happened on her last days on earth.

It meant I wouldn't have to be alone in this.

It also means another suspect. Another person who could have killed Siobhan. You have to be careful, Kerry. You have to slow down.

Quieting Frank, I took a step forward, walking onto the long, winding driveway.

Someone lived here; the footprints proved it.

Someone who could help me—who could hurt me, too.

But it was *someone*, at least, and I knew I had to try.

14

Siobhan

January 5, 2023
1:51 p.m.

Sweet light. Yes, fancy "film" folks really called it that. See, the common misconception is that a bright sun makes a good picture, but overcast is where it's at. Present, but not overpowering.

It was nearing two o'clock, a mere twenty-four hours since I'd run into Charlie. I'd spent the time devouring a set of screenwriting craft books, intent on mastering structure as well as sketching out a couple of storyboard ideas in my journal.

The plan was to catalog every bit of the place before I whipped out any INTERIOR or EXTERIOR—DAYS. Was it its own form of procrastination? Maybe. Allison would certainly say so. But let's just call it research, shall we?

As such, this afternoon was all about the pool and the surrounding grounds. Camera recording, I panned from the hotly contested dumpster area (still no trash in the yard, thank you!) and across the outbuildings, walking toward the pool.

Nasty, really, I thought, as my camera panned across it. In a good way, of course.

Pools were a horror-movie go-to, from the moody claustrophobia of the scene in *It Follows* to the vampire-fanged massacre of *Let the Right One In*. And abandoned pools? Even better. Practically their own subgenre, the unique terror of jumping off a diving board and finding nothing but empty, moss-covered concrete beneath. Spines cracking like twigs. But there I went, getting ahead of myself again.

Through the viewfinder, I took in the Twilite's pool. The wide-open concrete, NO DIVING painted along each edge. A deck free of chairs. One massive slab of nothing.

The cover itself was a deep, ugly teal and sagged beneath rain from who knew how many days before, dead, errant leaves here and there. I imagined, suddenly, a woman running, gasping and breathing hard, and then someone chasing her, the killer right behind her, and the empty pool right there . . .

Of course, the chase to get to said pool would be just as important, and I panned to the edge of the woods on the west side of the property, a couple of hundred feet up. With the camera, I took in the yellowed grass, the frost-kissed dirt, the trees up ahead, the road slicing through it all.

A killer walking on an abandoned road, lurking out in the woods—clichés were clichés for a reason.

Hold up. I was still maybe a hundred feet from the woods, but on the edge of the frame, I saw the outline of a car, mostly obscured by the woods and the curve of the road, only partially in view. Some kind of SUV?

The vehicle was too far up the road to be visiting the motel. Had someone pulled over? Gotten a bit lost? Was someone once again wondering if the place was open for visitors?

Rooted to the spot, I stood stock-still, waiting for the car to move.

It didn't. And then, something else. A figure. Deep breaths. Why would someone park and hightail it into the woods?

Or were the two even connected?

Could the shape in the woods be a deer, maybe even a bear? Things lived in the woods; that was normal here. I was being a city girl, wasn't I? Freaking out at every little sound, every little shadow? Every car pulled over to check Google Maps?

For Christ sake, it was broad daylight.

Only then, camera still on, the shadow moved, coming into the light, and I saw something—a flash of a black cap on top—a person. A man.

The person moved again. Walking, running, through the woods.

I racked my brain, thinking about any houses that could butt up to the motel, but Maisy hadn't mentioned any, and I'd driven both ways, seen nothing.

There was Denise, of course, that nosy-ass neighbor, but she was the other way down the road, and she was on the shorter side. This person—whoever he was—was tall.

"Hello?" I said, calling out. "Hello?"

But as I took a step forward, a rock clipped my toe. I stumbled, caught myself, then stumbled again. Fell. The camera launched forward as I caught myself with both hands.

"Shit," I said. I grabbed my precious camera, checking it for damage. Having to replace this thing would put a crazy dent in Charlie's money. Thankfully, it looked okay.

The man was gone by the time I pushed myself up. Car was, too.

What the hell? How had he gotten away so *fast*?

I was about to play the footage back, see what I could see, but then I heard the grumble of gravel in the lot. I looked up, bracing myself for the SUV I'd only just seen, but I spotted that awful woman's pickup pulling up instead, heading straight for the motel office.

"Christ," I said. "What now?"

Quick strides, like a New Yorker outwalking tourists in Times Square. My pulse was pounding, bracing for the confrontation. Maisy had said that if Denise bothered me again, I could call the cops, but was I really going to do that? Be *that* person? My shoulders tightened. Did I have another choice?

The door of the pickup opened, and a young man stepped out, throwing me off.

"Hi," he said, a smile stretching across his boyish face. He was early twenties, if I had to guess, with a nervous, earnest charm. "Tyler." He stuck out his hand.

"I—" I started, taking in the pickup. "I'm sorry, I thought you were someone else."

"Oh," he said. "My mom. We share the truck."

My eyes narrowed. He and his mother couldn't seem more different, but my hackles were still raised, prepared for the apple not to fall too far from the tree. "What are you doing here?"

"Should have started there, I guess," he said, grinning once again, this time sheepishly. "I've got to do some work on the boiler. Maisy said she told you. Said to come around two."

"Oh," I said. "Oh, right." Maisy had provided a list of contractor appointments in her handbook, and I'd looked on my first day in, before completely forgetting that there was one for this week. "I didn't realize you were the contractor."

"Expecting someone older, grayer, and not as clean-shaven?"

I laughed. "I mean, kind of? I'm sorry if that's, like, anti-contractor or something."

"I'll forgive you," he said. "We're not exactly a marginalized group."

I laughed, louder this time. "I'm Siobhan," I said. "And again—apologies for the mix-up. Do you need me to do anything—show you around?"

"Just unlock the door, unless it's open already? Maisy doesn't give me the keys."

"Right," I said. "Of course. Let me just get the master set."

I turned on my heel, walked quickly down to my room, and opened the door. The place was littered with story-board drawings and dirty clothes, plus an overfilling trash bin I hadn't dared take out should that angry, hateful woman pop up like a jack-in-the-box the moment I got to the dumpster. The woman who had a perfectly nice, perfectly lovely son. It didn't compute.

The keys, of course, were not on the front table where I'd promised myself I'd leave them to avoid situations just like these, but eventually I found them, tucked under a bra I must have tossed on the floor before crashing into bed the previous night.

Outside, the sun was beating brightly, and Tyler was

leaning against the side of his pickup, like a guy in a Hall-mark movie. You know, the one about the uptight city girl who gives up her job running the fashion brand to build a quiet life in Vermont. Well, if the uptight city girl was at least a decade younger than me. This guy was practically a kid.

"Thanks for your patience," I said, handing him the keys. "I'm not the most organized."

He smirked. "Which makes you perfect for the role of a caretaker."

"Hey," I said. "Until you showed up needing to do real work and all that, there was really no need."

We walked back around the edge of the motel and toward the outbuildings, then all the way to the right, which Maisy's map had marked as the boiler room. The dumpster couldn't be more than fifty feet from us, and I glanced at the space briefly, but Tyler didn't look that way. It took me a couple of tries, but eventually I located the right key and opened the door, flicking on the lights and leading him inside.

"I suppose this is what you're here for," I said, gesturing toward a large cylinder against one corner with pipes coming out every which way.

Tyler walked inside, but I hovered in the doorway. "You know, if it's not too much, would you mind looking in the laundry room, too? I'll unlock that door as well. I came in yesterday, and one of the washing machines was running through a cycle, but I'd never set it. I guess that can happen, right? Machines just trip out sometimes?"

Tyler's eyebrows narrowed. "I guess so. You sure you didn't accidentally hit it?"

"Yeah," I said with a nod. "I'm sure."

"Okay, well, I'll take a look when I'm done with this," he said. "No problem. Let me just get my tools from the truck."

He started to turn away, but I felt my pulse pick up again. "Hang on," I said. "Do you know of any neighbors?" I gestured. "Who live nearby?"

Again, the narrowed eyebrows. "Just me and my mom, really. And an older woman, down the road near us. We help her out sometimes, especially during the winter."

"No," I said. "Definitely not an older woman. It was a man, and I just saw him. Right on the edge of the woods that border the motel."

"Oh," he said, raising his eyebrows. "The other way, you mean. Well, there is Jeremy. He's very close, actually."

"Really?" I asked. "Because when I drove that direction, I never saw any other houses on the road."

"No," he said. "You wouldn't have. The property is very private. There's a small driveway that's easy to miss. Walk down about a quarter mile and you'll see it. But he pretty much keeps to himself. I haven't ever seen him near the motel."

"It wouldn't have been him, I don't think," I said. "But maybe someone coming to visit him? Because there was a car there, too. Maybe a contractor or a surveyor or something?"

Tyler's face tightened. He looked suddenly tense, uncomfortable.

"What?" I asked. "What did I say?"

In an instant, the look passed, and his face morphed back into its warm, open demeanor. "It's nothing," he said. "But I might as well tell you, just in case it does come up: There's a property dispute."

"Oh," I said. "Yeah, your mom did . . . mention it." I let him fill in the gaps. "But I thought it was between her and Maisy?"

"It's become a bit of a three-way battle," Tyler said. "Maisy thinks she has more land than she does, but our land goes right up to a little past that road, so yeah, Maisy is technically on our property, and it's driving my mom nuts." He raised an eyebrow. "But anyway"—he pointed the other direction—"Jeremy owns the woods on that side."

"I don't understand," I said. "Aren't there, you know, property lines?"

"Oh, for sure," Tyler said. "But we aren't in town proper. It can get a little hairy, I guess. So when you buy out here, you need to get a surveyor. Only Maisy didn't do that. Or she didn't use a good one. I don't really know. I just know Jeremy and Maisy are battling it out legally, and they've both had their own surveyors out here for that reason—" He shrugged. "My mom doesn't have the funds to do a legal battle, but she *is* right. Maisy's dumpster shouldn't be there, and would it really be so hard for her to move it? Personally, I think Maisy's just pissed because she believes she paid for something she didn't get. The motel was owned by a local family forever—a generation-to-generation kind of thing. But they never put stuff on our property. So I don't know if they made her think she had more than she did or if she just assumed. But she's wrong. And, like, I honestly don't even know why she cares so much. None of it prevents her from charging an arm and a leg for what used to be a run-down motel."

"Wow," I said, thinking of Denise chucking that trash. The anger, the bitterness in her voice. A touch of compassion I hadn't felt before. "And you still work for Maisy, with all that going on?"

"You sound like my mom," he said. "I probably shouldn't say this, but Maisy pays way more than she needs to. City people always do. So it's kind of hard to say no. I need the money. I'm saving—want to move to the city one day. Don't tell my mom, though."

I found myself smiling. "Don't worry," I said. "I won't blow up your spot."

He grinned back. "Thanks."

Still, my mind returned to the man in the woods. "The thing that's strange is, I called out to him, and I guess *maybe* he didn't hear me, but it was like as soon as he did, he just kind of disappeared. Weird, right?"

"I mean, it is weird, but if Jeremy instructed the person not to speak to Maisy, it might make sense? I've seen the guy he hired. Not exactly the friendliest sort."

"Was he tall?" I asked.

Tyler considered it a second, then nodded.

"Right," I said. "See, I got part of it on video. I'm making a movie, and I was already shooting when it happened. Do you mind looking to see if it *was* him? The surveyor guy? My camera's right in my room."

"Sure," he said. "I've got to go that way anyway for my tools."

I nodded, and we both left the outbuildings and headed back to my room. Tyler was right behind me when I opened the door, found my camera on the dresser opposite the bed. "I'm messy, too," I said nervously. "Another great quality Maisy couldn't pass up."

Tyler laughed, and we stepped out onto the covered patio.

I rewound the clip a bit, pressed play. Tyler stood right next to me, gazing into the screen. There was the pool, and the property, and then the edge of the woods. The camera panned slowly, showing trees and rocks and a whole lot of nothing, then stopped.

I rewound it, pressed play again. It wasn't there.

"Shit," I said, looking up at Tyler. "The film must have cut off."

He stared at me for a moment, and I could see the way he was seeing me, like I was freaking myself out for nothing.

"Sorry," I said. "It was probably just the property stuff, like you said."

"I really wouldn't worry too much."

"I know," I said. "You're right. It's just . . ." I sighed. "I guess I've lived in the city too long. I'm not used to being on my own. The silence is deafening, that sort of thing."

Tyler smiled gently. "You're not the only one, promise you. Half the jobs Maisy has me do, I swear it's just to have someone else around when things are slow. It's an adjustment, being here after the city. A different way of life." He raised his eyebrows. "Like I said, I'm trying to find a way out. Live around more *creative* folks."

"And here I was," I said, "thinking I could find creative nirvana out here in the woods."

"Oh, it's here," Tyler said. "But you really have to make

it for yourself." He hesitated, his eyes on mine. "Anyway, you want to take my phone number? I'm just up the road, much more helpful than Maisy, all the way back in the city."

"Oh," I said. "Yes. Thank you. That would be nice." I pulled my phone from my pocket and opened the contacts, then handed it to him.

"You need anything—anything at all—you call me, okay?" Tyler said.

I nodded, feeling a tiny bit of the loneliness evaporate. "I will."

15

Siobhan

A week. It had been a whole week.

I'd filmed every inch of the motel, I'd done countless drawings, I'd read craft book after craft book.

Now I was supposed to write.

I had to.

Up out of bed. Rinse out the kombucha glass in the sink. Brush teeth. Water on face. Jeans and a cozy sweater.

At the desk opposite the bed, I sat down, all business. I flicked through my notebook, the pages in no particular order. I was always just opening to one page or another and starting a sketch. Order would come in Final Draft, *promise*.

I looked at the drawing I'd done the day before, a body splayed across the bottom of an empty pool. A figure, fleeing into the woods.

Another page, this one of one of the women, one who could possibly become a main character. Returning to it now, it looked embarrassingly like Kerry, right down to the mole above her lip. Yikes. I had no idea where Kerry was, and I had no desire to know where Kerry was. I was done with drunks. It was too easy for them to break your heart. And yet *obviously* I missed her. Here I was, drawing her without even meaning to.

Another page. This one just a shadow of a figure, big and looming, dominating the frame. Another, the figure larger, spilling off the page, the charcoal even more sketchy. Like a child's nightmare. Another page, and more of the same.

See them like this, and all you'd really think was that someone had a morbid imagination. There was no narrative. Nothing even remotely approaching a storyboard. Just a through line of not even all that original deaths (freezer bodies! empty pools!) and ones that represented the distinct feeling of being watched.

One that hadn't gone away. Despite me telling myself everything was fine.

I pushed back the chair and stood, rinsed the charcoal off my hands, and brewed some coffee. I would go on my little walk, and *then* I would write. That was a good plan, right?

Of course, I *could* do my caretaking duties—about as good a way as any to procrastinate—but the rooms themselves remained entirely ordinary. Once I'd filmed them all, noting any differences in decor, in layout, cataloging which ones would be best for shooting in, going into each one every day had begun to feel like overkill. The thermostats were set right, there hadn't been any signs of critters, and they were all locked up tight. I figured if Maisy had omitted details—like a property dispute that led to not one but two angry neighbors—it didn't matter all that much if I *said* I was checking each room daily if I didn't.

Instead, in the mornings, I liked to pour myself a cup, add a good splash of half-and-half, and circle the grounds.

I told myself it was to appreciate the beauty of the rural land—one I didn't have easy access to living in Downtown Brooklyn, with the sounds of delivery trucks, city buses, and idling cabs much more common than songbirds or crowing roosters—but in reality, it made me feel a teensy bit safer. A little bit in control, a military captain securing the perimeter. Watching for anyone who may approach. For flickers of movement in the woods (one I'd spotted the day before and had chalked up to a deer, or at least I was telling myself that). For more trash bags littered on the lawn (so far, so good). For anything that felt out of the ordinary.

I slipped into my coat and grabbed my Thermos of coffee, opened the door, took a quick step, and—

Splat.

I crashed onto the patio, my Thermos shooting out of my hands and rolling into the gravel parking lot, my palms skinned and a tear already forming in the left knee of my jeans.

I checked myself for blood—nothing—then pushed myself up, my knees aching, turned back to the door.

It was a small, cardboard package, little more than nine by twelve inches—and yet enough to send me smashing into concrete.

"What in the world?" I asked no one in particular as I grabbed a dusty edge, lifted it up.

The mail typically went straight into a slot at the main office. One of my duties, one I wasn't shirking, was to sort out the junk, open and organize any deliveries, all that. I'd done it just the day before, but the postwoman came in the afternoon.

Still, I guess a package was different. Could be FedEx, UPS, an Amazon truck, one I somehow hadn't heard? And why here, way down in front of my room? The whole thing seemed strange, like it was meant, somehow, for me. There was no address on the back, only that silvery striped tape. I flipped it over, found the usual stamps and markings, then seized up at the name on the package.

Jeremy Gallo.

Jeremy had been the name of the next-door neighbor, the one who kept to himself, whom Tyler had mentioned.

I gave the package a quick shake. Whatever was inside sounded small, potentially valuable. I thought about leaving it, putting it in Maisy's office for her to deal with, but a part of me also relished the excuse to see the property, get a look at this man, confirm that he'd had a surveyor—or someone—come out the other day.

After all, I was set to be here another three weeks, and then another weekend after that. Putting that instance out of my mind, tying it into a neat little bow, would make me feel better, wouldn't it? Another tick in the *nothing-is-wrong-here-you're-just-a-fish-out-of-water-with-horror-on-the-mind* column.

Besides, I could explain to him that I wasn't Maisy. That I didn't care at all about some property line to-do. There was no need for people to run from me if I saw them in the woods.

I took a sip of coffee, tucked the package under my arm, and began to walk.

Up the gravel drive. Onto the road. Tyler had said the guy's driveway was only a quarter mile up. Just a friendly little visit. Correcting a UPS mistake.

There wasn't much of a shoulder, but the road unfolded rather straight up to the right. Wide enough shoulder that I didn't have to worry about getting smashed to bits by a car swerving to avoid hitting a deer and hitting me instead (another movie cliché).

One step and then another, across a bed of withered grass and crunched-up leaves. Woods butted up to both sides of the road, and the mountains peeked up on the left side, like they were watching me. The walk was a tiny bit claustrophobic, the evergreens and scraggly conifers blocking me like walls.

The sun was bright, making it feel almost warmish, and after a few minutes of walking, there it was.

I spy with my little eye a matte hunter green mailbox, sleek and rectangular and nearly blending into the trees around it. Stylish. Modern. Incredibly easy to miss.

A sigh of relief. The most likely explanation was that the delivery driver had cruised right past this box, not seen it, and landed at the motel instead. Maybe he'd noticed the address discrepancy, maybe he hadn't— either way, he'd left it at my door, the only one with a car parked in front. That meant no creepy strangers prowling around my room and dropping off mysterious packages. Good.

I hesitated at the mailbox, debating. The package was too big to fit in, but still. There was no reason I couldn't leave it here at the bottom of the post, having done my neighborly duty. I set it down, there among the grasses, was about to turn away when I picked it back up and stepped onto the gravel drive.

Shouldn't I know who this guy was? How much the

property dispute was bothering him? Then at least if I saw someone on the property again, I'd know what was up.

Surely I could handle some reclusive neighbor.

It was *fine*. Just fine.

The drive sloped immediately downward, then turned on a curve.

I looked back, could no longer see the road, which meant passing cars—rare as they were—couldn't see me. I ambled past the PRIVATE PROPERTY signs tacked onto the trees, remembering the stories that had dominated the news the previous spring, about people pulling cars into the wrong house and being shot point-blank, but I was determined not to turn back. To get this over with.

A few more steps, another curve in the road, and then—holy shit—there it was.

The house was such a surprise, the thermos of coffee and the dusty package nearly dropped from my hands.

I'd expected a country home, something run-down, paint peeling, wood porch sinking, the works.

No sirree. This was not *that*.

The house was a collection of shapes, sharp geometrical angles reaching up to a clear blue sky, evergreen trees framing it like some sort of modernist painting. Vertical wooden slats formed the face of it, a face that was mostly filled with enormous windows that looked into a living room dominated by a fantastic glass chandelier and a dining table that could have come straight out of the Museum of Modern Art.

The car, a BMW SUV that *could* have been the car I saw parked on the road, was nested into an open garage whose roof slanted from one side of the home and all the way to a ground manicured with some sort of shrub that was hearty enough to survive the winter, as it was still mostly green.

The whole thing looked like a child had stacked blocks every which way, and somehow, miraculously, it worked.

The home was almost a dare.

You say I can't build a house of trapezoids and triangles? Okay, I'm calling your bluff.

Smooth concrete steps led up to a matte hunter green door, the same exact color as the mailbox, and a single rectangular window atop it.

For a moment, one that made me question my own morality, I felt a bit safer than I had before. Some hedge funder from the city wasn't likely to be a gun nut who would shoot me on the spot, right?

But then, through the main windows, a figure. Tall and thin. I jolted, holding the package close, and in that moment, I wanted to turn on my heel, flee back to the motel, and leave the thing at his mailbox like I probably should have from the start.

It was too late; the door was opening. The man was stepping out.

He wore deep-blue indigo jeans and a clean black sweater that had to be cashmere. His leather loafers were the color of sugar caramelized in a Le Creuset pan.

"Can I help you?" he asked, his voice gruff, impatient.

My limbs tensed, and I felt silly, classist, for feeling more secure only a moment before. As if wealth and status prevented crime. Hell, if I'd learned anything from more than a decade in New York City, it was that a hedge fund guy was *more* likely to be a psychopath than just about anyone else.

I held out the box like an offering. "Your package was delivered to the motel. Just returning it."

The man's shoulders softened, and he took a couple of steps forward, and so did I. I passed him the package, and he took it with a ringless hand.

"Thank you," he said, looking down. "I was waiting for this."

"I could have left it at the mailbox, but I didn't want it to get taken. I didn't know if it was valuable or anything." I tried my best not to glance at the BMW, at the expensive-as-hell clothing, at the modernist house.

"I appreciate that." He was maybe six feet tall. Thin, but decently ripped. Probably the kind of Manhattan guy who got to the gym at five a.m., hours before the markets opened for the day. His head was shaved, his skin pale olive—maybe Italian, come to think of it the last name did sound a bit Italian, maybe from one of those old New York families, raised helping out at the family restaurant in Brooklyn before moving across the East River for a flashier life? Either way, he fit the profile of the guy I'd seen on my camera decently enough. He smiled, and I noticed a slight drift of his eyes down my body before landing back on my face. "Is there anything else?"

I felt myself blushing, feeling, somehow, a tension between us, a *something*, and I wondered if he felt it, too. But I knew I'd feel better if I cleared this up.

"I just have to ask," I started. "Were you out by the motel a few days ago? I saw a man, about your height, and I tried to say hello, but you might not have heard me . . ."

The man's shoulders seized up, and whatever energy had passed between us fizzled instantly. Pop! "Are you accusing me of being somewhere I shouldn't?"

"Whoa," I said, tossing up my hands.

"Because I don't appreciate the implication. It's my property, you know, right up to the edge of the woods."

"I know," I said, taking a step back. "I'm not talking about the property dispute. I have no skin in that game. Promise."

"Dispute." He scoffed. "The legal side of things is pretty cut-and-dry. And if Maisy had hired a surveyor to come do an inspection *before* she bought the place, we wouldn't have to be going through all this, would we?"

"Right," I said. "Like I said, I have nothing to do with that. But it *was* you, then? Or someone you hired?"

"I think we're done here," the man snapped. "Thanks for the package."

He turned on his heel and slammed the door behind him.

Leaving me staring, shocked and alone.

And maybe—scratch that, *definitely*—more freaked out than I was before.

16

Kerry

Frank would love this.

That was what I thought when the tucked-away home finally came into view, revealing an architectural master-piece. I wasn't as visually minded as Frank or Siobhan, but though I couldn't even describe exactly what about this house was so intoxicating, I knew he would *absolutely* adore it, same way I loved, say, the work of Shirley Jackson. Some things were just breathtaking, and this was one of them.

I followed the footprints up toward the door. There had been a moment, after getting my huge advance. A conversation, an idea floated, from me to him, asking if he wanted to scrap the marketing job and go to archi-tecture school instead. It had been a dream of his, always. He'd joked that, second to George Costanza, no one had wanted to be an architect as much as him. But he was a working-class kid, just like I was, and his under-grad had saddled him with enough debt to make additional schooling feel impossible. He'd made up for it by pursuing marketing at hip, cool places, like design firms and ad agencies, but Frank had wanted to really create something; there was always that untapped need.

In the end, he'd said he was too old to start over, that what he wanted to "create" was another human, with me, the money earmarked for IVF instead of career reinvention. Money that had come to nothing.

The house's windows were wide, and though I couldn't see anyone inside, something else caught my eye. The television, suspended above the mantel—it was on.

Power, I thought, oh my god, there's *power*, but how? There was no way this place was far enough from the motel to be spared from the outage. I looked around, trying to understand, and the answer presented itself, so obvious I should have thought of it immediately: solar panels.

I lifted my hand, knocked three times, my decision cemented. Whoever this person was, it was worth the risk, with the promise of actual electricity waiting just inside. Maybe they even had some kind of satellite-operated phone line. It seemed like something the kind of person who could afford this kind of house *would* have.

There was no response, so I knocked again, even harder this time. Someone had to be here. Where else would they go? I knocked one more time, then the handle turned, and a man filled the doorframe. He looked to be early forties, and his body was thick with muscles. Even at first glance, it was clear that he was strong enough to move a body, to drag Siobhan across the property, to heave her up into that freezer . . .

"I didn't hear you," he said, speaking first. "There's usually a bell when visitors drive up. Are you okay?"

"I walked," I said. "I'm staying at the motel next door. I'm the caretaker there, but I don't have power, and—and

I don't have cell service, and my phone is about to die—
and I'm stuck there, and I need to call the police."

"The police?" he asked, eyebrows narrowing.

"Yes," I said, trying to hold it together. "Someone is
dead. Someone's been killed."

I studied his face, looking for a tell, but all I could see
was the widening of eyes, a quick intake of breath, what
looked, on its surface, like surprise. "I'm sorry, *what*?"

"The last caretaker," I said. "I came in, and it was like
she'd never left, and then I saw her, and she was out there,
and she was—" My voice cracked.

"Wait a second. Siobhan is *dead*? I . . . I just saw her."

The name on his mouth sent a wave of shock up my
spine. "You *knew* her?"

"Not well, but—but she was at the motel, just the other
night." He shook his head. "I don't understand."

"I don't, either," I said.

He opened the door. "You want to come in?"

I hesitated only a moment, then followed him in, shutting the door tight behind me, and the first thing I noticed
was the warmth, more than that of a fireplace or a woodstove. Warmth seeping through the walls, coming out of
vents.

"You want something to drink?" he asked, walking to a
well-outfitted kitchen, an island in the center, an enormous Miele range shooting up to the ceiling like some
kind of altar. Everything in this place had been planned
down to the meticulous, moneyed detail, from the countertop espresso machine to the inset sink. "I'm Jeremy, by
the way."

"Kerry," I said.

He opened a pristine white cabinet and pulled out a small glass. "Water?" he asked. "Or something stronger? I have whiskey open."

You don't need to drink, Kerry. What you need is to keep your head on straight. I pushed aside Imaginary Frank's words. I'd never been good at living up to them before, so why start now? "Okay. Whiskey, sure," I said, trying not to sound too eager. "And I'd like to charge my phone, if that's okay."

"Of course," he said. He reached out his hand, and I dug in my pocket, relinquishing my device. He set it on a circular disc that was plugged into the kitchen island's outlet. My phone buzzed, indicating it was charging, then he returned to the cabinet and grabbed another glass. He set the pair on the countertop, poured us each a few fingers' worth.

The warmth, the obliteration, shot straight down my throat, reawakening my buzz—and pushing the fear, the grief, back down, where it belonged. Another quick sip, finishing the glass. Without being asked, Jeremy poured me another.

"When did you see her?" I asked.

Jeremy scratched at his chin. "Two nights ago, I guess?"

"You were at the party, then?"

"Briefly," he said. "But I left on the earlier side. Things were getting a little wild. Do you think it was an accident? That Siobhan somehow was drinking—using drugs—and got caught in the storm?"

Her body, frozen, shot back into my mind, and I took another sip, pushing it away. "No, I don't."

His face paled. "You don't think . . ."

"That someone hurt her? Yes, I do."

His eyes widened as they took that in.

"Who was still there when you left?" I asked.

"Some people from the city," he said. "And Tyler, who lives down the road."

I shook the glass, dislodging a bit of ice. "I met Tyler and his mom. I went that way to get help first. But Tyler says that he left early, too."

"Maybe," Jeremy said with a shrug. "He was still there when I headed out, but he could have left shortly after. He's a good kid. I guess not really a kid anymore, but when I bought the land seven years ago, he was only sixteen."

And Siobhan was only thirty-five, far too young to die. How could someone have done this to her? How was any of this fair? I took another sip. "What about the people who were from the city? Was one of them"—I thought of that lawsuit; I thought of all the pain Charlie must have caused Siobhan—"was one of them named Charlie?"

Jeremy scoffed.

"What?" I asked. "What is it?"

"Yes, one of them was named Charlie, now that you ask. Total douchebag, too. One of those guys who thinks he's this hotshot just because he can name artists and photographers you've never heard of. It was his friends— pair of French guys—who brought the drugs. Who turned the party into what it became."

"He's Siobhan's boyfriend," I said. "Or, well, he was. I don't really know exactly what was going on between them."

"He was an ex, all right, but he still seemed to think that

she was his," Jeremy said. "He made that *quite* clear. I got a bad vibe from him, right off the bat. Christ, do you think . . ."

Did I, *really*? I knew Charlie was hassling Siobhan for money, I knew he'd never made her feel good about herself—I knew, well, I *knew*—but did that really mean he could kill her? "I don't know," I said. "I found papers. A lawsuit. Charlie was suing Siobhan for twenty-five thousand dollars."

"What?" Jeremy asked. "Really? I got the idea that he was trying to get back with her."

An ache in my chest once again as the unfairness of it all hit me, as I realized how scared she must have been, how hopeless she must have felt when she'd realized what was happening to her. "Maybe Charlie was using the money to try to coerce her."

"Fuck," Jeremy said. "And like, on behalf of all men, I'm sorry. That's so fucked up."

"It is," I said, pushing the feelings back down as I sucked back more whiskey. "It *really* is. But I have to talk to the police again. That's what matters now."

"Again?"

"Yes, the neighbor—Denise—her brother's a cop. He came, but he and his partner . . . they didn't take me seriously. They left and then—" I thought of Siobhan, sitting in that freezer, prayed that the end had been fast for her, that she hadn't felt too much pain, worried that she had. "I found something that they have to see, but I have no way of contacting anyone again. My car—me—I'm not prepared to drive in this. I've got no cell service. The landlines are down. And Denise and Tyler are off at some neighbor's."

"Well, I can't help you make a call," he said. "Solar power doesn't do a thing for cell service, and my Wi-Fi router has plenty of juice, but if nothing's coming from the cable company, there isn't anything I can do about it."

My heart sunk, and I took another sip, half seeking obliteration. "Of course you can't."

"No, no, don't misunderstand me. I *can* help," he said.

"Wait, you can?"

Jeremy nodded eagerly. "I actually have a UTV. Got it for this purpose. Course I haven't had a real urgent need to use it. Up till now it's been little more than a fun toy of mine. The police station is just down the road, toward Denise and Tyler's, and then you take a left. Not more than a handful of miles, I don't think. The UTV is on the other side of my property, and I need to top it off with gas. You want to stay here, get your phone charged up, while I get it ready, and then we'll go over to the station together? I imagine you want to get there as soon as possible."

"Yes," I said, hardly able to believe him. "Yes, I do." For a moment, it was near impossible to take in, that the answer was right here, in the form of a solar-powered house and a utility vehicle. The fear subsided, making way for a new wave of grief. None of this would bring back Siobhan. She was gone, no matter what happened. No matter what the police found.

She was gone. I would never see her again. I took another sip of whiskey. It was so very unfair.

Jeremy set his glass in the large porcelain sink. "Let me go get everything ready. The police need to know this. All of it. And I can tell them what I saw, too."

"Okay," I said. "Thank you."

I grabbed the bottle that Jeremy had left as soon as he was gone.

Careful, Kerry. Easy, babe. Easy.

Shut up, Frank, I thought, lifting it to my lips. Siobhan was gone; her boyfriend may have killed her. Tears once again filled my eyes, dripping down into the drink, turning it salty. If this wasn't a reason to dive into a bottle, Christ, what was?

Absentmindedly, I reached for my charging phone, tapped to open Instagram, another thing to help me numb, before remembering that there was no service anyway, that a stupid thing like Instagram hardly mattered right now. Siobhan was dead. *Nothing* would change that. I chucked the phone back on the charger, took another sip, this one spilling from the glass, out of my mouth, down my shirt.

I pushed myself up, away from the counter, off the fancy stool, but I shoved a little too hard, the thing clanging back and forth on its four chrome legs. I grabbed the back, steadied myself, stopped the stool from wobbling.

I walked—stumbled?—over to one of those sliding doors secured to the wall with enormous iron bars. Behind it, I found a bathroom, with a wide window next to the open, waterfall shower, looking out on a gleaming sea of white. I imagined this man, muscles ripped across his body, standing here naked, water beading against his skin, against the roughened egg of his shaved skull, contemplatively looking out at his own slice of woods, one with the wilderness and yet entirely apart; protected, even, from the loss of power. I wondered if he lived here full-time or had something fabulous in the city, too, up in the sky, tempting us all to want it. I hated how jealous I could get, how I was always striving to prove myself to the people I met, ever the girl with student loans and no safety net and parents I couldn't just call up for financial help. Loving the city but always feeling like our time there was borrowed, like eventually we'd have to leave to make way for more trust funders, for wolves of Wall Street. Frank could so easily stay above the fray, could pull in his income, enough to pay for a semi-decent rental, at least, enough to have a baby if we wanted—just one—and be able to, mostly, pay the bills. Frank was content with his existence, but I always wanted more, more, more, proof that I fit in, and then, for a moment, I'd had it. All the enviable updates to send out through the ether and the promise, this time, that my ticket wasn't one that would expire, that I was here to stay.

And then I couldn't pull it off, could I? I couldn't write the book. My body couldn't make the baby. The desirable life I showed the world was little more than a lie.

I looked at myself in the mirror, my lips reddened and cracked from the wine I'd had before. The splash of whiskey wet against my shirt. Why was I even thinking about any of this? Siobhan was gone, locked in a freezer, her life stolen from her. Why did I care about all this bullshit? How could I still be jealous of this existence, even now? Why couldn't I just accept that Frank had been right to not want too much all along?

Why couldn't I consider that *I* was the lucky one here, that I could have another chance if I wanted one, and Siobhan couldn't? Why was I such a piece of shit, even when I was supposed to be grieving my best friend?

My head ached suddenly, and I needed something to quiet the pulsing in my temples. Something to *numb numb numb.* I reached haphazardly, up to the mirror, pulling it open to see three shelves of a medicine cabinet, a mirrored back surface making everything look doubled. I wanted Advil or—please, god—something stronger. My eyes scanned the bottles, but I found nothing more than vitamins, herbal supplements, fancy aftershave, wrinkle serums, and then—

Then—

A hairbrush, a cheap pink thing. One she said worked better to detangle than anything that cost way more. One she used to carry in her purse, to tackle the thick hair that fell beneath her shoulders—

My heart ticked up.

It could be a coincidence. It could mean nothing.

Then beneath the hairbrush, a rectangle of plastic, curved at the edges. An ID. It was face down, nothing but a jumble of numbers and a bar code, but then I leaned forward, looked up, through the glass shelf.

There she was, grinning under the words *NEW YORK STATE*, her mini hologram a second smile on the right.

And the words, so clear, at the top.

SIOBHAN SOPHIA JONES

17

Siobhan

INT. PANTRY—DAY

Katie and Claudia enter through the door,
approach the well-stocked shelves.

  KATIE
  There's got to be something decent to eat
  in here. Some wine, at the very least.

Claudia walks up to an oversize meat
freezer.

  CLAUDIA
  I swear my grandma had this exact model
  in her garage. I can practically smell
  the grape ice pops.

Slowly, Claudia lifts the lid—

A knock at the door, three quick raps. My shoulders
jolted, and I looked up from my laptop, where I'd been

toying with the freezer scene for the last hour, intent on getting some real words into Final Draft, while the *Halloween* soundtrack cranked out of my Bluetooth speaker.

See, I was writing, finally. And maybe it was slow going, and maybe it was imperfect. But I was doing it, wasn't I? The freezer dead-body seemed the most inspiring, and so it was a place to start, no? Kerry had once told me that when she was really stuck in her fiction, she'd fast-forward to the most exciting scene.

The curtains were open, and in an instant, I could see it was him, his large, muscled frame practically filling the window. The man from the day before. Jeremy Gallo. How long had he been standing there before he knocked, while my eyes were locked on my screenplay, the window leaving me fully exposed? And why was he here anyway? He'd made it beyond clear he didn't want to answer any of my questions yesterday.

Another knock. I shut off the music, opened the door, bracing myself for the confrontation.

To my surprise, Jeremy held a bottle of wine, cradled in his left arm like a newborn baby. His smile revealed clean white teeth, just a slight gap between the two front ones. "Peace offering? I was a total dick yesterday. It's a great bottle. One of my favorite Cabs." He held it out, and I hesitated slightly. "Oh shit," he said. "Do you not drink?"

"I don't *not* drink," I said. "Just . . . not as much these days."

"Dry January?" he asked.

I shrugged. "Something like that."

"My bad," he said, shifting his weight back and forth. "I shouldn't have assumed."

"No," I said, taking the bottle from him. "It's a lovely gesture. Thank you."

"It wasn't you, you know."

I tilted my head. "Sorry?"

"I mean, it wasn't you I was frustrated with. It's just this property thing; it's gotten a bit intense in the last couple of months."

"Yeah," I said. "I got that vibe from the other neighbor. She literally took a trash bag out of the dumpster and threw it on the motel lawn."

Jeremy guffawed. "That sounds like Denise. It's definitely got her on edge."

"I don't need to worry about her showing up here with a gun or something, do I?" A raised eyebrow. "Or you?"

"God, no," he said. "I leave all the gun stuff to the locals. No, thank you. I'm as boring as they come; my greatest weapon is a contract full of legalese. And Denise does have a rifle or two, I'm sure, but she saves it for hunting season. And the woman gets very, *very* angry if people try to hunt outside the approved months of the year. You don't have to worry about her. Besides, no one is angry at you, just Maisy."

"Easy for you to say. I haven't exactly gotten the warmest welcome."

"I know," he said. "We're all mad here, it seems." He laughed to himself. "And listen, if Dry January isn't exactly *set in stone*, that bottle there goes great with my homemade chicken cacciatore."

"You don't have to do that," I said.

"I don't have to, but my grandma taught me better than to treat you the way I did yesterday. And my early evenings are pretty laid-back. I'm a lawyer, in the finance industry. The markets close by four p.m., and then I'm free as a bird. Come over, around six? I promise I won't tell you to get off my lawn this time."

I hesitated.

"You're a writer, right? Maisy loves to get writers up here."

"I make movies," I clarified.

Jeremy laughed. "Wait, is that why this place sounds like the stuff of high school nightmares? That was from *Halloween*, wasn't it? That music used to terrify me."

I grinned. "It gets me in the mood. I'm writing a horror movie, actually."

Jeremy wriggled his eyebrows. "Who's the killer?"

A hand on my hip. "To be determined."

"Well, it looks like you're hard at work now," he said, nodding to my laptop. "And I don't want to interrupt, but maybe the promise of dinner will give you a little motivation to get through your next few scenes?"

The thought was tempting. And true. Even without all the weird shit that had been happening, it was hard to be alone all the time. Constant music and chatting to Spikey the succulent could only get me so far.

"How about this?" Jeremy said, seeming to make the decision for me. "I'm going to walk away before you get a chance to say no."

True to his word, he backed away, a smile on his face.

"See you at six, Siobhan."

*

It was dark by the time I left the motel, right on time. I walked up the road, hiking along the edge of the woods, careful not to walk too close to the asphalt as the occasional car flashed by, brights illuminating me, catching me in the headlights like a deer in a state of shock.

Hell, I could practically hear the eerie music playing as I walked, almost felt like Jamie Lee Curtis doing her best to evade Michael Myers.

I passed Jeremy Gallo's mailbox, nearly missing the turn it was so dark, wound down the curving driveway. The home in all its glory. Its angles and windows. Harsh yet harmonious lines. It gleamed like a diamond against the black night.

Before I could even knock on the door, it opened.

I jolted. "Hi."

"I realized that I invited you over in the pitch-black," Jeremy said, concern on his face. "I've been waiting at the window to make sure you got here okay."

"How paternalistic," I said.

"Hey, it's scary out in the woods alone. Well, maybe not for a horror aficionado like you. Besides, I don't want someone tripping and breaking a leg on my watch. A lawyer to a fault."

He ushered me into the warmth of the home, flames blazing brilliantly from a wide, cavernous fireplace on the left wall, etched perfectly into what looked like a block of marble, as if Michelangelo himself had come over to create it for this guy. I smelled tomatoes and garlic, basil and meat. Yum.

"Can I take your coat?" Jeremy asked.

"Please."

Turning my back to him, I faced a swath of windows that looked out on a wide expanse of darkness. We were in a shadow box. From the outside, you could see in, but from the inside, you could see so little, no farther than the patio lights illuminated. I thought, suddenly, of Drew Barrymore, answering the phone in that house while the killer watches her in *Scream*. The classic terror of being on display. Only with Jeremy here, it felt less frightening—more exciting.

Jeremy's fingers brushed the back of my shoulder as he took off my coat. He popped it onto a velvet hanger, tucked it away in the closet.

He turned back to me then, and yes, by George, he *was* taking me in. His eyes weren't exactly sweeping my every curve, but I could feel it anyway.

My dress was simple, black wool, nipped in at the waist and down at the chest. One of Charlie's favorites. I slipped off my leather boots, placed them on a mat, where a large pair of Sorels already sat. My feet in only stockings, the night already felt strangely intimate. Jeremy's were covered in the same camel loafers from the day before.

"Holy shit," I said, feeling the warmth on my toes. "Are your floors heated?"

Jeremy laughed. "Indeed they are."

"I thought that was something that only really happened on TV."

"The equivalent of a real estate unicorn?" he asked.

"Exactly," I said.

Jeremy beamed. "When you build your dream home, you know, you get to include a few unicorns. Anyway, the chicken's still simmering, but can I get you started on a drink? I make a mean old-fashioned. And if you want, I can do a mocktail version, no problem."

"Regular is okay," I said, full-up with date-or-not-date jitters. "We'll make an exception."

"Perfect." He led the way to an enormous kitchen island and pulled up a chrome stool, indicating for me to sit. A white Le Creuset Dutch oven was steaming on one of those stoves that blends seamlessly into the countertop.

Jeremy went to work. Whiskey, check. Bitters, check. Orange and maraschino. Check. Drinking for the first time since alcohol destroyed my relationship. Check check check.

It's pretty clear what this is, isn't it? I thought as I pressed my hands against the counter, stared at my chipped polish. Me, in a little black dress. Him, jumping straight to the cocktails. I half wanted to announce it, say it out loud. This is a date, right? I haven't been with anyone since Charlie. He broke my heart. I owe him money. It's complicated.

"So how was the rest of your day?" I asked instead, leaning forward slightly. "Advise a bunch of rich guys how to plump up their already fat pockets?"

Jeremy stirred the concoction with an elongated spoon. "Hey, whatever pays the bills, right?" He gestured around. "I didn't come from this, had to make it on my own."

"Well, you're a good-looking white man," I said. "Cis-het, too, if I had to guess."

His eyes caught mine. "Guilty as charged."

"So it's not like you didn't have a leg up."

"Fair enough," he said. "But like I said—" He grabbed what looked like an impossibly sharp knife and sliced through the edge of the orange peel, sending a fine mist of oil through the air. An instant tang. "I do legal compliance. So, you know, how *not* to break the law."

"Or how to skirt as close to the line as possible without alerting the SEC."

He smirked. "You know all our tricks, don't you?"

"I dated my share of finance guys in my twenties. Any straight girl in New York City did—a rite of passage."

"But now you stick with artists?" he asked, taunting me, just a bit, as he poured the drinks.

The irony about the city was that the people who worked in creative fields often needed money the least. Charlie worked in the art world, but he came from money. Men like Jeremy surrounded themselves with it, sure, but it was the ones like Charlie who used it so casually.

"Now"—I grabbed my glass, lifted it into the air—"I stick with myself."

We ate at an expansive black wooden table, my ass on a sculptural chair draped in sheepskin. The hide tickled my shoulder, like a series of tiny kisses.

My return to drinking wasn't a toe in the water but a full-on splash. After cocktails, we'd moved on to wine, Jeremy spouting words I'd heard, of course, but knew very little about—vegetal! tannins! oxidation! It tasted like a good red wine, nothing more, nothing less.

The food was incredible. Tomatoes on our tongues. Red sauce on our lips. We might as well have been vampires, sitting down to dinner.

Jeremy shared his backstory. That he'd bought the land here and started building years ago, that it had originally been intended as a weekend place, but after the pandemic, like so many, he'd moved to fully remote work and decided to live up here full-time. He inquired dutifully about my work, too, and I'd told him all about the festival. About Allison and her connections. How this was my chance. And I didn't know if he really cared, but he acted like it anyway. Made all the right faces. Asked all the right questions. It made me miss Charlie. Miss having someone to do this with, every night. Realize just how hard it was to be on my own.

Finally, the plates were put into the deep sink. The wines topped off. The fire was dying down, and Jeremy hadn't added another log.

Maybe the chemistry I thought I'd felt was just in my imagination, a result of finally having someone to talk to besides that poor succulent?

"I guess I should get going," I said, taking a last sip.

Jeremy looked at me a moment, and this was the chance. To do anything to change course. I wanted it, not just because being up here was lonely and occasionally scary. I wanted it because I wanted to be wanted by someone who wasn't Charlie. Who hadn't hurt me yet.

"I'll walk you, then," Jeremy said, pushing back his chair.

Here we were, once again, at the door. Him opening the coat closet. His hands holding out my wool coat, my arms slipping inside.

And then. *Then.*

His fingers, they lingered. Not forever, but enough to be a signal. Enough to create a little space, the tiniest opening I could fit my body through . . .

A quick turn on my heel, and there he was. His tall

frame. His kind eyes and crooked smile. Before anything could change—before either of us could lose our nerve—I leaned in.

Damn if he didn't meet my challenge, closing the space between us.

And then, it was like we were hungry all over again. Our lips parting. His tongue in my mouth. His hands pushed my coat right back off, then landed right above my ass.

A second later, I felt his teeth on the edge of my bottom lip.

Biting enough to hurt, but not enough to bleed.

18

Siobhan

Oh god, his bed felt good.

My eyes took in my surroundings. The mattress, empty on Jeremy's side. The sheets, silky and light as a cloud. A duvet that was somehow both cool and perfectly warm, spread all around me.

The bed faced an enormous window. I was looking out on thick woods, evergreen trees whose branches beckoned me, like a child's hooked finger asking a neighbor to come out and play.

The room was all white, apart from exposed beams on the arched ceiling, a perfect deep walnut that mirrored the floors beneath.

My head ached, and I realized how little I'd actually missed drinking. Hardly worth it.

A clatter of plates from the kitchen. The steam of an espresso machine. The aroma of coffee. A salty tang of bacon grease. I pushed back the covers, found my underwear and bra, plus my dress and purse, littered in a trail that led to the door—Hansel and Gretel's breadcrumbs.

Not wanting Jeremy to see me before I had a chance to freshen up, I slipped into the bathroom, which was accessible from both the primary area and directly from the bedroom. In the mirror, I surveyed the damage. Hair a mess, mascara smeared beneath my lids. Naked as the day I was born. I turned my body slightly. Caught the print of red on my backside. I pulled a small plastic brush from my purse, ran it through my hair. Added a bit of concealer beneath my eyes. Rinsed my mouth with water. Applied lip balm. Then I slipped into yesterday's clothes and popped everything else back in my purse.

"Hope you're hungry," Jeremy said from behind the stove, where he turned bacon in a pan.

"Very hungry," I said. "Like I said, I haven't really been drinking, so it hit a bit hard."

"I thought that might be the case." He pulled out a bottle of green juice from the fridge, poured a small glass for me. "Best hangover cure in the world. Proprietary blend."

I took a sip. "Delicious."

"And how about a latte?"

"I won't say no to that."

I watched as he ground the espresso, tamped it down, and hooked it in before running a rag up and down the steamer wand, cleaning it off. He seemed so wholesome, cooking for me, pouring me juice, making his perfect little lattes, and it was almost hard to reconcile this version of him with the one I'd been with last night. The one who'd bit my lip, circled his hands around my throat, smacked my ass—hard—once, twice, three times while I cried out in a strange mix of pleasure and pain as he entered me from behind and pushed my face down. As I found myself groaning. Wanting it.

Jeremy hadn't asked if I was okay with any of it. The hands on my neck had been slight, then more pressure,

168

and a bit more, until suddenly it was like I couldn't breathe, and I felt my heart racing, and I reached for his hands, but then they unclasped, almost like they'd never been there at all. And I wondered if I could have gone longer. Wished, maybe, I had.

His hands on my ass had been the same. It just happened—no warning—hard enough for me to cry out. Then again and again.

Charlie and I were all vanilla. The most we'd ever tried was role-play, and it had felt so ridiculous—like bad college improv—had sent us into fits of giggles, which had in its way been sweet.

Now, looking at Jeremy, delivering the latte, foam styled into a perfect heart, I wondered how far he would go if I let him. I wondered if somewhere, within this perfectly planned-out home, there was a closet of whips and leather and suspended swings. I felt a flush of heat from below, moving up through my body. A desire to pull him to me, for his hands to be on my throat once again. I reached for the latte, attempted to swallow the desire.

"This is fantastic," I said.

"I worked at a coffee shop in Chelsea while I was getting my MBA. Must have made thousands of them. A skill you don't forget. Muscle memory."

"A straight guy styling hearts in oat-milk lattes? They must have loved you in Chelsea."

Jeremy guffawed, then ran his hand over his head. "And I had all my hair then, too. Believe me, they did. The tips—" He laughed. "Let's just say the customers were more than generous. And I liked the work, too. Liked talking to people, doing things with my hands." He clenched and unclenched his fingers, as if they were itching to be back in that café. "But you can't survive—well, you can't live like I wanted to—making lattes. Contracts, it is."

The food was incredible. The eggs not too runny, not too hard. There were all kinds of fancy things to go with it. Herby butter. Lingonberry jam. Crispy, greasy bacon.

In horror movies, they so often made villains and sadists epicureans, gourmands. Hannibal Lecter and his famed Chianti.

But this wasn't like that, of course—this was harmless fun. A little pushing of my boundaries in bed. Overmedium eggs in the morning.

Soon, it was time to go, and Jeremy was helping me into my coat, leading me out the door and into the brisk winter morning, to a BMW he'd started with a remote five minutes before, a car not unlike Charlie's.

I could savor the luxury this time, because Jeremy hadn't broken my heart, had he? Wasn't threatening to take away money. Instead, the heat on my ass, the quiet yet powerful whir of the car's engine, it was something to be enjoyed: *I missed this.*

It was all temporary, I knew that. When I was back in the city, in the run-down sublet I'd found that was actually in my price range, there was no way Jeremy and I would be keeping in touch.

But that was good. Because I wasn't over Charlie. I wasn't ready for anything more serious than unexpected sex and chicken cacciatore.

And then, just as I was thinking of him, there was another BMW, waiting next to Allison's old Toyota in the motel parking lot. A mirror image of the one I was in.

Charlie, leaning against the car like he owned this whole place, his wavy blond hair shining in the daylight. His hands shoved into his pockets.

"Oh shit," I said.

I reached for the door handle without even looking at Jeremy.

"Charlie," I said. "What are you doing here?"

Charlie's eyes widened as he took in my day-old clothes, my messed-up hair and makeup. "Shiv, what's going on?"

"Is everything okay here?" Jeremy was out of the car now, his hands crossed into a power stance, the two of them eyeing each other.

"Who's he?" Charlie asked.

"Oh my god," I said, and I felt suddenly so foolish. A tall, thin man. What looked like an SUV. "Charlie, just tell me now, was it you in the woods?"

"What are you talking about, Shiv?" Charlie said, his face full of confusion. "In the woods? No, I've never been here before now."

"And how did you even know where *here* was?" I asked. "It's not like I told you."

"I—" He bit his lip. "I got the address from Allison."

"Why would she—"

"I lied, okay," he said. "I told her I had some things of yours to return. I didn't like how we left things the other day. And maybe I shouldn't have—"

"No," I said. "You shouldn't have."

"But?" Charlie said, his eyes finding Jeremy once again. "Who is he?"

"Hey, man," Jeremy said. "Let's just all calm down, okay?"

Charlie's face reddened. "Don't tell me to calm down, *man*." He looked Jeremy up and down. "So this is how you punish me? Find some hedge funder to fuck?"

"Hey," Jeremy said again. "Maybe it's time to shut your fucking mouth."

"Hedge funder who thinks he's a tough guy. Even better."

"Stop it," I said. My eyes ping-ponged between them, and I could feel it, the rage, practically rising in the air. I could smell the sweat, the testosterone, ready to escalate. "Both of you," I clarified. "Just stop."

Now Jeremy was tossing up his hands, backing away a step or two.

Charlie used the opportunity to turn to me. "You told me you still cared about me."

"I do," I said. "But I—"

"Some way to show it," Charlie said, his voice raising, his face pale with anger. His shoulders clenched up, and for a horrible instant, I thought he was going to do something crazy. Hit Jeremy. Hell, even hit me?

Then he seemed to deflate, and he turned quickly and slipped back into his BMW, whipping aggressively back and out of the parking lot.

Before I could say a word to Jeremy, he shook his head. "You don't have to explain," he said. "I'll go now."

Then he got into his own car, pulled out, too, only a few car lengths behind Charlie.

I watched them drive off until I couldn't see a hint of either of their cars.

Until I was, once again, completely alone.

19

Kerry

My pulse went crazy as I stared at Siobhan's driver's license in my hands, replaying all that had just transpired: the way Jeremy made sure to mention Charlie, paint the picture of a "douchebag" ex-boyfriend, dropping breadcrumbs I could follow instead of looking straight to him. The way he'd been so ready with solutions that had seemed too easy, too simple.

Did he even have a utility vehicle, or had he gone out for something else? A gun? A knife? Or was the vehicle indeed real, something he could use to drive me deep into the woods, leave me for dead?

Leave, a voice in my head argued. Not Frank this time. *Me*. My eyes caught the large bathroom window. Could I just slip out—

My phone, I realized. It was still charging in the kitchen. Ear to the door, I listened for Jeremy, heard nothing. I slid it open, spotted the phone on its magnetic charger. I bolted out, grabbed it and my coat, too, but as soon as I did, I heard the click of the front door, the shuffle of footsteps, headed my way. I rushed back into the bathroom, closed the door behind me, and locked it, too.

Zipped up my coat, then turned back to the window, sizing it up. It was big enough for me to fit through.

There was a handle at the bottom, and I turned it clockwise, cranking open the window—a few inches and then all the way, which looked like it would do. It would have to, I guessed.

More footsteps, approaching the door now. "You okay in there?"

"Fine," I said. "Be right out!"

I poked my head through the window, looking down. There was a drop, even though we were on the first floor—this side of the house was built against a small hill. Six feet, maybe seven.

Siobhan's ID popped back in my mind. The drop didn't matter now, did it? Jeremy had acted like he barely knew her, and yet her things were right there in his bathroom.

Facing him again wasn't an option. It was too great a risk. I grabbed the window, shimmying myself under it and pushing myself out—one leg and then the other, the shock of cold bitter after the respite, the whiskey, the warmth.

Looking down, the reality of what I was about to do sunk in: It wasn't six feet. No way. Ten, at least. Christ.

A knock on the door, my heart beating mercilessly.

A deep breath, my hands on either side of me, pressing into the open window.

And then . . . I jumped.

My body hit the ground with a solid thud, the snow cushioning my fall but not enough so it didn't hurt at all, pain shooting straight up my legs as I landed just outside of Jeremy's bathroom window, a shock of cold on my ungloved hands.

I pushed myself up, scrambling for purchase, and forced myself to move through the pain, one leg in front of the other. I looked back, checking the open window, askew on its hinge, then forward again. My legs hobbled through the snow, kicking up flakes and drifts, bits that had already gone icy, the moisture, the cold, seeping through the gaps between my boots and my pants.

My breath came in gasps, my heart racing furiously. I was not prepared for this, not for actual survival, nothing close to it. I had felt like I was floundering so many times this past year, but none of that had been real, had it? This wasn't some existential crisis or a panic attack.

Siobhan was dead. The man inside that house—he could have killed her.

He was big enough, strong enough.

He obviously had money, which meant he had resources, maybe even the sorts of connections you needed to get away with these kinds of things.

More than that, he was right here, living next door. I had been trying to figure out how someone could have moved Siobhan without leaving any tracks, but he could have simply walked over, through the woods, the snowfall heavy enough to cover his footprints.

It all made sense, didn't it?

A sound behind me, the call of a voice, and I turned to see an open door, him standing within. "Kerry," he said. "Kerry, where are you going?"

I bolted down the drive, my legs aching, my boobs bouncing underneath my heavy layers, the air biting at my cheeks, at my neck. At everything, exposed to the cold.

The chill of it pressed at me, filled my lungs, made it hard to breathe. To run.

Still, I did, and I could hear it, behind me—footsteps— but I went faster, rushing down the driveway, which curved back and forth, switchbacks.

How far behind was he? I chanced a look back, but he wasn't there. It was impossible to say, between the snakelike road and the woods thick with evergreens, with spindly branches weighed down, puffed up, with snow.

Despite the pain in my legs, the bitter cold on my hands, I pressed on, until finally the mailbox was in view, and at the road I gasped and veered left, rushing down the main road, retracing the footsteps I'd taken so naively less than an hour before.

My head pounded, and the sun glared against the blankets of snow. The whiskey he'd served me sloshed around in my stomach, and I wondered, for a moment, if there had been something else in it, too, even though I'd seen him pour the stuff. Had I seen him drink his own glass? I couldn't remember. The thought sent my stomach turning in on itself, and as I clambered forward, gasping for air, I felt the retches coming, uncontrollable. I stopped briefly, my bare hands on my knees, felt a lurch, and spat, but there was nothing.

Behind me, I still couldn't see him, and so I turned back toward the motel, kept running. Eventually, I saw its wide, tall letters etched out by snow. The awning, caved in.

Everything—and everyone—felt dangerous now. The strange young blond girl, the one I had chased. The lawsuit with Charlie's name on it. The threatening note that could have been from Denise. The binder full of our profiles, all of us rendered down to notes in Maisy's handwriting. Like it was all waiting there, hiding around corners, under beds, ready to reach out and snatch me, to serve me Siobhan's fate, too.

Still, I had nowhere else to go, so I jolted across the parking lot, around the office, down the long line of rooms until I found the last one on the left. Siobhan's. And mine now, too.

Fumbling for the key, I slipped it into the lock, twisted, and threw my weight behind it, my hands shaking—and aching, too—from the bitterest cold.

Then I was in, and the fire was warm, and I slammed the door behind me, twisting the lock. I pulled over the nightstand, propping it like a barricade. Then I thought, screw it, and I grabbed the bed, moving it desperately toward the door.

It was only then that I saw it, Siobhan's computer— it had been right here, shoved under the bed the whole time.

Her files. Her stories. The last emails she had ever sent. The remnants of a life that had been cut way too short.

Once I got the bed frame fully in front of the door, I pulled out my phone, typed out another text to Frank, praying that if I hit send, someway, somehow, it would go through.

This is bad. I need you. If you get this, call the police. Tell them to come to the Twilite Motel.

Then, still trying to catch my breath, heart racing, nerves shot, head sloshy, fingers cold, I reached for the bottle of wine, still sitting on the counter where I'd left it. I tipped it back and took a large, indulgent swig. Then I grabbed her laptop and tapped the power button.

The thing came to life.

20

Siobhan

January 10, 2023
12:23 p.m.

Despite Charlie's unplanned arrival and the way Jeremy had driven off like he was over the whole thing, despite feeling for a hot second like I'd been standing between two live wires, the intensity of Charlie's possessiveness vibrating against Jeremy's need to assert himself, I managed to get a full scene written that morning. One of the friends, alone in her room, convinced she's being watched. That a toxic ex has followed her and her friends to this remote spot (I know, I know).

Now I stood, flicking off the music on my speaker. I was behind on my caretaking duties—because of course I was—and now seemed as good a time as any to catch up. I moved through the rooms, checking them like I was supposed to. Nothing to see here, folks.

But as I approached the office, I stopped.

I heard a distinct buzzing coming from just around the corner, right past the office. My heart beat a bit faster, and I felt my stomach clench, seizing up.

There, on the side of the front office, was the trash bag, the one I'd finally gotten the nerve put out in the dumpster a couple of nights before. Only it was ripped to shreds. Torn by a raccoon, a fox—did it matter?

Everything was everywhere. Eggshells and chicken bones. Rotten salad greens and apple cores. A half pot of rice I'd had to throw out among torn tissues and paper towels.

My blood boiled with anger, with rage. That fucking woman. How dare she. She knew this would happen; she had to. She knew it would happen, and she'd done it on purpose.

The flies buzzed around hungrily, and I backed away, leaving it for now. I wasn't going to sink my hands into rotten trash unless I had a guarantee from Maisy that this wasn't going to happen again. I slipped my key into the door of the office—and stepped right into a mess of mail, a mix of bills, junk flyers, and catalogs.

My breath caught.

There, right on the top. A sheet of paper, words scrawled across it in bright red Sharpie:

TAKE CARE OF YOUR MESS

What the fuck?

Not only had she hauled the trash here, but she'd scrawled out a—what? A threat?—and slipped it through the mail slot? Was she really that incensed? About a dumpster a few feet over her property line? Christ.

And if she could do that, what else could she do?

For all I knew, she'd sent someone to prowl around here the other day.

Maybe she'd even turned on that washer—just to fuck with me.

Fingers shaking ever so slightly, I held the note in my

hand. I should throw it away, I thought. I should get rid of it.

Instead, I walked over to the front desk, set it on top.

Proof, should I need it.

That this woman was out of her damn mind.

Working through the caretaking duties in the rest of the rooms, I did my best to force the note out of my mind. Run water in every faucet . . . check. Examine mousetraps . . . check check check. In Room Three, I did find one that had gone off, a poor little guy sandwiched in wood and metal, and between gags, I decided I'd take care of it whenever I got around to tackling that awful mess of trash, which, realistically, was going to be on me.

Room One was the final one on my list.

It was the farthest room back, the one hardest to see from the front, the top point of the L.

I turned the lock, opened the door, and though I'd been through the motions so many times today that it felt rote, I paused now. Something was different.

Close door. Look around. Try to get bearings.

The room was decorated the same as the others. Bold tribal rugs. Chic white linens. Oak bed frame. Modern kitchenette. Wide-planked floors. Gaping maw of a woodstove.

It was the *smell*, that was it. A tangy musk. Could it be from the trash? But that was all the way down by the office, and I hadn't noticed it in any of the other rooms.

And it *didn't* smell like trash. It was distinctly human, like Charlie when he'd had too much to drink and sweated through the sheets. Quickly, I cased the room, checking closets, the bathroom, under the bed, looking for some-one's presence, but there was no one.

Was I imagining it? Definitely not.

My pulse sped up. The motel was closed. No one in, no one out.

I approached the bed. I needed proof.

At first, it seemed normal. The bed was made, the sheets tucked and everything, but then, not normal at all. The sheets were not quite right. They were loose in parts. The fitted sheet was rumpled. I leaned forward. And there was that smell. BO. Unmistakable. Like someone had slept here who desperately needed a shower.

I pulled back the sheet, spotted them instantly. Three long hairs. Blond.

"What the fuck?"

Looking around, it was like suddenly the signs were everywhere. Water droplets in the sink. Ash in the fire-place. A ring of water on the kitchen counter.

Someone had been here, and I wasn't sure they'd ever left.

21

Siobhan

January 10, 2023
8:15 p.m.

That night, I stared at my empty bowl in the sink. Refilled my glass of water.

"What now?" I asked Spikey the Aloe Plant. What *now*?

The day had been a mess, ever since I'd found the evidence of a visitor in Room One.

I'd called Maisy, but her mailbox had been full. I'd emailed her, too. Detailing all of it. The intensity the trash dispute had reached. The threatening note that had to be from that woman. Every strange occurrence, bulleted out in a list. I'd tried my best to work through it. I'd shot more B-roll, catching the pool, the property, the outbuildings, in different types of light. I'd added a sketch to my notebook—someone in the woods, lurking. I'd edited and reedited a scene in Final Draft. And then I'd dutifully made myself a healthy dinner, poured a glass of kombucha, and now, it was done.

Now, I was all alone in the dark.

"Just you and me, Spikey," I said to the plant, forcing a laugh.

A rustle from the next room—my hairs standing on edge—one of the many sounds I was always, always hearing, and I flicked through my phone, found an old indie rock album, blasted it.

Coming here wasn't *only* for the movie. I could have found a sublet that started earlier, written the damn thing in Brooklyn. Could have scouted locations on a weekend, shot on another. I didn't need a whole month at a remote motel in the woods to make this happen.

But the reason I'd jumped was because I had something else to prove, too.

Charlie had texted me. It had been December 11—a week after his birthday. A day after I'd thrown him out, insisting he stay with one of his friends until I got the hell out of the apartment come January.

This isn't gonna work, Shiv. You can't stand being alone.

And, much as I hated to admit it, it was true, wasn't it? I did hate it. Terribly so. And between Charlie and his social circle, Allison and her connections, Kerry and Frank and the loveliness of their company, I'd never had to really be on my own. Just me and my thoughts.

But then Charlie cheated. Allison flew off to the Caribbean for a shoot. Kerry disappeared from social media, stopped answering my calls. I'd texted Frank—*She's hit rock bottom, hasn't she?*—and he'd written back one word: *Yes.* Maybe I should have tried harder to be there for her, but I was fighting my own mess. And I was sick to death of alcoholics, anyway.

I was alone. And I hated it.

But what could I do to prove to Charlie, to everyone, to myself, that I could handle it?

Well, go off and be even *more* alone, of course. No friends. No internet. Nothing but me and my work.

Now, here I was, and it was harder than I'd imagined.

Spikey wasn't real company. The work wasn't enough to fill the interminable hours.

And there *was* something going on here. The notes. The presence. The shredded, rotting trash. The proof of someone in that room.

I'd come here to write a horror movie, but I'd never wanted to be this inspired.

I'd never wanted to think someone was actually watching me, to feel like I was crawling out of my damn skin.

Before I could stop myself, I grabbed the landline, dialed Allison's number, which I'd written down in my notebook. Turned off the music.

It rang four times, then went to voicemail. Her cheerful voice, even in recorded form, was like a balm. God, I missed her. I missed *people*.

The beep came, and I couldn't help it.

"Allison, call me when you can. I'm lonely, Al. I'm lonely and this place is only making it worse."

A gust of wind whipped around the place, and music off now, I heard a *pat-pat-pat* outside.

Like footsteps.

"I'm lonely, and I'm scared, too."

A sound woke me, later that night.

Bang bang bang!

Three solid thuds, wrenching me from an awful, restless sleep.

My body jolted, and I sat up in bed.

Ears perked up, I listened, heard nothing but the patter of rain, slamming against the room like drumbeats. Had I imagined the banging, dreamed it? All I could hear was the steady thrum of a storm, before a crash of thunder, followed, mere seconds later, by a flash of lightning.

It could have been the sound of an animal, a critter overhead, could have been a branch falling against the roof, could have simply been the thrum of the rain.

Could have been one of the many noises that were always taunting me, always unexplained. Like the footsteps when I'd called Allison. I'd gone out the moment I'd hung up the phone, but no one was there.

I took a slow, deep breath, my eyes struggling to adjust to the dark. I fumbled on the nightstand until I found my phone, but it was dead—the damn charger had come out of the wall. I plugged it in again, watched to make sure it was working.

Listened again for the sound. Nothing more than the rain.

I pushed myself out of bed. Stumbled in the dark over to the kitchen. Flicked on the light and grabbed a glass. Filled it straight from the tap. I swallowed back the water, poured another glass, and drank that down, too.

Then I dropped it, the glass landing on my right toes, sending a shock wave of pain through my body, before clattering against the tile floor and shattering into bits.

Because the sound was back—*bang bang bang*.

And, unmistakable now, the door handle started to jiggle.

The door began to shake . . .

22

Kerry

February 2, 2023
3:02 p.m.

Door barricaded, locked away in Room Thirteen, I stared at my friend's computer, at a desktop that was clean and organized into practical folders, a single file there at the bottom left.

TheLastRoomOnTheLeft.fdx

I double-clicked the document, and the Final Draft software opened, filling the screen.

A screenplay, of course, what tied everything together. The camera. The sketches. Couldn't make a film without a screenplay.

A page came up, the cursor blinking, and even now, even after everything, I felt that catch in my chest, the pressure of that blinking cursor. This wasn't mine to write, though. I could read instead. So I did.

INT. MOTEL ROOM—NIGHT

Katie slams the door behind her, twisting the dead bolt and engaging the chain lock. She's wet from a rain storm, her hair

dripping, caked to the sides of her face,
and she walks the perimeter of the room,
locking windows, checking behind the shower
curtain, then returns to the door, pulling
a piece of furniture in front of it,
barricading herself—

My shoulders jolted, and the hairs on the back of
my neck stood straight up. It was like I was reading
about myself. Even the name—Katie—was so much
like my own.

How had Siobhan known this was all going to happen?
It felt like she had almost planned it, somehow ordained
it. Yet that wasn't possible, of course. This place wasn't
magical, wasn't haunted. She'd been killed, by *someone*. It
had nothing to do with what she was writing; it couldn't. I
kept reading.

Katie's phone rings, and she digs in her
pocket until she finds it.

KATIE
(voice shaking)
Hello?

WOMAN (OS)
What is it, Kat? You don't want to be
friends anymore? You think you can just
erase me, pretend I don't exist? Drown me
out with wine?

I swallowed, the realization dawning.

Pretend I don't exist. Drown me out with wine.

Wasn't that exactly what *I'd* done to Siobhan? I'd blocked her, stopped answering her calls. I'd pretended she hadn't existed, because it had been easier that way, easier to put it all out of my mind.

```
KATIE
It's not like that. I—

WOMAN (OS)
Because I do exist, you know that. You
can't just delete me. I'm right here.
Right here with you, even now.
```

Katie looks up to see the handle turning,
the door beginning to shake—

I slammed the laptop shut, my heart racing. I didn't want to be reading this. It felt like some kind of twisted revenge fantasy.

More wine, that's what I needed. I lifted it to my lips, gulping it back. It didn't matter what she'd written, did it? Siobhan is *gone*, I thought desperately, another sob crawling up my throat. Murdered by someone who'd dragged her body into a freezer, left her there. The grief was overwhelming and mixed, inextricably, with shame, a cocktail brewing inside me. The fact of Siobhan's anger had been there in front of me, practically flashing on the screen. And I would never get to make it up to her. I hadn't been there for her when she'd needed me, and now I never could be there for her again—someone had stolen that from both of us.

Jeremy. Had he stopped running, or had he followed me here? Would my barricade stand up to his anger, his brute strength? Was he about to burst in any moment, punch me in the face, knock me unconscious, drag me through the snow, leave me out there to freeze? He could get Siobhan's body back out of that freezer—I was the only one who'd actually seen her, after all—dump both of us somewhere in the woods. By the time the snow melted, however many days from now, by the time we were found, the police would make assumptions, our bodies too far decomposed to tell the truth. Two women, city girls, who wandered out of their lodgings, got in—literally—over their heads, the snow swallowing them whole.

Don't just sit there, Kerry, Imaginary Frank practically begged. *Do something.*

I had to keep moving, maybe back to Denise's, who surely had to have returned by now from the neighbor's. I could find my way through the woods, guarantee that Jeremy couldn't intercept me on the road. Tyler could drive me to the police station. I could tell them what I'd found. I could tell them everything, I could prove it this time, I could—

I froze.

It was too late; it was too damn late.

There, in front of me, as if pulled straight from the Courier text of Siobhan's screenplay . . .

The door. The handle was turning. The door was shaking.

Bang bang bang. Bang bang bang.

Jeremy had found me; Jeremy had already come.

My pulse pounded in my ears, and I was frozen to the spot—paralyzed, terrified—

And then, a voice.

"Help me! Please, god, let me in!"

It wasn't Jeremy; it was a woman.

A woman who sounded almost like . . .

I scrambled around the bed, rushed to the window, pulled back the drapes.

There, a vision through the picture window. Surrounded by snow. As if yanked from that freezer, somehow reanimated, as if revived from the very dead.

A rush of joy of fear of disbelief of happiness of magic of knowledge, somehow, that she wasn't really gone.

Because there she stood, banging hard against the door to Room Thirteen.

Siobhan.

23

Siobhan

January 10, 2023
11:38 p.m.

I watched, completely freaked, as the handle jiggled beneath someone's grip.

Bang bang bang.

Eyes casing the room. Had to find a weapon. I grabbed the wine Jeremy had given to me. Brandished it like Thor's hammer.

And then: "C'mon, Siobhan, don't tell me you're asleep already."

I stopped short, wine bottle tight in my grip.

"Siobhan, it's me! Let me in, it's pouring out here!"

"Allison?" I asked.

I rushed to the door. Undid the chain. Whipped it open.

My friend was wet as a drowned rat. "Good lord, woman, I really thought I was going to have to sleep outside."

"Come in, come in," I said. She stepped across the threshold, dripping. Set down her suitcase. She immediately began de-layering, tossing it all onto a chair like she owned the place. Allison was always incredibly comfortable wherever she went, even in a situation like this. "What are you doing here?"

She smiled for the first time, her red-coated lips, somehow smudge-proof, morphing into her classic charming grin. "Surprise! It was supposed to be a smoother arrival than this."

"How did you even—"

"Can I get some water?" Allison asked. "I'm absolutely parched."

She floated over to the kitchen, opened a cabinet, grabbed a glass.

"I've got kombucha, too," I said. "And a nice bottle of wine I haven't opened yet." I held it up, still in my hand. "It was my makeshift weapon when I heard the door banging."

"Oh shit, I really freaked you, didn't I? I'm the worst. But just water, thanks. I'm exhausted."

She sat down on the bed, tossed her body back. "Cozy," she said, before sitting up, bouncing a couple of times. "This feels like memory foam. Is it?"

"I think so?" I said. "But what are you doing here? Did you get my voicemail?"

Allison's eyebrow scrunched up. "Voicemail?"

"I called you," I said. "Desperate with loneliness. Honestly, you should probably just delete it. It's embarrassing."

Allison checked her phone. "Ahh, there it is. I didn't hear the call. Must have happened once I was already on the train. Service was in and out."

"Wait, you were already on your way here when I called you?"

She beamed. "Yes, ma'am. I got an email from Amtrak, advertising discounted prices on fares, and decided on a whim. There was only one train left, the last one of the night, leaving from Penn Station at eight o'clock."

Allison was always going on about fate and destiny, about manifesting her own luck. In truth, chance did seem to favor her more times than not. I'd always chalked that up to her charisma, her beauty, more than anything else. "I'm glad you're here, but why didn't you call me? I could have picked you up from the station. I mean, lady, it's your car. I owe you."

"I know, I know," she said. "But I really wanted the surprise to hit. Problem is, there are no Lyfts and Ubers at the train station. You have to use local cabs, and they're all booked up in advance. How was I supposed to know? After a while, I started to freak out and did try to call you. I wrote your number down somewhere but I couldn't find it, so I looked up the main number for the motel, but no one answered."

"It probably went straight to the front office."

"Anyway," Allison said, "I *finally* was able to get in touch with a cab company to bring me here, and then the drive was a good thirty minutes. And then I get here, walk right up to trusty Bessie, and you're in a deep sleep. I mean, my fault for arriving so late! But still. Weren't you always a night owl?"

"I was," I said. "But with no internet and no distractions, it's kind of hard to be. Plus this place gets weird at night. Staying up too late freaks me out. But enough about that." I pulled her into a hug, holding her tight. "You're so impulsive, you know that? But in the best way. You are still not allowed to listen to that voicemail, but suffice it to say I needed you. I've been lonely and freaked out and—"

"And here I am," Allison said. "And you get to tell me everything that's been going on. Please don't skip a thing."

So I did. I went over it all. The reappearance of Charlie and his face-off with Jeremy. The footprints outside the pantry and the running washer. The creepy woman and her obsession with my trash. The note that might have been from her—or might have been from someone else. The blond hairs that had been in the bed in Room One. The loneliness that was baked into every passing day. I even told her about naming the aloe plant.

"Yikes," Allison said, when I'd laid it all out. "Can I meet the famed Spikey? Where is she?"

I laughed, pointed over to the window.

Allison turned back to me, eyes narrowed. "In all seriousness, though, you should have called me way sooner. I mean, your ex is hanging around, you've taken a new *lover*," she said in her deepest, most absurd voice. "You're talking to plants and all sorts of legitimately weird stuff is happening. What does Maisy say about that, by the way?"

"A whole lot of nothing," I said. "Her mailbox is full, and she hasn't emailed me back."

Allison rolled her eyes. "Yeah, I mean, she's no great friend of mine or anything. She's a connection from a director I knew years ago. She asked me to post it because she knows I have a big reach with the newsletter. I thought this would be such a good opportunity for you. I'm sorry it's not working out."

"No, don't get me wrong," I said. "It *is* good for me. I'm doing the work—I mean, I'm trying at least. It's just been a lot of emotions. Beyond all this weird stuff, a lot of it is just me, struggling to be on my own."

"I get that," Allison said. "I really do." She reached out a hand, took mine in hers. "Everything with Charlie, god, it's been awful, hasn't it?"

I felt tears swim in my eyes. "It would be easier if I didn't care about him, but I still do. I miss him, terribly. I miss being with him. But I don't know how to trust him again. I don't know that I can."

"Yeah," Allison said. "Please don't tell me you're thinking about taking him back."

"I'm not," I said. "But listen, I've been meaning to ask you—why are you and Charlie still in contact?"

"In contact?" she asked, shoulders jolting. "What do you mean?"

"He said you gave him my address up here. I mean, I know he told you that he had stuff to return to me, but don't you think you should have run it by me first?"

I paused. Allison was staring at me, a blank look across her face. Not one of guilt but one of confusion.

"What is it?" I asked.

"He said that I gave you the address *up here*?" Allison asked.

"Yes," I said, a chill starting to crawl up my spine as I spoke. "I mean, didn't you?"

"I did, actually. Few days ago. And I'm sorry, you're right. I should have checked with you, but he said you meant to send it to him but hadn't yet emailed or something—I figured it was due to the lack of service. But, Siobhan, I gave him your address in *Brooklyn*, the sublet that starts next month."

My heart began to race. "You did?"

She nodded. "Yeah. I actually didn't tell him you were up here at all."

"You didn't?" My heart beat a bit faster. "But then how did he get it?"

Realization was already dawning on me, the pieces fitting together, answering my own question. The coincidence of it all. The way he'd been there when I went to town. The way he'd been here again, just as I was coming back from Jeremy's . . .

Allison stood, crossed the room in three quick steps, then secured the chain lock, pulling the door to make sure it was locked tight.

"Honestly?" she said. "I really don't know."

24

Siobhan

January 15, 2023
10:59 a.m.

INT. BATHROOM—NIGHT

Katie flicks on the light, illuminating the white subway tiles. She spots a smear of blood against one wall. Quickly, she pulls the shower curtain back with a screech of metal-on-metal.

  KATIE (screaming)
  Oh my god. Oh my god. Oh my god.

Claudia runs into the bathroom.

  CLAUDIA
  What is it?

  KATIE
  Becky, no. Please, Becky, no.

Becky lays supine in an empty, waterless bathtub. Blood is pooling from her temple. Her eyes are shut. Claudia runs to her,

kneels down, and waves her hand in front of
Becky's mouth.

    CLAUDIA
    Wait wait wait. She's still breathing.
    Help me. Help me help her!

Katie kneels down, beginning to help her
friend lift Becky from the tub.

"Ding ding ding!" Allison cried with glee as her phone
played its usual melody. She sprung from her seat at the
small desk and ran up to me. Flicked my laptop closed
with one hand.

"Al—wait—I was—"

"No no no," she said. "We stick to the schedule, right?
That was the end of your Power Hour. Final Draft
autosaves anyway, trust me. Now we walk. And do our
caretaking duties. Habits, right?"

I opened my laptop and quickly saved a backup file to
my desktop. Then closed it again and stood from my
makeshift desk at the kitchen counter, which I preferred
to the small one by the window. That one was Allison's
when we were doing our Power Hours side by side.

"All right," I said. "We'll do the routine."

Al had explained to me, the morning after her late-
night arrival, that she'd spent her whole plane ride back
from the Caribbean reading a book about habits. Unlocking your full potential, all that jazz. She'd proposed a
plan—she'd stay at the motel, and we could both work on
our creative projects together. Me, the horror short.

Allison, a one-woman show that her agent had been on her to finish.

The schedule was this: We woke at eight, showered, and got ready. Had breakfast and coffee and talked over each of our plans. Then at ten a.m., we began our first Power Hour, where we had to essentially stare at our screens for an hour and force the writing to come out, no matter what. It wasn't that I hadn't been trying to write before, but social creature that I was, I found it easier to do when Allison was in the room with me, even if we weren't allowed to talk. At eleven, we did our caretaking duties, followed by a brisk walk. One o'clock, lunch. And two, our second Power Hour, which I could also use to work on storyboarding or shooting B-roll. From three p.m. on, we were free to keep working or take a break—either way, we had to be ready to do it all again the next day.

It had been five days of this, and it was actually working. No more meetups with Jeremy, the handprint he'd left on my ass almost entirely faded by now. Sure, I'd woken more than once in the middle of the night, sweat soaking the sheets, realizing I'd been dreaming about sleeping with him again. But I figured it was likely for the best.

"You think you'll actually finish in time?" Allison asked as we stepped outside. In the distance, I caught a glorious view of the mountains, already snowcapped at the top even if there was still no snow on the ground.

"As long as you're here, for sure," I said. "Now shall we be caretakers?"

Allison smiled, then took a gulp of coffee. "Let's."

Since she'd arrived, I hadn't skipped a single caretaking duty—not even once. She insisted on it. Part of her new obsession with habits. No more sleeping on the job.

Now, as we worked our way through the rooms, I had to admit she was right. The routine was good for me—good for the movie, too. It got my mind wandering. Creative juices, all that. Plus, with Allison here, I was no longer scared of my own shadow. Or human presence in what should have been an unoccupied room. Whoever had come—for whatever reason—they were long gone by now.

Or at least I thought so.

We opened the door to Room Six, the one closest on this side to the office, and there it was. Again.

The scent. Human. Sweat. Bodies.

"You smell it, right?" I asked, stepping across the threshold. "This is *exactly* what it was like last time. I knew I wasn't imagining it. I knew—"

Allison pointed ahead, her face pale, as if she'd seen a ghost.

Though the room was dark, the drapes still pulled shut, the littlest bit of light showed that the bed wasn't made. In fact, it looked like someone had only just stepped out, and next to it, a small duffel bag, beat-up combat boots, and—

"Oh shit."

There she was, standing in the door to the bathroom, the daylight from the bathroom window bathing only the right side of her face in light. It cast across hollow cheekbones, the wide forehead of a heart-shaped face, speckled with the remnants of adolescent acne, as if this woman—girl, really—had stepped out of some sort of teen slasher movie.

My heart raced, and behind me, I could hear Allison taking steps back until she tripped, her body running into the table near the door, tipping a small succulent over with a clang.

My eyes stayed locked on the girl. "You can't be here," I said. I gestured to the bag by the bed. "Whatever this is, whatever you're doing, you can't be here. You have to leave. *Now.*"

For a moment, she didn't move. Was still as a statue, and in that moment, I wondered if something was wrong with her, if she'd reached some catatonic state and I should be helping her, not throwing her out. But then she leapt into action: Scurrying across the floor. Slipping feet that weren't even socked into her combat boots. Pulling on an oversize sweatshirt I hadn't even noticed crumpled in the corner. Grabbing the duffel bag and tossing it across her arm.

Her hair was wet, her skin damp from a fresh shower, her clothing rumpled, but still, her beauty seemed to precede her. Long ice-blond hair and large doe eyes. She was one of those people who would get discovered by a model scout at the mall.

"Why are you here?" I asked, my heart softening a bit.

She looked close to tears, but she didn't answer. Just took quick strides, making her way through the door, out into the parking lot.

Allison watched her go, then turned to me. "That explains it, then. Everything that was freaking you out. The sounds. The presence you found in the other room. Hell, the washing machine, too."

I couldn't take my eyes off the girl. I watched as she headed up the road, veered to the right until we couldn't see her anymore.

"What is it?" Allison asked. "I mean, don't you feel better? Knowing you weren't losing your mind? That it was just some girl?"

"I don't know," I said. I couldn't quite place what exactly was bothering me. I took a breath, trying to put my finger on it, and then it hit me, smack in the face. Fear. But not fear *of* her. Fear *for* her. A feeling so strong, it was baked into my bones. Like something had happened to her or something *was going to* happen to her. And we weren't doing a thing to stop it.

This girl didn't need to be chased off; she needed to be protected. I was somehow sure of it.

"We shouldn't have let her go like that," I said finally. "What if she really needed our help?" I looked at Allison, my eyes widening. "What if she's in some kind of danger?"

Allison was back near the bed now, pointing once again.

There it was, poking out from beneath the mattress, a glint of metal. Allison knelt, pushing back the bed. A knife. Skinny, sharp, and long. The sort of knife you could use to gut a fish.

To gut a lot of things.

"I think if anyone was in danger just now," Allison said, "it was us."

We did what we should. We called the cops, and a pair of them had come by, chalked up the whole thing to "addicts and partiers" and, a perennial favorite, "kids these days." One of the guys had taken down the girl's description, bagged the knife as evidence. Told us to call him if we saw her again.

Around four, I finally managed to get Maisy on the phone, and the woman had admitted she occasionally had trouble with people sneaking into the rooms during the off-season, had mentioned drugs as well, something she conveniently forgot to tell me when she was sending me the link to the Twilite's carefully curated Instagram.

By dinner that night, Allison seemed intent on putting the episode behind us.

"I'm glad we know at least," she said, twirling a bit of pasta on a fork. "She's probably just on pills or something. The knife is for cutting up her drug tablets, I don't know."

"Drug tablets?" I asked, laughing. "God, you sound old."

"I don't know what kids do these days!"

"And now," I said, "you sound like the cops."

"Well, either way, she's gone now. Fade to black. Whatever."

But I wasn't so sure. Something about it felt so wrong, chalking up what was going on with this girl to drugs when it could be any number of things. And did it matter if it was drugs, anyway? Did that make her beyond compassion? I kept returning to the look on the girl's face, the way the moisture had crept into her eyes. I couldn't shake the feeling that I should have helped her. That she had needed it, in some deep, real way.

It was the same way I felt about . . .

"Siobhan?" Allison asked. "You okay? You look like you're going to cry."

"Sorry," I said, playing with a bit of pasta on my plate. "I don't even know why I'm thinking about this right now."

"About what?" Allison asked.

"The girl just . . . she reminds me of Kerry."

Allison reared her head back. "Kerry *Walsh*?" she asked. "Funny to hear her name out of your mouth."

"Why?" I asked.

Allison hesitated, then narrowed her eyebrows. "Okay, well, you distinctly told me not to ask you about her or talk about her at all. That you were done with alcoholics after Charlie. And, like, I don't really disagree? The few times I met her, that woman did not know when to stop drinking."

"Right," I said. "Yeah, I did say that. But I guess it's less that I was done with her and more that she fell off the map. Just completely disappeared from social media. Even after she had this big following. All her accounts gone. Then she wouldn't answer me at all. And I asked her husband if she'd hit rock bottom, and he said yes, and I didn't really try after that. But maybe she needed me. Maybe I should have worked harder to help her. I don't know if she's in rehab or in some program or—"

Allison practically rolled her eyes.

"What?" I asked.

She shook her head, sighing.

"Al. *What?*"

Allison sat up straighter. "Okay, first of all, that girl you're so worried about is an adult human who *broke into the motel with a knife*. Let's not romanticize the whole thing."

"Yeah, but—"

Allison lifted a hand. "Please. Just hear me out. You're

way too trusting. You're always giving people the benefit of the doubt. Kerry didn't *disappear* from social media, Siobhan."

"What do you mean?"

"Her accounts are alive and well. I see all her posts."

I stared at her a moment, my mind spinning in circles.

"If you can't see them, that means she blocked you."

"What? *Why?*"

"That I don't know," Allison said. "Because she's a selfish drunk and she doesn't have your best interests at heart? Charlie, but in friend form? But here's the other thing: I don't know if she hit rock bottom or what, but if she did, it's a pretty nice one."

"What is *that* supposed to mean?" I asked.

Allison leaned back in her chair. She shook her head, and then—"Listen, I haven't been totally honest with you."

"Out with it," I said, pausing mid-bite. "Please just tell me, whatever it is."

"She's coming here, next month. Kerry is the next caretaker."

My fork clattered against the plate. "What? But how did she even . . . ?"

"She subscribes to my newsletter. She actually did before she even met me through you. Told me the first time we met."

"God, Allison, you and your successful Substack."

"I know," she said. "Maisy asked me if I knew her, and I said not well but we had mutual friends. I think Maisy was enamored by her following because she told me after how excited she was to welcome her."

"Why didn't you tell me?" I asked.

Allison raised her eyebrows. "Remember? You told me not to talk about her."

"Not if there's something pertinent like that!"

Allison took another bite of pasta. "I really didn't want you to get distracted."

"But that means when I come back to shoot next month, she's going to be here. Didn't you think that—"

"To be honest? I wasn't sure if you'd be ready to shoot. So I figured, cross that bridge when we come to it."

"Thanks for the vote of confidence," I said.

Allison set down her fork, took my hand in hers. "I'm sorry," she said. "I shouldn't have doubted you. Because you're doing the work. And I'm so, so proud of you for it. And the rest of it, it'll work itself out." She squeezed my hand. "I'll talk to Maisy, okay? Make sure Kerry knows to steer clear."

Her eyes locked on mine, her grin mischievous. "Leave it to me. I'll make sure you never have to see Kerry Walsh again."

25

Kerry

Siobhan was standing in front of me. Siobhan was pale, and her lips were halfway to blue. A dirty down jacket was wrapped around her, the front of it covered in what looked like vomit.

And yet she was here. A corpse, reanimated.

At first, nothing but joy, but relief, because here she was. Tears sprang to my eyes, because the friend I'd thought was gone was here, standing right in front of me.

But at the same time, my mind began to spin, remembering the way the cops had looked at me, so very, very doubtful.

What you think you found.

There had been a body out in the snow, a hand I'd seen through a window, and then there hadn't.

And then there'd been a body in a freezer, something I was so sure of, wasn't I?

And yet . . .

Yet . . . when I'd seen her in the freezer, I was drunk. Was it possible? Was there any way I'd made up the whole thing, pulled it out of the recesses of a boozed-out, over-medicated mind?

Siobhan stepped across the threshold, without waiting

to be asked in, took quick strides until she was in front of the woodstove, knelt down, and leaned forward, so close I worried she might burn herself, and for a moment, I imagined her on fire, running around like something out of one of her horror films, because she was not supposed to be here. She was not supposed to be in this room, in front of me. Breathing heavily. Soaking up warmth.

And yet, I was so very glad that she was.

"I thought you were dead," I said, tears streaming down my cheeks now. "I . . . I *saw* you." My heart raced as I closed the door behind me, blocking out the draft. My voice cracked, and a sob crawled up my throat. "Christ, I *saw* you."

"Kerry," she said, her eyes piercing mine. We hadn't seen each other in two months. Not in person, not even through our screens. And yet here she was, saying my name. Alive.

Could I have imagined it all? Was it really possible to hallucinate a dead body like I'd hallucinated those two lines on the pregnancy test?

But to hallucinate it . . . twice?

For my eyes to lie to me, for the very sense of reality I'd always been sure of to be cracking all around me, crumbling like a bad foundation?

Did it matter, so long as Siobhan was here? So long as her life wasn't cut short like I'd thought?

"Kerry," Siobhan said it again.

I rushed to the fire and knelt down, too, and I wrapped my arms around her, squeezing her tight, holding the weight of her, the realness of her. I could feel it, the coldness in her clothes, the stiffness of her limbs, and I could smell it, too. The vomit and a tinge of urine. A distinctly human sort of decay.

And yet, here she was. Real. Here she was, proving everything that I'd thought over the past twenty-four hours was wrong.

Here she was. *Alive.*

"You're freezing," I said. I stood, pulled a heavy wool blanket off the bed, wrapped it around her shoulders, pulled it tight.

Her hands were gloved, but her eyelashes were frosted, her lips chapped and cracked. She stared at me, and for a moment, her gaze was so intense, I thought maybe she'd somehow forgotten how to blink, as if that part of her had been broken, an instinct left to freeze out in the snow along with everything else. But then she did, and her lips parted.

"What happened to you?" I asked. "God, Siobhan, what *happened*?"

"I—I don't—" she started. And then, her voice half a croak: "Water," she managed. "I need water."

I stood, rushing to the sink and filling a glass, then returned to my friend, lifting it to her mouth. She took it with a shaky hand, downed it in a couple of gulps. I refilled it. She did it again.

She stared at the fire a bit longer, then turned to me again. "My head," she said. "It's killing me."

I jumped up again, wanting to get her some painkillers, but I remembered my stuff was in the other room. So I went to the bathroom instead, looked through the mess of toiletries until I found a small travel bottle. I walked back to the fire, poured three pills in Siobhan's hand.

"I can't get warm," she said, as soon as she'd swallowed them.

"You need to get out of those clothes," I said. "Into something dry."

Here she was, very real, very not dead. Here was my friend. A friend who needed my help.

"We'll get you cleaned up," I said, desperate to help her, however I could. Desperate to somehow turn this around, to right it.

"We'll make this better. Promise."

Twenty minutes later, we were in the bathroom. The shower curtain was pulled back, and steam was rising from the claw-footed tub. There was still no hot water since the power was out, so, after popping another anti-anxiety pill that seemed well-earned, all things considered, I'd heated water in the kettle I'd propped on top of the woodstove while Siobhan attempted to eat a couple of crackers. I'd filled up the tub slowly, kettle by kettle, pot by pot, until there were at least a few inches full, enough to partially submerge in.

Now, I poured in a last kettleful, a bit of hot water splashing back, singeing my hand, then set it on the tile floor. "I think that should do it."

Standing across from me, Siobhan held her hands out to the sides like a child waiting to be undressed. I pulled off the down parka. She was lucky she hadn't choked on her vomit, in the state she was in. She was lucky she wasn't dead.

But she was. You saw her. You saw her stiff with rigor mortis. In the snow. In the pantry. In the freezer. Dead. How far have you gone, Kerry? How far from sanity have your vices led you this time?

I put the outerwear in a pile on the floor, and Siobhan reached for her jeans, slowly unbuttoning them, as I shushed the voices in my head. Not Frank this time, but me.

Carefully, I knelt, working the material over her hips and around her butt, her silky cream underwear wet and cold. I kept going, pulling the jeans carefully down her legs, like a snake shedding its skin, until she winced, and I did, too. Her knees were bloodied and crusted, as if she'd fallen on both of them at the same time, rocks—or something—cutting through the denim. Dirt was matted in the wounds, and the one on her left knee looked to be filling with a creamy white pus that was almost certainly infected and would only get worse unless we cleaned it up.

Siobhan winced again.

"I'm sorry," I said, looking up at her. "I'm trying to be gentle, but your knees are banged up pretty bad."

I kept pulling down the fabric until it pooled onto the tile. She stepped out, reaching her hands to steady herself on my shoulders, and then lowered herself to the edge of the tub so I could pull off wool socks that were matted with sweat.

Siobhan stood again, carefully lifted her hands over her head. I lifted her black V-neck sweater, something that felt soft and sumptuous and intended for cozy holiday parties, ski weekends, nothing like this. Underneath, I found bruises, yellow and purple and blooming up her right side. I tugged it fully off and gasped as I saw marks, three clear ones, across her back. Like someone had hit her—lashed her, really. *Hard.*

I didn't ask—there was too much to ask—only put a

hand on her shoulder, making sure it was okay. "Should I—your bra and underwear?"

She nodded.

I walked around her, carefully unhooked the three clasps, then loosened each strap, letting the bra dangle down her arms and fall to the floor.

I moved to her underwear, pulling them down slowly, then offered a hand to hold again so she could step out.

Then I stood, meeting her eyes, avoiding her dangly veined breasts, the burst of pubic hair between her legs.

I knelt down, placed a wrist into the water, which had stopped steaming but was still hot enough. "I think that's good."

Siobhan sucked in a quick breath as her toes hit the water. One leg and then the other. Her hands held tight to my arm as I lowered her body in.

I had the strangest feeling then, that I had spent so long wanting, dreaming, of being a mother, and now here I was, mothering.

Mothering Siobhan, who was supposed to be dead. Siobhan, who was alive but very, very broken. Siobhan, who didn't even realize all the debts I owed her.

She let her arms fall to her sides, and she leaned back, resting on the back of the tub. Carefully, I scooped up handfuls, pouring them over her shoulders, her elbows, her forearms, her bloodied knees.

I thought again of the baby I'd dreamed of bathing, of the smell of powder and new skin and what it would feel like to massage oil into a pair of chubby arms you and the love of your life had created. The hole inside me that I'd tried to fill up with booze and bad decisions.

I thought of all the time I'd spent looking into other people's worlds and wanting wanting wanting. All the things I'd posted to social media, trying to show everyone else that my dreams were coming true, too. Even though they weren't really. Far from it.

Still, here I was, being a mother, in my way. To a friend who needed me. A friend I thought I'd lost. A friend who the universe had given me another chance to care for.

"Thank you, Kerry," Siobhan said, as if reading my mind.

I waited until I'd wet her hair, until the tub was dingy with soap and grime and Siobhan's blood. Then I put a hand on her shoulder, and I looked my friend in the eyes.

"What do you remember?"

Siobhan's bottom lip began to quiver, and I reached into the tub, cupped some water in my left hand, poured it over one of her shoulders, then did the same with the other. "It's okay," I said as I did it. "You're with me now. But I have to know what happened. There was a party. Right?"

She nodded. "I was drunk. High. I remember going to bed, but then—then I was in the boiler room."

"The boiler room? The one next to the pantry?"

Siobhan nodded.

"Wait, this whole time? But how?"

Siobhan's eyes widened with alarm, fear. "What do you mean *this whole time*? Last night—"

I stared at my friend, wondered exactly what had happened to her. "Siobhan," I said, firmly but calmly. "The party wasn't last night. It was two days ago."

She stared at me. "But that can't be. I—"

"What is the last thing you remember?" I asked.

"I was in bed, and—I got scared, and I went out to see where everyone went. And the door to the boiler room was open, so I walked in, and—" She shook her head. "God, I was so drunk. It's just flashes. I must have hit my head in there. It's killing me, still."

"But for two days?" I asked. "And you never left that room?"

Siobhan closed her eyes tight, opened them again. They'd filled with tears. "I—I didn't know it was that long. It was so dark. I woke up, and I could feel the heat, and I knew it must be the boiler. And then I woke up again, later, and I heard rustling, and there was vomit—everywhere—and I tried to call out, but I had no voice, I just, I *couldn't*—I was so tired. I don't even remember going back to sleep."

"But how did you—"

"The last time I woke up, and it was cold. The boiler wasn't working anymore."

"There's been a storm. Everything's lost power."

"That's when I forced myself to get up. I was worried I would, I don't know, freeze in there."

"You did the right thing," I said. "You could have—"

Died. And it was such a wild thought, because only an hour ago, I thought she had.

Siobhan's head tilted forward. "I just want to *sleep*."

"No," I said urgently, a hand on her elbow. "You probably have a concussion. Aren't you not supposed to sleep when you have a concussion?" My hand found my pocket, looking for my phone, to put in a request to Dr. Google, before it hit me, once again, that I couldn't do that right now.

Siobhan looked down, then up at me. "Where is she?"

A chill ran through my spine. "What did you say?"

"Where *is* she?"

"Who?" I asked.

"She should have been looking for me." Siobhan stared at me like a poor lost puppy. "If it was really two days, I mean, that's why I left the room in the first place, to find her, to see where she'd gone. Whether the party was over or still going, she should have been there. She's who I was looking for, when I saw the door to the boiler room open . . ."

I stared at her, trying to understand. "Siobhan. Who? What are you talking about?"

"I passed out," she said. "You're right, I probably did have a concussion. But she should have been there. She should have been looking for me," Siobhan said again. "She should have *found* me."

"What are you talking about?" I asked again, desperate now. "*Who* should have been looking for you?"

When Siobhan finally spoke, it was like the most obvious thing in the world. "Allison."

"Allison?" I asked, leaning closer now. "Allison Romy? Your friend?"

"Yes," she said. "Where is she?"

I heard my gasp before I felt myself take it. "Allison was up here with you?"

Siobhan nodded. "For the last two weeks. It was her idea to have the party. To celebrate our last night here. But then we had an argument and . . . I stormed off. And I kept drinking, and we didn't get a chance to work it out, and I know she was mad, but that doesn't mean she wouldn't worry, that doesn't mean she wouldn't try to find me, to *help* me—"

Already I was standing, backing away from the tub. "Hold on," I said.

"What is it?" Siobhan asked.

I turned around, fled the bathroom, pulled on my snow boots and my puffer. In seconds, I was once again out in the snow, the sun blinding, glistening off the blanket of white.

I followed my steps around the motel room, beelining back to the pantry, my heart racing.

I was terrified, horrified, and yet I had to know, didn't I? I had to know for sure.

That I wasn't imagining it all. That I wasn't halfway to losing my mind.

I shoved the key hard into the pantry door, jiggled until it turned. I wrestled the door open, swallowed back my fear, approached the freezer.

Noticed what I hadn't before. Frozen veggies, cuts of meat, piled on the bottom shelf on the opposite wall. Whatever had been in the freezer before cleared out to make room for the body. No stench, nothing—it was too cold, even outside the freezer, to rot.

Proof, wasn't it? That my mind hadn't simply conjured the image.

Still, I had to see. I placed my hands on either side of the lid, and then, with a huge tug, I lifted it.

There she was. Face down. *Real.* I hadn't imagined it. I hadn't imagined a damn thing. I wasn't losing my mind. It wasn't the booze and the pills and the desperation. It was all real. Impossibly, horrifically real.

The brown hair. The red-coated press-on nails.

I shoved my gloved hands on one side of her body, felt my heart race, felt my blood pumping, felt the hardness of her, the heaviness, the rigor mortis, the frozen skin.

She feels like frozen meat, I thought depravedly, bile threatening to crawl up my throat.

She was a human, a woman, a person who had never deserved this, and she felt like a piece of frozen meat.

The vomit came then, and I turned to the side, puked—red wine—onto the pantry floor.

I wiped my mouth and turned back to her.

I had to see. I had to know.

I tugged and tugged and then, with a final, desperate scream, I gave a good wrench, and she turned.

There she was.

Allison.

Staring back at me.

I hadn't been imagining things. I hadn't been losing my mind.

There had been a dead woman, but it wasn't Siobhan.

I backed away, and the freezer door fell shut on its old, rusty hinges.

Allison was dead, there was no denying it. She'd been chucked, face down in a freezer, like she wasn't even human.

Who had killed her?

26

Siobhan

"You're almost done with the screenplay, right? Like you're seriously almost across the finish line?"

Allison and I walked briskly down the road that led back to the motel, a pickup zooming past us, mountains big in the distance. They were even more snowcapped than they had been a week before. Winter was coming. The sky was gray, sunlight only just breaking through.

"It's hard to believe, but I am." I kicked at the few inches of snow that had fallen over the past week. Turned it into icy gravel. Took quick steps to keep up with Allison's power walk.

"That's what happens when you stick to the schedule."

I raised an eyebrow. "Or the magical power of your company."

"How sweet," Allison said. "The Great Allison shows up and all your problems disappear."

I didn't tell her that in truth my feelings of being watched had only intensified. The writing had gotten easier because of the schedule, sure, but also because I was leaning right into the unease, heavy and weighted in the pit of my stomach. The sense someone was watching me, which never quite seemed to leave. I'd be sitting there, typing away. Feel someone behind me. See a shadow. A flash of movement out the window. Nothing I could pinpoint. Nothing to confirm. Little hunches, ones I couldn't shake.

"Siobhan," Allison said now, breaking my trance. "You okay, girl?"

"Sorry," I said, shaking myself out of it. "Mind just wandering."

Allison cocked her head to the side, eyeing me. We followed the curve of the road, and it looked like she was about to say something else when a voice stopped me.

"Siobhan."

Allison stopped short. I did, too.

There he was, standing in front of his mailbox, only a few feet in front of us, his muscled arms bulging beneath a wool sweater, his face—and head—clean-shaven. Eyes daring, like he was thinking about his hands on my neck right here in broad daylight.

My blood ran hot, and it was like I could feel the mark on my ass glow. "Jeremy."

Allison's gaze ping-ponged between us.

"I haven't seen you around," he said. "I even went by the motel the other morning. Your car wasn't there."

"Oh," I said. "My friend's been up. This is Allison, by the way."

Allison smiled, but Jeremy barely gave her a glance. That in and of itself was thrilling. Yes, we looked alike in a lot of ways, but she was way more beautiful than me. The kind that made both men and women fall for her almost instantly. There was something appealing in the fact that her charms didn't work on him, not like they seemed to work on everyone else. "You been all right? Anything more—er—from your ex?"

"Oh," I said. "No. He's—I'm sorry you had to see that. It's embarrassing."

"No," Jeremy said. "I'm just glad you're okay. You should—" He hesitated. "You should come over again." His eyes flicked briefly to Allison. "Both of you. I'll cook."

"We'd love to," Allison piped in, before I could say a word. "Both of us are take-out addicts, and we've certainly reached our culinary limits. Tonight, maybe?"

My eyes widened, but Jeremy only grinned. "I can make that happen. Seven o'clock?"

"That's perfect," Allison said. "We'll see you then." She turned away before I could add anything else. I offered Jeremy a quick smile before following behind her.

"What in the world was that?" I asked.

She walked briskly, leaving Jeremy behind us. In moments we couldn't even see the turnoff to his house. She kept up a good pace until the motel and its tall letters were once again in our view.

"He *obviously* wanted to fuck you, Siobhan," Allison said matter-of-factly. "Again, I mean."

I felt my face flush as we turned into the parking lot. "So we should just offer me up to him on a platter, then?"

"Correct me if I'm wrong," Allison said, "but you haven't had a second tryst because Charlie basically cockblocked you? Haven't you earned a little fun? I, for one, am tired of looking at your mug and your mug only every single night. Spikey the Aloe Plant isn't going to do much for either of us. You deserve it. Unless he's a creep or something, and you want nothing to do with him?"

"No, but I—" I stopped, swallowing my words.

Denise's truck was idling in front of the motel.

"I told you you shouldn't have parked there," I said. "That's *her*."

There had been no more standoffs over trash, thankfully. But when I'd told Allison that I was having trouble getting good shots with her car in the way, she'd taken the liberty of moving it herself, driving it down the gravel road and parking it behind the dumpster.

"Please," Allison said. "I'm not scared of some kooky neighbor. Let her throw more trash our way. It's a *driveway*. You're obviously meant to park there."

My pulse slowed as I watched Tyler step out of the truck instead.

"Thank god," I said. "It's just Tyler. He's her son, and he falls really far from the tree. Decidedly normal."

We approached, and he looked up, smiling at both of us.

Allison grinned right back, taking him in.

"Tyler," I said. "I didn't see you on the schedule."

"No," he said. "Maisy had asked me to come over and seal up one of the baseboards when I got a chance. I've been slammed but figured it was as good a time as ever. If you can let me in?" he added. "No keys."

"Oh," I said, reaching into my pocket. "I mean, as long as Maisy said it's okay."

"She did. But definitely give her a call if you need to. Last thing I want is to get you in trouble."

"No," I said. "It's fine." I reached into my pocket and found the key ring. "Which room?"

"Four," he said. "But ideally, I'd like to check them all.

Because if there are any other gaps, it's easier to do all of them at once."

"Right," I said. "Well, here you go." I handed him the key ring. "Go to it, I guess."

His eyes lingered on Allison. Unlike Jeremy, he did not in the least seem immune to her charms.

"I'm Allison," she said, before I could introduce her. "Siobhan's friend from the city."

"Tyler," he said. "Nice to meet you."

She grinned, her red lips showing off perfectly white, straight teeth.

"Well," Tyler started, "I should get to it."

Allison looked at me and only hesitated a moment. Then she cleared her throat. "Hey, Tyler," she said.

He turned back so quickly you'd think he gave himself whiplash. "Yes?"

"You know Jeremy? Down the road?"

Tyler shrugged. "A little, I guess."

"We're going there for dinner later." She grinned mischievously. "You should come with."

That night, we walked briskly over to Jeremy's, just before seven o'clock, a flashlight guiding our way.

"I can't believe you invited Tyler," I said. "He's like . . . a kid."

"I'm not going to *do anything*," Allison said with a smirk. "But at least this way I don't have to be the third wheel while you two eye-fuck each other all night. Plus, he's got to be mid-twenties. *And* he's cute."

We turned at the mailbox, made our way up the

"Well," Allison said, clasping her hands together, "as much as I love a little drama, I do at least need a drink for it."

"Great idea," Jeremy said, turning on his heel. "Follow me."

I let my no-drinking rule slide once again. Jitters, nerves—you get the idea—and the first drinks went down easy, caramel whiskey and spherical chunks of ice clinking against the sides of lowball glasses. Jeremy moved on to a bottle of red as dinner was served. Braised short rib, tender and succulent. Creamy mashed potatoes. Bright green peas. Allison led the conversation, regaling Tyler with tales of her career, from her biggest roles to her latest shoot. Tyler lapped it up like a dog at a water bowl, beaming in the light of Allison's energy, seemingly content to have moved beyond discussions of property lines and what his mother should or shouldn't do.

Soon enough, the plates were cleared, more wine poured. Allison even pulled out her THC vape pen, which she'd been offering me since she got here but I ... took winding drive. It was still and quiet and eerie, only the *crunch-crunch* of gravel and the *whoosh* of the wind.

Finally, the house came into view. Lit from within like a modernist moonscape.

"Remember, this is just dinner," I said. "I'm not staying here tonight."

Allison raised an eyebrow. "Whatever you say, love. Whatever you say."

I was about to knock when I noticed the two men's body language. They were standing opposite each other, Jeremy stretching his frame, Tyler almost cowering, shoulders hunched.

Unfazed, Allison walked right up to the door, knocked three times—*rap rap rap*.

"Hello," she called. "It's us!"

The two men turned, our arrival jolting them out of their conversation. Tyler stood still, a deer in headlights, but Jeremy moved for the door. "Hello," he said. "Come in. Please."

"You beat us, Tyler," Allison said as she sashayed in. She tossed her purse onto a modern hall table like she owned the place. Shrunk out of her jacket. "But I'm so glad you came! We didn't even see your truck in the driveway."

"My mom needed it," Tyler said distractedly. "So I walked."

I stepped in behind her, Jeremy moving to take my coat, his hand brushing my shoulder slightly. A shiver crawled up my spine, a good one this time.

"I was just updating Tyler on the—"

"Lawsuit?" Allison asked, her ears practically perking right up. She positioned herself next to Tyler and elbowed him playfully in a way that made his cheeks flush red. "What is this, small-town drama?"

Tyler's mouth flattened to a line. "My mom has a right to be upset, you know."

"Of course she does," Jeremy said coolly. "Like I told you, we're on the same side. Maisy is in the wrong. I know that. You know that. The laws of New York State make that beyond clear. Now we just have to make it official with the county. And we will. But all I was saying was to leave it to the lawyers. Your mom threatening Maisy isn't going to help anything."

"She didn't threaten her," Tyler said. "And we don't have a lawyer, remember? Who are we supposed to leave it to? Besides, it's our land. Our family's been here for generations. We aren't—" Tyler's eyes flitted around the absurdly modern, obviously richly outfitted space. He didn't finish his sentence, but he didn't really need to. *We aren't interlopers. We have a right that you don't.* "Can you blame her for being mad? We never had this problem with the last owners, and they were there forever."

"I was merely suggesting," Jeremy went on, "that trying to argue with Maisy—outside the court, at least—isn't going to get us anywhere. Even if you don't have a lawyer, if your mom is going to file any petitions herself, that's *still the right strategy*."

Tyler... still

what I'd found on Charlie's collar. But it was impossible, of course. She'd left early.

And she wouldn't anyway. She was *Allison*.

I pushed the wild, weed-paranoid thought from my mind, took in my friend. In real life, she was just as stunning, as captivating, as she was on-screen, maybe more so. And I could feel the men appreciating it. Relishing it. Jeremy's eyes checked in with me, but even he couldn't help but stare at she went into a story I'd heard far too many times already, about a shoot in Toronto that had required snow machines, the way she'd never felt childhood magic like she did except when she was watching fake snow puffed into the air.

A flicker of jealousy sparked deep in my belly as I watched her release a plume of steamy smoke, looking half like Lauren Bacall, so easily charming these men. She had arranged this, had opened her perfectly lined mouth and spoken this unusual dinner into being. I had thought this afternoon that it had been for me. That she wanted Jeremy and me to have another chance to hook up. But now, as she made graceful gestures to mime artificial falling snow, I wondered if that was really true.

Allison needed her hit of male attention, wasn't that it? That was what this was for. No more, no less. The truth of it prickled my nerves. Why, after all, did she get everything? The cool career, the Substack newsletter that made an actual income. Beauty that would always, always make me look plain in comparison.

And attention, so much attention. She grinned again, smacked her red lips together.

I shifted uncomfortably in my chair, the minutes moving slowly now. Molasses dripping, that kind of a thing. What next? Would Jeremy get up and announce dessert, or could we just pack it up and leave?

I was suddenly tired of *The Allison Show*. Tired of always feeling less vibrant in comparison.

Tired of the feeling that if Charlie had been with someone like her, none of this would have happened.

I glanced down to my hands, nail beds peeled and cracked like they got when I was a bit anxious. When I lifted my head back up, Jeremy was looking right at me.

"So she's the actress, but you, Siobhan, are the real creator, right? I mean, you're the one making the movie."

"Oh," I said. "I mean, I haven't actually made it yet—"

"Oh stop," Allison said. "She's very nearly done. It's happening for her. It really is this time."

Guilt washed over me—*whoosh*. How could I have sat here stewing about her when she was, as always, singing my praises? Pushing me to do what she knew I wanted to do so badly?

"I mean, it's a bit like playing god, isn't it?" Jeremy asked. Under the table, his foot found the edge of mine, running up my ankle, to my calf, then back down. I felt a flush of happiness. Jeremy wasn't distracted by Allison. His eyes were on me.

"It is a bit," I said, leaning forward in my chair. "Kind of like you're building a shadow box and then taking the lid off, looking right in."

As soon as I said it, my muscles tensed. I sucked air into my lungs, a quick gasp.

Because there in the window, staring at us.

Her icy blond hair. Her svelte body. Her piercing eyes.
There was the girl who'd been squatting in the motel.
The girl we'd chased off.
The girl with the knife.
Watching.

27

Siobhan

I blinked, adjusting my eyes to the darkened window, but as soon as I did, the girl was gone.

I pushed myself out of my chair. Legs scraping against the polished concrete of Jeremy's dining area. Wineglass tipping. *Splash.*

Jeremy jumped up, running to the kitchen island to grab a dishcloth to tackle the spill. I went the other direction, toward the window where I'd seen her.

I got so close my breath made condensation against it, like a kid on a school bus in winter.

Could I see a thing? No. Nothing more than a few feet of frosted grass, lit by the almost-full moon.

"Did no one else see her?" I asked, whipping around to face them.

Jeremy tossed the rag over the stain. They all looked at me.

"She was just here," I said. "Here, looking at us. *Staring* at us. Watching us, like, like—"

A shadow box . . . taking the lid off, looking right in.

"Who?" Jeremy asked.

"That girl," I said to Allison. "The squatter girl."

I rushed past them. Into the main room, to the front door.

"What are you doing?" Allison asked, following me now.

"I'm going to look for her. She might need help. She can at least tell us why she was staring like that."

"Whoa whoa whoa," Allison said carefully. "You cannot just go running out into the dark chasing a girl we know brought a *knife* to the motel."

"A *knife*?" Jeremy asked. "Wait, what?"

Allison brought him up to speed, and his eyebrows shot up. "Then I agree with Allison," he said. "You shouldn't be chasing someone like that. You're sure it was the same person?"

"Yes," I said. "I know what I saw."

"Well, then, we can call the police if—"

"I don't want to call the cops!" I said. "I just want to see that she's okay. What she wants, what she—"

"I'll go."

We all looked to Tyler, who'd been quiet until then.

"I've lived here the longest. I know all the neighbors. If someone's out there, it's best it's me, okay?" He stood a little straighter. "Safest, too."

Allison and Jeremy hesitated. I didn't.

"Yes," I said. "Please. Just make sure she's okay. See what she wants."

Jeremy opened his mouth, and for a second, it looked like he was going to protest. Then he turned to Tyler. "Do you need a flashlight?"

Tyler shook his head. "I keep one on me."

We all watched as he walked out the door, shut it behind him. For a moment, you couldn't see him, couldn't see anything, but then there was an orb of light, outside the living room window. Tyler walked to the right, circling the place, waving the flashlight back and forth, a pendulum swinging. It was eerie, watching him do it. Reminding us—full stop—just how many ways there were to see into this house.

He circled the grounds twice. Then he was back at the front door, crossing the threshold.

"There's no one out there," he said. "I was thorough."

"We know," Jeremy said. "We saw."

"Whoever she was, she's long gone now. But I can ask around. Maybe my mom has some idea." Tyler's eyes caught mine. "I really don't think you have to worry too much."

I nodded. "Okay."

Allison sighed dramatically. "Well, now that that's done, shall we have another drink?"

A moment, a tipping point, where we all stared at each other, deciding how the night would proceed. For a hot second, I just wanted to go. Get out of this place. Go back to the motel and sleep sleep sleep.

But Jeremy's eyes caught mine, and I could see want in them, and I thought, Fuck it. That girl didn't need me, just like Kerry didn't need me. Here I was, letting them both distract me from an escape I actually deserved.

"Let's do it," I said, knowing what it likely meant, knowing it and wanting it, too. "I mean, why not?"

It was the middle of the night, and my back was on fire.

Hot and raw, burning with the pain that hadn't gone away. Waiting for me, after a deep, drunken sleep.

Jeremy was in bed next to me, his body emanating warmth. His breath, in and out, stale from the night's drinks, from the weed we'd passed around—first Allison's pen and then a joint put together with an antique cigarette roller, all brass and practically gleaming with old-timey romance.

I slipped out of bed, made my way to the en suite bathroom. Turned on my heel and looked at my naked body in the mirror. I was covered in red marks, an angry pattern from the top of my shoulders down to the base of my spine.

It was another thing Jeremy hadn't asked about, had just done.

When it was close to midnight, Allison and Tyler had left, Allison claiming she needed sleep, Tyler offering to walk her back to the motel, the fact that I was staying here unsaid but understood.

And then, we were in the bedroom. Jeremy was opening a closet, pulling out a black leather whip, holding it gingerly in his right hand.

He pushed me against the bed, and *snap*, it was happening. *Snap snap snap snap snap.*

Now, looking at the marks, I felt a flush of heat rushing through me. I had read about S&M on Reddit threads, in ladymag essays. Talked about it with friends over the years. Jeremy wasn't going about it the way you should, with consent at the forefront. Jeremy was just doing it, and I was letting him.

And I loved it, even if it was fucked-up.

A crack of a branch. I jolted, turning away from the mirror, looking out the window that was uncurtained. Peering out on the woods.

I thought, again, of that girl. Decided, this time, that it

was nothing more than a woodland creature. That whatever was going on with her wasn't mine to figure out—not my monkeys, not my problem—turned back to the mirror, staring at myself once again.

Relishing every mark.

Jeremy was up soon, and then the bed was made. Whip put away. All evidence of what had happened tidied and erased. Poof and it was gone.

There were lattes at the kitchen island. Eggs cracked in a pan. Fresh herbs stripped and cut with kitchen scissors. Tomatoes sliced with one of the many knives from a massive butcher block.

But something was bothering me. I tried to place it as I watched Jeremy switch from one knife to another. Something was wrong with this picture. I finally put it together as he was slicing into a second huge, juicy tomato.

"That slot on the bottom is empty. The skinny one on the left," I said, pointing to the block.

Jeremy smirked. "You inventorying my kitchen supplies?"

"No," I said. I replayed the image like rewatching a movie. "The girl from last night. She had a knife at the motel. It was skinny. It looks like it could have fit there."

Jeremy frowned. "No one's been in here. I can promise you that. Since I came up full-time, I'm always here."

"Don't you have cameras?" I asked.

"Only a doorbell one. Not many people come by this way."

"Well then, you don't know, do you?"

He tilted his head to the side as he laid out tomatoes,

layering them between fat slices of mozzarella and leaves of basil. "You seem really bothered by this girl."

"I am," I said. "And I don't really get why you're not? She was outside your window last night. *And* one of your knives is missing. Doesn't that freak you out?" I forced myself to pause. "Could it be in the dishwasher? The knife?"

Jeremy laughed.

"What?"

"You can't put these kinds of knives in the dishwasher."

"Okay," I said. "Sorry I don't know all the ins and outs of expensive-knife care."

"Hey," he said, his face softening. "This has really got you worried, hasn't it?"

I nodded.

"Look, I went to a dinner party in the city couple of weekends ago. Brought a few knives down so I could slice up a roast I made. Because yes, I like nice things, and yes, I can be a bit meticulous. I probably left it at my friend's place. I *promise* you. You're safe here. There's nothing to worry about. The motel? I don't know. It doesn't sound like Maisy has the best security. But here, no one is coming in. I assure you."

I let out a breath. "So do you think I'm being paranoid?"

"No," he said. "Not at all. I'm just saying, I really wouldn't worry." He leaned across the island, pulling my face close with his right hand. He kissed me with an open mouth, biting my bottom lip just slightly. "I'm sure it's nothing more than one of those strange coincidences." He pulled back, smirking. "Something you'd probably write into your screenplay."

*

238

Back at the motel, I hopped into the shower. Let the water run warm against the marks on my back, then got into comfy clothes. Guzzled water. Drinking, man. Really didn't miss it.

Allison was at the door before I even had a chance to open my laptop, two mugs of coffee in her hands.

"You little hussy," she said, handing me the coffee and coming inside.

She took a gulp, sunk onto the bed. "So? We're a bit off schedule today, but I hope it was worth it? I want details."

I felt myself blush. "Well, he made me breakfast. Fried eggs and caprese salad."

"Isn't that nice?" Allison said, smirking. "Anything else you want to divulge?"

I thought of the leather whip, of the marks on my back. "A lady never talks." Then I sat on the bed next to her, nudged her with my shoulder. "And?" I asked. "What about you? You had Tyler eating out of the palm of your hand. I think that's the most time he's ever spent with Jeremy, by the way."

"I know," Allison said, her eyebrows narrowing. "What was that about? They full-on looked like they were going to kill each other when we arrived. This property-line thing is no joke, I guess."

"Did Tyler say anything about it on the walk home?"

"No," Allison said. "He spent the whole time talking about how cool it was to be around creative people like us. Turns out, the boy wants to be a writer. Can you believe it? I *never* would have guessed. But he did have some intel, actually."

"What's that?"

"The girl. He thinks it might be a friend of his who's got controlling parents and a shitty ex-boyfriend. Said she crashes here sometimes when she's trying to get away from it all but that we shouldn't worry. McKenzie something. He said he'd talk to her."

"A shitty ex-boyfriend?" I asked. "So maybe she *does* need our help."

"And what are you going to do, Siobhan? Fight the guy?"

"No," I said. "I guess not. I just feel bad for her."

Allison took another sip of coffee. "There are girls all over the world with crappy ex-boyfriends, you included. There's nothing to be done. It's a fact of life."

I hesitated but decided not to push it further. Allison was right—what *could* I really do? "So did anything happen? Between you and Tyler, I mean?"

"Come on, Siobhan," Allison said, eyebrow raised. "He's, like, a kid."

"Hey," I said, "you're the one who invited him."

"Yeah, so?" Allison traced her finger in circles along the edge of the mug. "Can you blame me for wanting a little male attention? It's nice to be adored."

I burst out laughing.

Allison's gaze trained on mine. "What is it?"

"Come on," I said, taking a sip of coffee. "Like you've ever had trouble getting male attention."

She stopped tracing. "What is *that* supposed to mean?"

I tilted my head just slightly, took another sip. "You know what it means. Guys go crazy for you."

"And you, too," Allison said. "I mean, neither of us are bad-looking."

I rolled my eyes, then stood from the bed. "You don't

have to pretend. You command a lot of attention. You kind of seek it out."

"Seek it out?" Allison asked. She stood, too, adjusting the hem of the black tee that hung perfectly across her body. "Seriously?"

"It's not a bad thing," I said, my heart beating a bit faster. "It's just . . . an Allison thing."

Her face fell. It was the same exact expression I'd seen on one of her acting reels, but it wasn't fake this time; it was true, genuine hurt. "An Allison thing." She took a deep breath in, let one out. "Siobhan, I have feelings, too, you know. And you think just because I'm—"

"Gorgeous," I blurted out. "Successful, every guy's dream—"

"This is what I mean," Allison said. "*This*. You say this stuff about me like I'm not even a real person. I don't have it any better than you."

My eyes really did widen then. And though I felt bad for hurting her, of course I did, she wasn't seeing this clearly at all. "Oh, you don't?"

"How do I? Seriously?"

"Look," I said. "I'm sorry for saying anything. Obviously we don't see eye to eye here."

"No, really," Allison said, a hand on her hip now. "Tell me. How do I have it better?"

I caught her eyes, and it was clear she wouldn't let up. "Fine," I said. "You're a real actress. In real movies. You have a huge following of people who listen to you, who respect you. You know everyone. Your newsletter makes actual money. And to top it off, every man—and about half the women—who meet you fall instantly in love with you. I mean, is that enough? What do you want to do with your one wild and precious life, that's what you're always quoting. And you're the one who's out here *doing* it."

Allison walked over to the kitchen counter, set her mug down, and pressed her hands against it. When she turned back to me, she wasn't crying, wasn't angry, just looked . . . deflated. "We've been friends for so long, and I swear it's like you don't know me at all. You think I want to be Newsletter Girl? You think that was my dream? You think I want *She Had a Really Popular Substack* carved on my tombstone?"

"No, but your acting—"

"I'm thirty-six, Siobhan. Ten years ago, I was going out for main roles. Now, my agent wants to send me out for the divorced mom of the ingenue. And those parts are hard to come by, too! I had my chance, and I worked my ass off, and I was so, *so* close to actually breaking out, and it didn't happen for me. And now it's too late. The one-woman show I'm writing? It's because nothing else is working. It's a Hail Mary. For a career that's stalling and might soon be over."

"Don't say that," I said.

"But it's true. And you can tell me about this woman or that woman who was discovered after forty, but the reality is, it almost never happens. You want to make movies? Well, guess what: There isn't an expiration date. No one is going to look at your face and every tiny little line and pore and tell you that you need Botox and fillers—but done in a way that no one will ever know you had Botox and fillers—just to be able to go out for stuff. No one is chronicling your every pound. No one is telling you that the parts for 'women your age' are hard to come by. And now, even the smaller roles in the B-films, they're drying up, too. Do you know why I actually came up here?"

My eyebrows knitted. "Why?"

"I learned that I didn't get a role that I really thought was on lock. Same director as the movie I was just shooting. And he all but promised me. They cast a twenty-seven-year-old instead. Said they wanted someone more unknown, as if I am not completely unknown, too. What they meant was they wanted young."

"I'm sorry," I said. "I had no idea."

"No, you didn't," Allison said. "And you don't. I don't have a partner. I don't have someone who's begging me to take them back. Yes, a lot of men want to fuck me, but who cares? Half of them, they're practically offering up some quid pro quo so I can try to get my headshot moved to the top of the stack. No thanks. The other half just see a face like mine and they want to prove to themselves that they can bag the *hot girl*."

"I'm sorry," I said. "I should have asked. I was just . . . I was always jealous. I assumed."

"Yeah," she said. "A lot of people do. But what life looks like on the outside and what it looks like from the inside are very different things."

I stared down at my hands. "I know."

Allison looked for a moment like she might actually cry, but then she picked her coffee back up, took a rather large gulp, forced a smile. "Look, Siobhan, I don't want to fight. What I wanted to talk about is my great idea."

"And what's that?" I asked.

"A party," she said. "On our last night here. To celebrate how far you've come."

"A party?" I said, turning the idea over in my mind. "I don't know. Maisy's instructions clearly said no parties."

"They also said no guests, and here I am. She's not going to know. And if she does, who cares? She's so desperate for the motel to have creative clout, she'll let you shoot your short here no matter what happens. I promise you. You deserve it. A celebration. You're so close to being done. We can ask Jeremy and Tyler, whoever we can drum up."

An idea popped into my mind then. "Maybe I could ask Charlie."

Allison scoffed. "Why would you ask Charlie?"

"Because I don't like how things ended with us, the last day I saw him. I want us to have real closure. And to finally come to some agreement about this money stuff. I feel bad how it's all gone down."

"*You* feel bad?" Allison asked. "Seriously? He's the one who cheated on you. On his damn *birthday*, no less."

I stared at her, tilted my head to the side. "I didn't tell you it was that night."

"What do you mean?" Allison asked. "Didn't you?"

"No, I didn't. I told you we broke up, that he cheated."

"Oh," Allison said, looking down into her mug, as if suddenly fascinated. "I mean, I guess I assumed. Everyone was drinking. And you told me you split only a few days later."

My heart started to beat a tiny bit faster.

"Whatever," Allison said. "The point is, he cheated on you. He followed you. And you want to invite him over to celebrate? Alongside the guy you're currently fucking?"

Could I tell her? That the opportunity to make Charlie jealous felt so tempting? So delicious?

Or the secret, even deeper? That maybe, sometimes, I *did* want to take him back? And now that he'd fucked someone and I'd fucked Jeremy, maybe it felt like we could start fresh? Clean?

"You're not actually thinking of getting back together, are you?" Allison asked, her eyes back on mine now.

"No," I said, maybe too quickly. "It's just . . . we kind of need him, don't we? We can't have a party with only Tyler and Jeremy anyway. He's doing this thing at Storm King, and I bet he can bring some artsy types."

Allison stared at me a moment, and her mind seemed to turn something over, but then she tossed her hands in the air, as if it wasn't her battle to fight. "If it's what you want," she said, "then we'll invite him. The point is, you're down for a party?"

"Yes," I said. "We just can't get too wild, okay? Because we'll be leaving the next morning."

"We'll be good little hostesses with the mostesses, I promise," Allison said. "And the next morning, we'll clean it all up, and we'll check out exactly when we're supposed to, and no one will be the wiser." She grinned. "It will be like the whole thing never happened at all."

28

Kerry

Carefully, I opened the door to Room Thirteen, saw it all, somehow, through a new lens once again.

The wineglasses in the corner. The drug paraphernalia lining the counters. Not one but two suitcases half packed next to the bed. Siobhan's suitcase, of course, but Allison's, too.

I walked slowly toward the bathroom, my heartbeats picking up speed as I did. Inside, it all hit different, too. The false nails, spread across the counter; those had been Allison's, not Siobhan's. The makeup, the products, had likely been shared that night; just two friends getting ready for a party together. Pretending like, maybe, for a night, they were younger than they were. No idea that that night would be Allison's last. My god.

And among the realizations, the thankfulness, too. That it was Allison and not Siobhan. That my friend had been spared, even if it wasn't right or fair, even though the thought made me burn with shame, because, god, Allison hadn't deserved it, but I was glad that of the two of them, it hadn't been Siobhan.

Siobhan was still in the tub, had barely moved an inch

from where I'd left her. She was staring straight ahead, near-catatonic.

"Siobhan," I said softly, like I would to a hurt animal, something cowering and shaking. "Siobhan."

She turned to me, shook her head. "Where did you just go? Why did you leave me?"

Breath caught in my throat, because I hardly knew where to begin, what to say, and Siobhan shivered. "You must be cold," I said. "Let me heat some more water for you, and then—then we can talk."

"You're not leaving again, are you?" she asked, her voice an alarm bell. "Please don't leave me."

"No," I said. "I promise. I'm not leaving. I won't leave. I'll be right in the next room."

She stared at me a moment, almost like even that was too much, but finally she nodded, and I retreated, thinking again of the child I would probably never have, because, in her state, Siobhan *was* like a child. Seeking comfort and security, direction, to be told what to do.

A child whose heart I was about to break. Allison had been her closest, oldest friend.

In the kitchen, I flicked on the tap and let the kettle fill all the way, then set it atop the woodstove, the water droplets on the side sizzling as they touched the hot cast iron. As the water warmed, I tried to make sense of this new reality—not only what it meant for Siobhan, for my friend, but what it meant for both of us, still stuck here, without power, with someone out there, someone who could hurt us, too . . .

Allison Romy was dead. It turned everything I thought I'd learned upside down: the lawsuit from Charlie, the threatening note, Jeremy's lies about how well he'd known Siobhan. How did it all fit together, now that Allison was the victim? Who had wanted to hurt her, and *why*?

And would they stop now that they knew I'd seen her? Or was I a mess to clean up—Siobhan, too?

"Kerry," Siobhan called from the other room. "Kerry, are you coming back?"

"Be right there," I said. Absentmindedly, I reached for the kettle, the handle burning hot against my bare palm. I let it go, the kettle dropping to the stove with an awful clang.

"Kerry," Siobhan said again. "What's going on?"

"Sorry," I said, quickly grabbing a pot holder, carefully lifting the thing again, making my way back to the bathroom.

Siobhan was shivering and had her arms wrapped around her body, covering her breasts now. Her eyes were wide as a puppy's, and she looked like all she wanted in the world was to be held tight, never be let go. Slowly, I poured a bit of water into the front of the tub, careful not to scald her.

"What is going on, Kerry?" Siobhan asked, her bottom lip quivering. "It's bad, isn't it? It's really, *really* bad."

I set down the kettle, glanced in her direction, and as I did, the thought I'd had earlier—that I was glad it wasn't Siobhan—while still true, felt even crueler. Someone had stolen Allison's brilliant, vibrant life. Snuffed out her light. It was horrifying, so deeply unfair.

"I thought you were dead," I said softly. "Do you get that? I really thought it was you."

Siobhan looked up at me, her eyes wide, and I took a deep breath. "Because I thought I saw you. Because I found a body. A body I thought was yours."

Siobhan began to shake her head. "No."

But I kept going—I had to. "So when you said Allison was up here—I had to look, to see if it was her."

Siobhan sucked in breath. "No," she said again.

"I'm sorry," I said. "Allison is dead."

Siobhan shook her head viciously. "No," she said. "Don't say that. Don't *say* that." Tears sprung to her eyes, and she began to gasp for air, almost like she was about to hyperventilate. "It's not possible. She can't be. She can't be—". A sob escaped her, and her shoulders caved in, her naked body practically folding in half as the grief took her over. "No, it's not fair. It's not *fair*."

"I know," I said. My arms were around her now, and I didn't care if I got wet; all I wanted was to hold her, to somehow make it better, even though I knew that was impossible. Least of all from me.

Finally, she pulled away. "Where is she?"

"You don't want to—"

"I do," she said. "Just tell me."

"The freezer," I said. "Someone . . . someone put her there."

Another gasp. Another bout of tears.

When she looked up again, her eyes begged me for answers. "Who did this to her?" she asked. "Who would hurt Allison?"

"I don't know," I said. "That's what I'm trying to figure out."

There was silence between us, and I was painfully aware

of the rush of wind outside, of the chill in the air so far from the woodstove.

I cleared my throat, trying to force myself to think clearly. "Who was there that night? What happened?"

Siobhan took a deep breath. "Just a few people. It was small."

"Siobhan?" I said. "Allison is dead. And whoever did it, they could still be hanging around. You have to tell me. Everyone."

"Okay," she said, nodding slowly. "Okay. Let me get into some clothes."

Siobhan put a hand on each side of the tub. She pressed against the porcelain, pushing herself up, then found a towel on the rack and quickly wrapped it around her body as she stepped out, water dripping everywhere. She walked from the bathroom, and I followed. She knelt down in front of her suitcase, rifling through it. Shrinking out of the towel, she pulled on underwear and a bra, and even though I looked away, I could hear the wince as she did, could practically feel the way the pain was affecting her body.

"It was, I don't know, six or seven people," she said. Her voice, her breathing, had calmed. Like she was exhausted and spent, had used the last of her energy just getting into her clothes.

"Okay," I said. "Who?"

"Me and Allison," she said, her voice catching on her friend's name. "I'm sorry," she said. "I just . . . I can't believe it."

"I know," I said. "But you have to focus. Please. Who else?"

"Jeremy. He's——"

"I know who he is. I jumped out his window, right before you showed up, ran through two feet of snow because I was convinced he killed you."

"What?" Siobhan asked. "Wait, why?"

"I went to his place to get help, and he made like he barely knew you, but then I found your ID in his medicine cabinet."

"It must have fallen out of my bag when I was over there," Siobhan said. "I asked him to bring it to the party, but he forgot. He was going to give it to me on our way out of town. Obviously"—she gestured around—"that never happened."

"So why lie?" I asked. "Why pretend?"

"Well, I don't know, you told him I was dead, right? Maybe he didn't want to get caught up in it. I mean, I'm here. He didn't hurt me."

"You were sleeping together?" I asked.

Siobhan nodded.

"Your back . . ." I said. "Did he . . . ?"

"Yes," she said. "It was consensual, though."

"Was it?"

"Yes, Kerry, okay? And I don't think Jeremy would hurt anyone," she said. "Not like that."

"All right. Who else was there?"

"Tyler—he's the other neighbor."

I nodded. "I met Tyler, too."

Siobhan's eyebrows knitted. "You did?"

"Yes," I said. "And Denise, his mother. I went that way first, after I found the body. They helped me get in touch with the police, and Tyler drove me back here. Denise creeped me out. For a moment, I thought maybe she had something to do with it."

Siobhan swallowed. "She was pissed at me because she says the damn dumpster is on her property, and she was mad that Allison had parked her car there. She had our car towed, the day of the party. It's still in some impound lot, probably. We were going to get Jeremy to drive us the next day, but again, obviously that didn't happen."

"It's clear the woman was mad at you."

"Yes," Siobhan said. "But mad enough to kill over? And why Allison? Besides, Denise wasn't even there that night."

"Okay," I said. "But Tyler was."

"Tyler's a puppy dog," Siobhan said. "I don't think—"

"Siobhan," I said. "Allison is *dead*. Someone had to do it."

Fresh tears pricked her eyes then. "Sorry," she said. "It's still—it's hard to believe. I just—I don't see how—"

I ran back through everything that had happened. "There was a girl. Young. Blond. Was she there that night?"

Siobhan's eyes widened. "You saw her? I thought she was long gone."

"Definitely not. I saw her today. Who is she?"

"I don't know," Siobhan said. "A squatter, I guess. Local girl. Tyler was going to talk to her, get her to stop coming around. That's what Allison said. But we did find her camped out in one of the rooms. She . . . she had a knife hidden under the bed."

My eyebrows shot up.

"I really think she only had it to protect herself. She looked scared, honestly. When we saw her."

"You *and* Allison?"

Siobhan nodded.

"She looked scared of me, too. But that doesn't mean she didn't have something to do with this. She could be scared *because* she's guilty."

"She wasn't even at the party," Siobhan said. "And you think that little thing could move—" She swallowed. "Come move *someone* into a freezer? She must be a hundred pounds soaking wet."

"No," I said. "I don't know. What about Charlie?"

Siobhan's eyes widened. "What about him?"

"He was there, wasn't he? That's what Jeremy said. With friends."

"Yes," she said. "He was."

"And he must have been angry—" I started. "I mean, you must have been on the rocks, you two." I paused awkwardly. "I found a lawsuit in the office. He was suing you for thousands of dollars."

"Wait," Siobhan said. "What are you talking about?"

"The lawsuit," I said. "Against you."

"Can I see it?" she asked.

I stared at her a moment, then pulled the papers from the pocket of my coat. Siobhan reached for them, desperate. She flicked through, her eyes widening again.

"You really didn't know?" I asked.

She shook her head, and I could practically see the gears turning. "You found this in the office?"

"Yeah."

She scoffed. "Piece of shit didn't even have the nerve to hand it to me himself. He must have brought it that night. He gave me money to make my movie. He wanted it back."

"Okay," I said. "Is it possible that Allison found that out, that she confronted him in some way?"

Siobhan looked down at her hands; more tears dripped from her lashes, and when she finally looked up, her eyes were pleading. "I don't know. I don't have an answer. I don't know what happened to Allison. And I don't know what to do now. But I—" She paused.

"What is it?" I asked.

"Just don't leave me again, Kerry," she said. "Please."

"I won't," I said. "I'm staying right here."

"That's not what I mean," she said. "I know . . . I know you pulled away from me, and I know you were drinking a lot, and I know, maybe, because of how I'd tried to stop you before, you knew I would come down hard on you or whatever, so I don't blame you for what you did."

"What I . . . did?"

"For cutting me out," she said. "Because I don't even care. Frank told me you'd hit rock bottom, and when Allison explained that you blocked me, that she could see your stuff but I couldn't, I mean, I was mad, but it doesn't even matter anymore." She shook her head. "Charlie broke my heart, and now Allison—" Another sob escaped her. "Allison is *dead*. And I'm scared out of my mind, and you're all I have. So whatever caused it, don't do it again, okay?" Siobhan trained her eyes on me. "Promise me you won't. I need a friend more than ever."

I reached out my hand, took hers in mine.

"I promise, Siobhan. I promise."

29

Siobhan

"To friends," Allison crowed, grabbing the Martini shaker we'd found tucked away in a cabinet. She tapped her nails on it, long and coffin-shaped, ones we'd painted together that afternoon: falsies for her, au naturel for me, but bright red for us both. "And we'll be commemorating tonight with the Allison Special. Secret recipe. Tasty. Strong. Fucks you up in all the right ways."

She grinned, her eyes widening with mischief as she approached the kitchen counter, where she'd lined up all that she'd collected that afternoon, poking through the rooms until she found enough coupe glasses to go around. Her eyes were lined heavily but effortlessly with kohl, her cheeks smeared with coral cream blush, her lips that classic Allison red.

She sloshed pink liquid into each glass, and I looked around the room, took them all in, while Allison moved the shaker like a maraca.

Jeremy had arrived first, promptly at 8:02. He'd forgotten my ID, which meant I'd have to go and get it the next day—I'd realized it was gone when Allison and I had stocked up on bottles of wine for the party the day before. I'd warned him then that Charlie was coming, that we needed to talk through a couple of things, and though he hadn't exactly looked pleased, he'd smiled eventually and opened his nice wine before tucking himself in a corner, savoring it.

Tyler arrived next, his normal mop of locks gelled just slightly, in a button-down instead of his usual work hoodie. He'd grinned sheepishly and offered us a bottle of cheap wine, which Allison had taken with delight before pulling the boy into a hug. Now he was hovering near my friend, grabbing a cocktail the moment she poured, helping to pass them around.

And then Charlie. Charlie and his friends.

"Hotel party," Charlie said now, taking a seat next to me on the edge of the bed. "So retro."

He'd come with a pair of perfectly coiffed French guys he'd met at Storm King, Étienne and Pierre. Étienne was tall and lanky, Pierre stout and round, a Franco version of Bert and Ernie. The pair had headed straight to the bathroom, emerging with twitchy noses, hands readjusting their sweaters. Fairly aggressive for not even nine o'clock. Now, they were on their phones, flicking through Instagram in tandem.

Turning to Charlie, I raised an eyebrow, took a sip of wine. Watched as Étienne attempted to pair his phone to the Bluetooth speaker, insisting that there was a new French trap track we just had to hear. "You work with what you've got."

"They're a lot, I know," Charlie said. "But when they heard I was going to a hotel party, Pierre said it sounded 'delightfully *américain*.'" Charlie made air quotes. "They insisted on coming."

Tyler walked over then, handing us each one of Allison's concoctions. I finished the wine in my glass, and so did Charlie. Quick as anything, we made the switch. As if the drinks were runners in a relay and our hands the passing batons.

The first sip hit me hard. "Damn," I said.

"I guess at a hotel party, you have to get drunk, right?" Charlie asked.

"Well, it's a motel, for one. Roadside. Different vibe."

Charlie raised his hands. "Touché. But it's decorated so meticulously you know they're charging hotel prices."

I nodded. "Fair."

Charlie took a gulp as Étienne finally hooked his phone to the speaker, aggressive French lyrics blaring. Jeremy shot me a glance—"You good?"—and I said yes with my eyes.

"I really didn't think you'd call me," Charlie said. "I'm sorry about before."

"Jealous ex is really not a good look for you," I said. "I'm not your property, you know."

On the bed, Charlie inched his thigh a touch toward mine, and I tried my best not to care, not to feel the heat building in my body. "I know," he said. "But it still hurt. Seeing you." Charlie's eyes flicked momentarily over to Jeremy, who had moved to the kitchen, topping off his own wine, his back to me.

I turned to Charlie, the drink making me bold. Outside, frost was collecting on the window. There was a chance it would snow. A storm was coming tomorrow, but after Allison and I would be gone. "How do you think I felt, the morning after your birthday?"

Charlie winced.

I lowered my voice, just slightly. "And I know Allison didn't tell you I was up here. How did you know, before you showed up that day?"

A flush of red crept across Charlie's face.

"Just tell me. Because right now, I have to assume you followed me from the wine store."

Charlie reared back. "No, no, I didn't do that. I'm sorry if you thought that. That's why I said Allison told me; it seemed simplest."

"So how?"

"It was in your email."

"Wait, what?"

"I know, I know. It's not good. That's why I lied. You used to check your email on my laptop sometimes, and you never changed your password." He shrugged. "I just wanted to feel close to you. To know what you were doing. But, yeah, the motel details were in there."

"Jesus, Charlie. That's fucked-up."

His eyes went to his hands. "I know."

I shifted on the bed as one of the French guys once again changed tracks. "Is that *why* you left Berlin? Is there even a Storm King thing at all?"

"Come on," Charlie said. "If there wasn't a Storm King thing, how would I have conjured two artsy French coke-heads out of thin air?"

I burst out laughing, I couldn't help it.

"I didn't make any of it up, but I was planning on thinking of some reason to come and see you, and then there you were, at the shopping center of all places. It felt ser-endipitous, didn't it?"

"I didn't want any of this, you know," I said, my stomach roiling. "I didn't want to be here. I didn't want us to split up. None of it."

Charlie half smiled. "And yet, look at you. Allison told me you wrote the whole screenplay. That you're going to be able to shoot soon. It's what you always wanted, isn't it?"

Not like this, I thought, cursing myself for still loving Charlie. How much I wished I could change everything. Somehow take him back, flaws and all. "Yes," I said instead. "I'll be able to shoot in a month. And I'm right on budget, too."

Staring at him, I practically dared the man to ask me again, to demand his money back. Charlie only took a sip of his drink, then smiled, his leg inching closer again to mine. "Should we go outside?" he asked. "I have Parliaments."

I only ever smoked when I was drinking, but I loved to do it with Charlie. Something about it was so sexy, so perfect. After a glass of wine or two, we used to steal out of Kerry and Frank's apartment, between rounds of their silly strategy games, suck on Parliaments, and kiss like we were teenagers. God, I missed it.

"Come on," Charlie prompted, nudging me. "Old time's sake."

I eyed the door. "It must be twenty degrees out."

"Fuck it," he said. "Let's go."

I laughed, but I let him link his hand in mine, pull me up off the bed.

"Y'all okay?" Allison asked, eyeing us as Charlie moved for the door.

I nodded. "Smoke break."

I slipped into my coat and followed Charlie out front, shutting the door behind us.

The cold whipped at my face instantly. "Christ," I said. "It's freezing."

Charlie pulled the pack from his back jeans pocket. "This will warm you right up."

He grabbed a cigarette, handed it to me, then placed another between his lips. Pulled out his Zippo, flicked to make a flame, raised a hand to block the wind, lit the thing effortlessly. Then his eyes caught mine, and he gave a subtle nod, and I leaned forward. When the tips of our cigarettes touched, I sucked in before pulling away, feeling the rush hit my lungs, my head. Coughing a bit like I always did, then taking another drag. I reached out a hand to steady myself, and Charlie grabbed it.

"I haven't had one of these in a while," I said.

Charlie laughed. "You're better off. Trust me."

I took one more drag. "What are we going to do about this money thing, Charlie?"

He shook his head, like I'd disappointed him somehow. "You know what I want to do about it."

I inhaled again. "And what's that?"

"Get back together," he said. "Obviously."

"Allison doesn't think I should consider it. She didn't even want me to invite you."

"Allison?" For a second, he looked so shocked that I'd said her name, even though she was there, standing in the next room, even though we both had the taste of her drink on our tongues. But then his face rearranged itself. "She's your friend, Shiv. She just wants to protect you."

"I want to protect me, too."

"I know," he said. "I *know*. But it will be different this time."

"How do I know you won't just fuck someone random in a bar?" I asked.

Charlie sighed. "I'm sorry, Siobhan. I won't."

"But what's going to change?"

"Honestly," he started.

"Honestly?"

Charlie took another drag, almost as if for courage. "Listen, I can't lie about it anymore. It wasn't someone random."

"What?" I asked, my heart pounding brutally. "Who was it, then?"

"It doesn't matter."

"Charlie," I said. "Of *course* it matters."

"What matters is that I'm going to make sure I'm never, ever around her again." Charlie's eyes caught mine. "I love you, Siobhan. I never stopped."

Before I could say a word, before I could process what exactly was happening, Charlie was leaning in, his lips brushing mine. For a moment, I let him do it. I let myself pretend that this was all okay, that we were still Charlie and Siobhan, that the world made sense like it used to.

But then I opened my eyes, and I saw her, through the window into Room Thirteen.

Standing there. Staring. Her eyebrows knitted. Her face clenched with derision. With disgust.

Allison.

30

Siobhan

"Come on, your turn, Siobhan," Allison said as I took another sip of drink, my head buzzing from the cigarette, from the weed, from Charlie's kiss, from the drink that Tyler had topped off the moment Charlie and I'd gotten back inside.

The camera—my camera—pointed straight on me. Allison hadn't said a word about Charlie and me, but she'd insisted on documenting the night. A character in a found-footage horror film. Part of me was almost inspired, was thinking how I could work a bigger, more intense party scene into my film, synapses firing, even if my head was already starting to spin.

I'd pulled away from Charlie's kiss, and when he'd refused to tell me *who*, I'd stormed off, insisting I wanted another drink, and in the last hour or so, the party had taken on a different, new life. The coke had been brought out of the bathroom and into the kitchen. Allison's THC pen was being passed around like a sacrament. Her cocktails were hitting, hard. And then someone—I didn't even know who—had suggested we play Never Have I Ever, as if we were at some basement party in high school, and the Frenchies wouldn't let it go, saying it sounded *très américain*.

Now everyone was looking at me, and I could barely hold a train of thought.

"Yeah, Shiv, let's go." Charlie elbowed me, and when I looked at him, his eyes were so impatient, so cutting, that I struggled to remember why I'd felt like maybe I could forgive him. And all I wanted to know was *who who who*. Who had he slept with? Who, besides him, had broken my heart?

And then they were all chanting, "Shiv, Shiv, Shiv, Shiv!" And I just wanted it to stop. To pause. To reset.

Only Jeremy was looking at me, eyes kind, mouth not moving. Knowing that maybe I wasn't entirely happy with how things were going.

So I took a sip of my drink, and it didn't even burn, was only sweet, sweet escape. Then I cleared my throat, looked straight ahead even though I knew my words were meant only for one person.

"Never have I ever cheated on someone."

An instant pall set over the room, and in the corner of my eye, I saw both Étienne and Pierre drink before Étienne gave a casual shrug and Pierre merely laughed. But then I turned to Charlie, and to my surprise, his eyes were trained on Allison, and it was only as he saw me staring that he lifted his drink to his lips. Across the room, Allison set down the camera, took a drink herself.

What the hell? Was I the sole person going through life never stepping out on my partners? Had it just been one giant free-for-all of cheating, and I was the only one who abstained? And then I thought, *why* had Charlie and Allison been looking at each other so intently?

With the weed twisting my thoughts, little things started

to stand out. The way Allison had known that the cheating happened on the night of Charlie's party, even though I'd never told her that. The lipstick she always wore, same color as on his collar. The way she hadn't wanted me to invite him, hadn't wanted me to get back with him—was it because she knew that eventually, if I kept him in my life, it would come out?

Allison had been drunk that night, too. She had left early, I thought—but she could have hung around, couldn't she? It was all so fuzzy.

Was I stupid, naive?

Had they both betrayed me, and I was a fool for believing in either of them?

Jeremy didn't take a sip. Tyler didn't, either.

They weren't cheaters. How incredibly refreshing.

"All right," Allison said, lifting the camera back up. "That was a bit . . . pointed," she said, without even looking at me. "Let's lighten it up, shall we? Never have I ever . . ." She took a beat to think. "Gone streaking!"

Allison looked around the circle of us, waiting for someone to drink. No one did.

"*Vraiment?*" Pierre crowed. "Isn't that also *très américain?*"

"You could remedy it," Étienne said.

"Hell yes you could!" Allison cried. Already, Étienne was leaping from his seat, grabbing Pierre, and people were standing, following. The door was opening, and Charlie was laughing, and all of us were realizing that, yes, we were about to head out into the bitter, frigid cold to watch a rotund French art curator run through a motel parking lot buck naked.

Outside, the sky was dark, illuminated only by starlight.

The first touch of snowflakes was falling through the air. Charlie hovered near me, but I found I couldn't look at him. Was I absolutely losing it for thinking this way? Or to not have thought it all along?

In the barren parking lot, Pierre began to de-layer, taking off his sweater first.

"So cultured, your friends." I looked up to see Jeremy, standing next to Charlie now. "Very mature."

Charlie looked like he wanted to tell Jeremy to fuck off. Instead, he slipped his hand in mine, grabbing it.

I pulled my hand back, muttering something about needing gloves. Walked away from both men, to where Allison was filming, camera trained on Pierre as he pulled an undershirt over his head with a piercing shriek, revealing a round, hairy tummy that made him look almost like a hobbit.

"The great Siobhan." Allison turned to me. "Come to watch the show?"

"Enough of this," I said, and I reached for the camera, but Allison pulled back, stepping out of my grasp.

"Hey, hey," she said. "I'm documenting."

"No one needs to see this," I said. "I'm serious."

"What is it, Siobhan?" she asked. The camera was still trained on me, and her eyes were challenging, cutting. "Did your reunion with Charlie not work out as planned?"

I reached up then, my voice sharp. "Turn that fucking thing off."

Once again, Allison stepped back, refusing to do what I said. "What, did he promise you he'd never do it again? I mean, do you really think that's true?"

"I don't know," I snapped. "Do *you*?"

Her hands slipped down, the camera trained on the ground instead. "What's that supposed to mean?"

Snowflakes were really coming down now, forming a halo around Allison's perfect face. Yes, she had spun me a whole sob story about never making it, but she was still the biggest star of us all.

"I never told you it was on his birthday."

Allison rolled her eyes. "Yeah, I put two and two together. Sue me."

I bit my lip. "You know, there was red lipstick on his collar. Your exact color."

"You really think Charlie and I . . . ?" She laughed out loud, an awful, mean-girl cackle. As if Charlie were so far beneath her she'd never even consider the prospect.

And in that moment, I had a bizarre vision of lifting my hands to her throat. Of squeezing the life right from her. Of how beautiful it would look on film, the night and the stars and the snowflakes all around us . . .

I shook myself out of it. "Why were you looking at him, during that game?"

Allison reared back. "Why was I looking at *him*? I mean, I should think that was obvious, wasn't it? You said it as a dig at him. Who else was I supposed to look at?"

"Okay," I said. "Then why was he looking at *you*?"

Behind us, Pierre began to unbutton his pants.

Allison turned, lifting the camera again, but I swatted at her hand. "Stop that."

"Christ, Siobhan, you're going to break the thing."

"Why was he looking at *you*?" I asked again.

"I wouldn't *touch* Charlie," she said. "You should know that."

"The lipstick," I said again.

"So?" Allison said. "You think I'm the only woman on earth who wears red lipstick? Do you even hear yourself?"

"You didn't want him to come tonight. You don't want us to get back together. Because you're worried, you're worried that—"

"Yeah, Siobhan, I fucked your loser alcoholic boy-friend. For shits and giggles."

"Fuck you," I said.

She smirked. "Right back at you."

Rage filled me then, practically exploding from my fingers. Allison stared, my camera still in her hand, even if it was pointed at the ground. Perfect, beautiful Allison, who could get any man she wanted. I didn't know what set me off more, that she could have slept with Charlie or that she was so far up on her own fucking high horse that the prospect of it was laughable, as if the man I'd loved, who had hurt me more than anything, was worthless to her. Was so far beneath her as to make her cackle with disdain.

It's not fair, I thought. It's not fair that you have the looks and the talent and the world by the balls. It's not fair that I'm only finally making anything for myself by riding your coattails, your connections. It's not fair that you show me what a pathetic, jealous little shit I really am. It's not fair that you opened up to me, and yet I still feel this way.

And it was like I could see it again, reaching up, circling her neck with my hands. Letting violence explode from within me.

"Everything okay?" There was Tyler, breaking the spell

in an instant. Looking at her with his puppy-dog, I've-never-seen-anyone-more-beautiful eyes.

I didn't answer. Didn't let myself look at Charlie, whose gaze was trained on me, or Jeremy, who was looking, too.

I marched right back through the parking lot, straight to the door of Room Thirteen.

And inside, alone, the music Étienne had put on still blasting through the Bluetooth speaker, I went straight for the booze, grabbed the bottle of vodka, tipped it straight back into my mouth.

Drank until it burned.

31

Kerry

Siobhan's hand was still in mine.

I promise, Siobhan. I promise.

But I pulled it away. I couldn't do this. I couldn't just pretend . . .

"What is it, Kerry?" Siobhan looked at me, sitting on the edge of the bed. She was so desperate for me to take care of her, but she didn't know. She didn't *know*.

Without a word, I walked across the room, to the kitchen, to a bottle of wine that had not yet been drained. I poured myself a glass and drank down half of it.

You don't need the wine, Kerry. You really don't.

But Frank didn't understand. Nothing was harder to face than shame.

And nothing took away shame like obliteration.

Siobhan's eyes widened as I poured myself a large glass, as I tipped it back, letting it slosh down my throat.

"I can't lie to you," I said. "I can't just sit here and pretend."

Siobhan shrugged. "So drink, Kerry. I don't care. What you do with alcohol, it's your problem, not mine. It's not my place to judge."

But it is, Siobhan. God, if you only knew.

I took another sip, craving again the escape, and I stared at her for a moment, hating that I was going to destroy her, but I didn't know another way. "I'm not a good person, Siobhan."

"What are you talking about?" she asked. "Of course you are."

"No," I said. "I cheated on Frank. Frank, who never deserved anything like that. We're separated, we'll probably be divorced soon, and it's all because of me."

Siobhan took a deep breath. "Okay."

I took another big gulp of wine, already feeling the way it was swimming in my head, thought of that night, that stupid, awful night that had changed everything. Of all the different coincidences that had led me—her, all of us—to that night. So many things could have gone differently. Frank could have come with me after all. Siobhan could have stayed, escorted Charlie home. Allison could have never been there, buying the whole room rounds of shots. And me, of course me. Because it was my mistake, my choices, my pain.

"I didn't block you because you tried to get me to stop drinking," I said.

Siobhan's head tilted to the side. "Then why?"

More wine, sloshing into my mouth, as I went back to that night in a way I hadn't let myself do since the morning I told it all to Frank.

To the night of Charlie's birthday.

We were all drinking, all singing, all packed into one of those karaoke rooms. The night was winding down, and I'd tripped, nearly dropping the mic into a pitcher of beer, and the look on Allison's face, who was already on her way to leaving, it was so cutting, so naked with judgment. She didn't know me well, did she? I was Siobhan's friend, not hers. And she, apparently, was the kind of woman who could order shots for the bar and somehow keep her respectability intact. And so, shortly after she left, I stood, too. In words I'm sure were slurred, I announced that it was a good idea for me to go home, too.

How different would things have been if I had?

Would my friendship with Siobhan have ended?

Would Frank and I have split up?

Would I have ever come up here?

Was there some alternate universe where I had just gone home, woken up with a hangover, decided to get my shit together without having to hit rock bottom, apologized to Frank for everything I'd already put him through, committed to our marriage, committed to my career, finished my book, stopped drinking for long enough for us to do another round of IVF?

Some sliding-doors reality where the world wasn't dark for me, but hopeful?

I looked at the glass in my hand, took another sip, felt it trickle down my throat.

Who was I kidding? This was who I was. A screwup. A drunk. Someone who took took took.

Because I didn't leave when I said I would. I stepped out of the private karaoke room, walked through the crowd along the bar, until I found a seat in the corner where no one from the party would be likely to see me. Ordered myself a gin and tonic. Dug around to make sure I had my things. Phone, keys, wallet. The drunkard's constant refrain. Phone keys wallet phone keys wallet. So easy to lose one of them if you didn't constantly remind your-self not to.

And then my fingers brushed against a smooth plastic cylinder. I pulled it out. The lipstick, of course. It was Allison's, I was pretty sure. Had no idea how it had gotten in my bag—but that was how drunks were, always collecting things, your hands turning to Velcro, things you'd use to put together a timeline the next morning. She'd probably dropped it, and I'd probably grabbed it to give it back to her, then forgot.

I uncapped the lipstick, sipped my drink, thought I would never be brave enough to wear it, sipped my drink again, slathered it on anyway, sipped my drink again. Ordered another. Sipped sipped sipped.

"Kerry?"

I'd jolted, turned, and then there he was. Charlie.

"You look *different*."

"Oh," I said. I pressed my lips together, felt the smooth cream of the rouge on my mouth.

"Not in a bad way," he added.

I bit a red lip, ran my tongue across my teeth to make sure it didn't mark.

"I thought you'd left," he said.

You know how when you're drunk out of your mind, how fun it is when you see someone you know? Like hearing a familiar riff on the radio that stands out among the rest of the noise.

"You caught me," I said. "I guess I wanted another drink. Don't tell Frank."

He lifted a finger to his chiseled chin. "Mum's the word."

"Where's everyone else?" I asked.

"Gone, too," he said. "So I guess *you* caught *me*."

I looked at Charlie, picked up the wanting, but not for what you think: a wanting for the party to keep going. When you live your life like I do, you get exceedingly good at picking that up in other people. You can see very clearly who will indulge you and who won't. And that, in and of itself, almost sobers you up a little bit, sorts through the holes already forming in your mind, in what will be your memory of this night, and gives you clarity. Focus. Because another drink is about to be in your hands, cold with clinking ice and promising you pure escape, pure annihilation. And when you find someone who won't judge, who will indulge, well, it's absolute *bliss*. "Another round, then?" I asked.

Charlie didn't even answer, just motioned to the bartender, and I was so happy, so exceedingly happy, that I'd bought myself another stay, another hour at least until I would have to go home, to see Frank, to face the mess I'd made of my life, to disappoint the people who cared about me yet again.

"Kerry," Siobhan said now. "*Kerry*. Why did you block me, then?"

I finally let myself look at her. At the friend I had betrayed like it was nothing, telling myself that it was better, far better, to have me out of her life. Telling myself that she deserved so much better than me, because, let's face it, she did. Everyone did.

"I blocked you so you could be free of me," I said.

Her eyes narrowed, and she took a slow, deep breath. "Why would I need to be free of you?"

It could have all been harmless. It could have been one of those nights you told your friend about later. *Okay, so I actually went to the bar to get another drink and Charlie and I ended up closing the place down. We talked about how much we both love you, and he helped get me into a cab, and I went home. Hilarious, right?*

I kept telling myself, as one round turned into another, as Charlie suggested shots, and I said yes, that that was all it would be. But alcohol, it took things, things that were so small as to be harmless, and made them bigger, made them take over completely.

I loved Frank, I did, but I liked how Charlie and I were the fun ones on our couples' game nights. Sure, Siobhan might have a glass or two and steal outside with Charlie to smoke, but eventually he and I would find ourselves in the kitchen, raiding the fridge, the liquor cabinet, looking for whatever could give us more.

Nothing had ever happened. But it was nice, I guessed, for that part of me—fun, party Kerry, Kerry who laughed loud and talked loud and sometimes dropped things but turned the world Technicolor—to be appreciated, not resented. Because Frank used to love it about me, back when I had it under control. And when I'd see sadness and pity and maybe a tinge of disgust from both Frank and Siobhan, well, there was Charlie to give me a knowing look, like, *How did we lasso ourselves to these grandmas? What's the big deal? It's just another drink. It's just a little fun.*

And so, that night at the bar, when Charlie asked why Frank wasn't there, when I told him Frank didn't really drink these days, didn't really like *me* to drink these days, when Charlie shared that Siobhan was the same, that she hadn't even stayed out on his birthday, that it had disappointed him, it really had, it was impossible not to look at each other. To smile. To feel like, Okay, at least we don't have to pretend when we're together.

"But you're here," Charlie had said, and I could feel his knee close in on mine, just a millimeter—touching, but not touching—like it wasn't even happening.

"Yes," I said. "I'm here."

Now, I looked at Siobhan, let the lies fall away for the first time. "When I left karaoke that night, I didn't leave. I went to the back of the bar. I didn't want to go home yet and face Frank. I knew he would be disappointed in me. I had promised him that I would only have two drinks max. We had a whole system. I would wear two hair ties on my left wrist and move them over to my right as I drank." I winced, thinking of it now, how helpless Frank must have felt. Because if you were the kind of person who *needed* a hair-tie system, then of course you were already too far gone. "Charlie didn't leave, either. He found me at the bar."

"Did you—" There were tears in her eyes now. She couldn't finish the sentence.

I took another gulp of wine.

Sitting at the bar with Charlie, I kept thinking about how I should pull my knee away and how I wasn't. And then there was a pressure on my bladder, an excuse to break contact. And I stood up, and I was already stumbling. It was one of those tiny all-gender stalls.

I found my way in, did what I needed to do, looked in the mirror, stared at the red lips, at this person, wild and selfish, with a mind toward utter destruction.

And then the door cracked open, and there was Charlie.

He stepped inside.

"We shouldn't—"

But his lips were on mine, and I didn't push him away. And I kept telling myself over and over again that I could.

Only the thing was, what if I didn't? Charlie and I were both such fuck-ups, such awful, terrible people. All we did was hurt the people who loved us, made them worry, made them codependent, made them try to save us.

And what if there was a way to stop that all, to save them both? Because in my drunken state, it felt almost like it would.

Hands up my shirt. On my waistband. His pants unzipping. One of those freebie condoms.

This was an opening, a door, a door that led straight to rock bottom. No take-backs. Because I would tell Frank in the morning, and it would destroy him, destroy us, and then he wouldn't have to love me anymore, and I wouldn't have to disappoint him anymore. And his heart would be broken, but it would be shattered all at once, instead of the death by a thousand cuts that an alcoholic inevitably put their loved ones through.

I had been looking for a way out, a way to stop owing anyone anything.

And Charlie was it.

So I let it happen, and it was so fast, and then it was over, and even in my drunkenness, I had the wherewithal to do it, to slip the condom wrapper in the pocket of his overcoat, praying that Siobhan would find it in the morning, that she would be free, too.

"It wasn't about you," I managed, forcing myself to look Siobhan in the eyes. "Well, it wasn't about me and you. I was hurting Frank, and Charlie was hurting you, and together, if we did this, I knew it would destroy both relationships. And there wouldn't be pressure to be good anymore—a good wife, a good friend. I could just be me. Someone who hurts people. Someone who fucks up. It was a rock bottom."

Siobhan's lip was quivering. Tears were streaming down her cheeks now. "It was you, then. It was you."

I didn't deny it.

"I thought . . ." She sucked in a breath, catching in her throat. "I didn't think it was *you*."

Heat lifted into my face, shame practically leaking out my pores, because I wished I could say something—anything—to defend myself. It had been the same with Frank the next morning, when I told him all that had happened, laid it out, not skipping a single detail, right down to who it was with.

Only with Frank, there had been relief. I had come so close to destroying him so many times that it was freeing to actually do it, to finally be done with that chapter of my life, to cross a line that I couldn't uncross.

"Get out," Siobhan said, shaking me from my thoughts.

"Siobhan."

And then her words were frantic, charged—a yell, a scream, a cry of desperation.

"For god's sake, get *out*!"

32

Kerry

"Please," I said, but Siobhan was screaming. A terrible screaming punctuated by sobs.

"Get out! Get out! Get out!"

So I did. I rushed out the door, but even my room felt too close. I didn't stop walking until I was in front of the office, until I couldn't hear her horrible crying anymore. Couldn't hear her heart breaking all over again.

It had been just as awful as I'd imagined. No, not just as awful—worse.

Now Siobhan knew what I had done. She had lost Charlie. She had lost Allison. And now she had lost me, too.

The wind bitter, I opened the door, slipped back into the office, shutting it tight behind me. And then something wild happened. The lights flickered on and off, and I was hit with a buzzing sound.

On, off, buzz, and then . . .

They were on. I waited a second, not wanting to get ahead of myself if they were just going to go right back off, but they stayed. Not a flicker, just light.

Power. Finally. *Power.*

I rushed to the thermostat, cranked it high, thankful we'd have real heat again.

I returned to the desk. I grabbed the phone sitting there, but despite depressing the hook on and off a good five times, there was still nothing. Okay.

I pulled my phone from my pocket. It had charged a bit at Jeremy's, but not very much. I whipped open a drawer and retrieved an iPhone charger, popped it into the wall, saw the green battery symbol appear. Success.

I tried 911 again, but it wouldn't go through. I still didn't have a single bar of service. Shit.

I tapped open my texts, looked at the one I'd jotted out to Frank. It hadn't sent, so I tried again.

> If you get this, Frank, I need help. Call the police. Tell them to come to the Twilite Motel off Route 208.

I set down the phone slowly. Tried to orient myself. Siobhan and I should have been sticking together now, because the killer could still be out there, eager to get rid of us before life returned to its post-storm normal, and yet, due to my actions, we were on opposite sides of this old motel, each braving it alone.

Before I'd told her my horrible secret, she'd barely said a word. No clue as to who had killed Allison—or why. Because Siobhan had blacked out. She couldn't remember. She couldn't—

I froze.

There, in front of me, was Siobhan's video camera. I reached out, lifting it up gingerly.

What if there was an answer here? What if there was proof of what happened, some kind of clue about what to do next? I looked at the power jack, messed around in the drawer of cords until I found one that fit, plugged it in. For a second, nothing happened, but then there was a familiar ding, the sound of an electronic turning on. A yellow light flickered, indicating it was charging, but impatient, I flicked open the screen.

It worked.

I stared at a mess of thumbnails, each one a bit of film.

The last one showed Allison, with a time stamp underneath.

2/1/23, 12:51 a.m. 14s

Fingers shaking, I pressed play.

Allison's face filled the screen, her red lips breaking into a grin, the sky black behind her, the motel sign barely lit by the moonlight in the background. "Helluva night, folks. This is your tour guide, Allison, signing off. Siobhan, I'm sorry if I was a bit of an ass. I promise you—you have nothing to worry about with me. Hopefully you will find this all very funny in the morning. Peace out."

Then a scream, and the camera must have fallen, because suddenly there was a frame or two of the gravel parking lot and then black. And then Allison's voice: "Fuck—"

A crunching sound of gravel, and the camera went black.

I watched those fourteen seconds three more times, hoping to get a clue, realizing that this was possibly Allison's last moment on earth, captured here on this screen, and just how wild that was. How morbid. I wanted to crawl into the frame, somehow stop whatever was going to happen to her.

Who had come up behind her, startled her? Who had flicked the camera off?

I went back to the thumbnails, found the video before it.

1/31/23, 11:05 p.m. 35s

I tapped, and I was once again back in the parking lot, except Allison's face wasn't filling the screen this time. Instead, the camera was pointed outward, shakily following a figure—buck naked, skin white in the moonlight—rushing across the parking lot, while shouts and screams made a soundtrack.

I watched it twice, trying to see exactly who was in the crowd, but it was near-impossible to make out, just a smattering of the backs of heads. A flash of hair that could have been Charlie, but could have been Tyler, too. Or just as easily one of the French guys Siobhan had mentioned. It was too dark to parse out the color.

I returned to the thumbnails, found another, this one black.

1/31/23, 11:01 p.m. 2m 3s

At first, I saw little more than the parking lot, figures in and out of the frame. And then, the camera was trained on a man in the distance, undressing while people cheered him on.

The camera turned, and there was Siobhan, filling the frame, her eyes narrowed. Angry.

"The great Siobhan." It was Allison's voice.

But Siobhan wasn't having it. She was mad. She was reaching for the camera, saying, "Enough."

The frame kept darting away, and Siobhan kept reaching, the two friends snapping at each other, trading barbs.

I had to pause—rewind—pause—rewind—to figure out what was going on, what they were really fighting about, in the darkness of the night, with the shakiness of the camera, with the background noise obscuring.

Then I caught it—finally.

Allison: "Did he promise you he'd never do it again? I mean, do you really think that's true?"

Siobhan: "Do *you*?"

Allison: "What's that supposed to mean?"

Siobhan: "There was red lipstick on his collar. Your exact color."

Allison: "You really think Charlie and I . . . ?"

My heart began to race as I rewound, played the interaction back again.

Siobhan had thought Allison was the one who had betrayed her, that Allison had slept with Charlie. Siobhan thought she had every right to hate her friend, to . . .

I pressed play, watching as the women yelled at each other, as Siobhan reached desperately, drunkenly, for the camera. As Allison kept pulling it out of her reach, taunting her.

And then Siobhan was saying "Fuck you," and I could hear Allison's voice: "Right back at you."

Siobhan's face filled the frame. I hit pause and looked, using one of the buttons to zoom in. Her face was white with anger, her eyes smoky with hate.

Her own words, from only moments before, suddenly made so much sense.

It was you, then. It was you. I didn't think it was you.

A chill crept up my spine, despite the heat now pumping out of the split unit near the ceiling.

I pressed play again, but there was only a voice—"Everything okay?"—then the camera cut off.

I knew Allison didn't die then. There were two clips after, the last one with her signing off before someone surprised her.

Was it possible that Siobhan was the one who came back, that she was the one who startled Allison at the end of the night?

That Tyler and Jeremy had both been telling the truth? That they didn't stay late? That it came down to Siobhan and Allison at the end, and Siobhan was sure—convinced—that Allison had betrayed her?

Siobhan wasn't a violent person, was she?

I remembered the drawings. The body in the freezer, sketched out right in her notebook, a hint of what was to come? How would it have even played out?

Booze flowing, drugs passed around. Someone suggests a dare—to streak through the parking lot of the motel. Everyone spills out into the cold. Snowflakes are already beginning to fall.

There's an argument—the one I saw—and Siobhan *does* storm off, plies herself with even more booze. And then the people outside, they keep partying. The guy streaks. Allison catches it. The camera goes off. People start to peel away; it's getting late, now, and it's getting cold. And then, there's Allison, having said goodbye to

288

everyone, and she turns the camera on herself, and she "signs off." But then, someone startles her.

It's Siobhan.

The argument begins again, but Siobhan is angry now, furious. Allison starts to walk away, but Siobhan follows. Maybe it wasn't even meant to be anything. Maybe it was just a push, a shove, an accident, and then—Siobhan stumbles away, somehow finds herself in the boiler room, Allison's body out there in the snow, where I find her. And then the alcohol wears off, and Siobhan emerges. Sees her friend out there in the snow. A flash, a memory. She knows she's done something terribly, terribly wrong. And the body, the evidence . . . it's out there, just waiting to be found. She has to hide it, and in the haze, the freezer is the only place that makes sense. So she uses all the strength she possesses to drag Allison's dead weight, the snow falling steadily, but then she's so tired, and she just wants to sleep a little bit more, and the boiler room is right there, right next to the pantry, cozy and warm . . .

No. It was wild, outlandish. And how did the camera get back in the room where I found it? And why would Siobhan have made up a whole story about falling asleep in bed first?

I rewound the tape again, zeroing in on Siobhan's face, white with rage; it felt over-the-top, unreal. Altogether unbelievable.

But was it impossible?

For god's sake, get out*!*

What would Siobhan do—what *will* she do—now that she knew it was me who betrayed her, not Allison?

33

Kerry

A sound outside, like footsteps, and I jolted, looking out the front window, whose curtains were still drawn open. It was beginning to get dark, the sky splashed with pinks and purples, and then I saw her, bent down, beneath where the structure had caved in.

That girl again. Blond in her combat boots. So young. Young enough to perch precariously under a half-caved-in awning weighted down by snow.

"What are you doing?" I asked as I whipped open the door. "You're going to get yourself killed."

Her shoulders hunched up, and she whipped around, her eyes widening.

Before she could run off again, I walked forward a couple of steps, grabbed her wrist. "Hey," I said. "Wait."

Her breathing was coming fast now, and despite an air of I-don't-give-a-shit plastered across her face, applied thick like too-heavy makeup, I could feel her arm shaking beneath my grasp.

"I'm not going to hurt you," I said, letting her arm go. "But you can't be out here, digging around in the snow when the roof is ready to fall on top of you." I took a deep breath. "What are you doing here?"

Her weight shifted, and her eyes darted back to the snow. Then I saw it: a glint of metal.

At first I remembered what Siobhan had said, only minutes before—*we found a knife*—and I was sure that was what I was looking at, but as I stepped closer, I could see that the image I'd conjured was all wrong. The metal . . . it wasn't sharp; it was round.

The girl saw where my eyes landed, but I jumped for it before she did, lifted it in my hands.

A ring of keys, just like the one Maisy had given me.

I looked up at her, my stomach turning in on itself, my heart beating fast as I remembered that whoever had killed Allison would have had to have access to the pantry at the very least, and here was a whole set of keys, ready to unlock any and every door.

I struggled to rationalize the vision of someone carrying a body across the snow with the waifish girl in front of me. The words in my mouth were like ash, but still, I had to get them out. "Did you do it . . . did someone help you?"

Finally, the girl spoke, her voice that upstate twang, a mix of old-school New York City and an obvious rural upbringing. "No one *helps* me. I help myself."

"Did you kill her yourself, then?"

Her eyes widened, and I saw in them what looked like genuine surprise. "*What?*"

"There's a body. In the freezer in the pantry."

"All right, Poy-rot," she said, raising her eyebrows in disbelief. "Whatever you say."

My head tilted to the side, and it took a moment for it to click, and then it did. *Poirot*, she meant the Agatha Christie

detective. Only she ⟨...⟩
because she'd never h⟨...⟩
one trying to educate th⟨...⟩
station, trying to grasp s⟨...⟩
me, suddenly, of myself, goi⟨...⟩
ing out every paperback classi⟨...⟩
desperate to escape into a book, t⟨...⟩
own. That was what used to drive ⟨...⟩
to dive into, drinking up Dostoevsky⟨...⟩
how to pronounce Karamazov until yea⟨...⟩ ⟨...⟩ge.
Now I chased Instagram validation and ⟨...⟩ drink.
The thought both sickened me at how far ⟨...⟩ ⟨f⟩allen away
from myself and softened me toward the girl.

"It's not a joke," I said carefully. "It's real. A woman has
been killed. Her name was Allison. I found her out in the
snow this morning, and then I went out to get help, and
when I came back, she was gone. She didn't deserve anything that happened to her. And whoever did it is still out
there. And if you had nothing to do with it, all that means
is that we're *both* in danger until we can get some help."

The girl shivered, and she opened her mouth, shut it
again, then let her arms drop to her sides. "I didn't know
that," she said. "I . . . I didn't see anything like that."

"What did you see?" I asked. "And what are you doing
here? You still haven't told me."

Instead of answering, she pulled her arms close,
crossed them in front of her. A gust of wind whipped at
both of us, and above us, the awning once again began to
creak.

"Come inside," I said. "The heat is finally back on.
Lights, too. Come inside and explain yourself."

me to hand these keys over to the
ce of your trespassing."

she said. "Okay."

held the door for her, ushering her in, not wanting her
out of my sight for a moment, sure she'd try to run again,
and this girl might not have seen a body, but she knew
something that could help decipher this—I was sure of it.

Once inside, I shut the door behind me and nodded to
a file cabinet on the opposite wall. "Come on," I said.
"Help me with this."

At first, she looked like she was going to argue, but
then, reluctantly, she went to the other side of it, and
together, we pushed the thing, legs scraping against the
hardwood, until it was in front of the door. I secured
the chain lock, too, and then adjusted the curtains so
there wasn't even an inch of space. I didn't want anyone
to be able to see in.

For a moment, I wondered if I should get Siobhan, if
she should be part of this, too, huddled here with us, but
then I thought of her sobs, the way I'd destroyed her. And
I thought of what I'd seen on that camera, too . . .

I went to my phone on the wall, checked the service
again. Still nothing.

"Is your phone working?" I asked the girl.

"I don't have one," she said.

"You don't have a *phone*?"

She looked almost embarrassed. "My parents took it
away."

"Oh," I said. My voice softened. "How old are you?"

Her body stiffened.

"Look," I said. "We're stuck together now, until we can get some help. I'm Kerry. I was supposed to be the caretaker here for the month of February, but everything got off to the wrong start. Obviously. I'm thirty-nine, a whole lot older than you, and I'm trying to figure out what's going on."

The girl made her way over to a cream-colored canvas sofa, took a seat on the edge closest to the door, as if she might bolt up at any moment. I sat down a few feet from her, giving her space, my eyes on the door, making sure the knob wasn't turning so much as a millimeter.

"McKenzie," she said finally. "But everyone calls me Mac. I'm twenty-one."

I raised an eyebrow.

"Fine. Eighteen. But I *am* eighteen. Really."

"Okay," I said. "And you're not in school or anything? I mean, I guess that's obvious."

"No," she said. "My parents, they were going to help me with college, but . . ."

It took me a second, and then it hit me. "Wait, McKenzie? You're not the girl—the young girl who applied for the caretaker position? I saw you in Maisy's binder. You had orange hair, though."

The girl went beet red. "It seemed like a good opportunity to get away from my parents. But Maisy didn't pick me." She raised an eyebrow. "Surprise surprise."

"So you're—what—squatting? You steal these keys and—"

"I didn't steal anything," she practically spat. "I'm not a thief."

"Then how did you get these keys?" I asked. "They're not yours."

She crossed her arms. "They are, actually. Well, my family's."

"I'm sorry," I said. "I don't follow."

"It's not my fault Maisy didn't even get someone to change the locks."

"Your parents—"

"Yup," she said. "We were the original owners of the Twilite Motel. My great-grandpa started it in the fifties. Moved up here from Queens. It was really popular then. Lotta Irish folks. They like to stay with other Irish, I guess? I don't know. By the time it got to my dad, it was a money suck. I mean, I used to play in all the empty rooms, growing up. And there were a *lot* of empty rooms back then. And not this nice, either. We almost lost everything because of it. It was a *whole thing*. But then Maisy came along, ready to take it off our hands. Of course, they had no idea how much she was going to charge for the rooms after. Pisses my dad off. He should have known, though. It was obvious she was going to pour city money into it. Still, she could give him a break about the property lines. Especially since she's charging everyone so much."

"The property lines?" I asked. "You mean the dispute between the neighbors?"

"There's that, yeah, but Maisy was threatening to sue my dad if she loses that lawsuit. Because she says he lied about the property before selling it."

"Okay," I said slowly, taking in this new information, wondering how it all connected to Allison—and if it even did. "And that's why you've been hanging around here?"

She shook her head.

"Then why?"

"My parents are difficult, okay? They're super strict—their house, their rules kind of thing—and they found, you know, my birth control, and they saw, you know, some texts on my phone, between me and—" She stopped herself. "Anyway, they totally flipped out. And it's not like they threw me out or anything, but they took my phone, and they said they weren't going to help me with college, and it's just—it's made living with them impossible. And so I come here sometimes. To get away. I think my dad is catching on, though, because I saw him here a few weeks ago. You might have seen him, too." She tilted her head to the side. "I guess the other girl would have seen him, not you. You just got here, right?"

I nodded. "Right."

"I didn't see anything, though, I promise. Just you. And the cops, earlier today."

"What about two nights ago?"

"Oh, you mean the party?"

"Yes," I said. "Were you there?"

"No," she said. "I went out with my friend that night. But I heard them talking about it. A couple of days before. The two women."

"Did you ever see them arguing?"

She shook her head.

"So you don't know who could have—"

"I really don't," she said, cutting me off. "I promise you. I didn't kill anyone, and I didn't want anyone to die."

"What about the knife?" I asked. "Siobhan said you had one with you."

"Oh. That. Yeah, I guess I got scared the first night I stayed here. There were so many noises. So—" She shrugged. "I took a knife. I kept it under the mattress. I don't know, it made me feel safe. But when the women found it, they took it. See—at the beginning of January, the woman, she didn't really check all the rooms that much, but then when the other woman came, they did. So I couldn't come around as much."

I believed her, which didn't get me any closer to knowing who had killed Allison.

"Here," I said, pushing the keys toward her. "I'm going to be out of here as soon as I possibly can. It's not my business what you do with them."

The girl reached for them, but I let them go a second too soon, and they clattered to the floor.

"Sorry," I said, as she leaned over, reaching for the keys, her jacket riding up, exposing a few inches of pale skin.

Pale except for the marks, red and angry, cascading across her skin.

My heart seemed to stop. They were the same marks I'd seen on Siobhan's back.

"What is it?" she asked when she looked back at me.

"Your back," I said. "Who did that?"

Her face went red again, and she zipped her lips together. "Don't worry about it."

"It was Jeremy," I said. "Jeremy did that to you?"

She rolled her eyes. "It was consensual, okay? And it's none of your business anyway."

"He's old enough to be your father," I said.

"God," she said. "You sound just like my dad."

I wanted to argue; I wanted to tell her that it was fucked-up, that a man his age—he had no business. With Siobhan was one thing, but a girl—this was a child.

Then it hit me: What if Allison had found out? What if the girl wasn't even eighteen? What if she'd threatened to tell Siobhan? What if Jeremy had wanted to stop her?

I didn't have time for any of that, because the girl was looking at the wall now, where my phone was suddenly vibrating, coming back to life.

Service was back.

I rushed for the phone, my heart already racing. The service was indeed back, and it was a lot better here in the office than it had been back in my room. I actually had three bars.

A series of notifications popped up at me—all from Frank—but I ignored them.

Instead, I tapped into the phone. And I dialed 911.

We had to get out of here.

Before it was too late.

34
Kerry

Words were coming out of my mouth, though I hardly knew what I was saying.

Dead body. Someone moved her. Spoke to the police already. Help us, please help us.

After rattling off the motel's address, the dispatcher told me that they'd already received a call for help at that location, to "hang tight," that the police were on their way. Once she let me off the phone, I returned to my notifications. All from Frank.

Kerry, you okay?

Kerry, what is this?

Kerry, call me!

I've called the police, but I'm coming up, too.

Leaving now. Stay safe.

My heart swelled with a mix of sentiment and shame. Here was Frank, ready to save me once again, even though I didn't deserve it. And me, back to my old vices. Drinking to escape. Lips stained from red wine.

"Are they coming?" the girl asked me, breaking my train of thought, and for the first time, I didn't think of her and her mystery; I thought about how I must look to this girl, this teenager. A woman approaching middle age, smelling of booze. I was supposed to have it all figured out by now. Shame shook me again, but I pushed it back.

That didn't matter. What mattered was safety. Survival.

"The police?" she asked.

"Yes," I said. "My . . . *ex* called them already. They're on their way. Should be any moment now."

The girl shook her head, quick as anything.

"No," she said. "No no no." She stood, the ring of keys in her hand now.

"Wait," I said. "Where are you going to go? *How* are you going to go? It's brutal out there, still. Power's only just been restored. You don't even have a phone."

"I know my way around," she said.

"But it's getting dark out. What if you trip, fall? What if something happens?" It was inexplicable, but I found myself suddenly wanting to protect this girl, wanting to be the type of person you could come to in a crisis, one who would help, not judge. "You could die out there."

The words hung between us, unsaid but acknowledged all the same: *Someone already has.*

"I'll take my chances," she said, tucking a stringy bit of hair behind her ears. "I'm not messing around with a bunch of asshole cops."

Such bravado. Such assurance. Such fearlessness. I'd had that, too, once, hadn't I? Before I spent so much time trying to run away from myself?

This girl, she was running away from real things— asshole parents, asshole cops. She wasn't yet trapped in the messed-up devices—and vices—of her own mind, her own choices.

She crossed the office in a few quick strides, heading for the door, and I felt, suddenly, that I had to stop her, had to prevent her from going out.

"It could have been Jeremy," I said.

She didn't turn.

"He could be the killer," I said, daring her to ignore me.

She hesitated, and then she looked back at me. She was so very young, and I wished I could protect her from this world. But of course, we adults had already failed her, and she had the marks on her back to prove it. Consensual, my ass. A man in his forties and a girl desperate for escape from her overbearing parents— violence strong enough to leave marks? She might have thought she was consenting, but the power dynamic made that nearly impossible. It wasn't as simple as saying "okay." It rarely was.

"I'm not just saying that, you know. It makes sense."

She crossed her arms, the keys jangling between her fingers. "How? And don't start with the S-and-M stuff. That's different. You can kink-shame all you want, but that doesn't mean shit."

Kink-shame, I thought. Something about the words on her young lips broke my heart a little bit. I could practically hear the way Jeremy had convinced her that she was very, very grown-up for doing whatever she did with him, made her feel like she knew more than any of the adults in her life who had so failed to protect her.

"It's not that," I said. "Are you really eighteen?"

She rolled her eyes. "What, are you going to card me?"

"Because you don't look it. Did Jeremy card you?"

Her eyebrows scrunched up. "No, why would he?"

"Which means he knows that you could have been lying, as girls who want to be treated as women sometimes do."

"I wasn't, though."

"Does it matter? He was willing to take the risk, wasn't he? And I bet he told you that you couldn't tell anyone about what you two were doing, that people wouldn't get it, that they'd *kink-shame*," I said. "That they wouldn't understand that age is just a number. You're a smart girl. Surely you knew that at least some of those were lines."

I could see that I'd flattered her, calling her smart. "So what? Doesn't mean I didn't want it. I did."

"It means he knew enough of the risk he was taking to encourage you to keep it quiet. And what if someone found out? Siobhan, the January caretaker, she was sleeping with him, too, you know. She's got the same exact marks all over her back."

The girl hesitated, and I could tell that she'd known, but that it was hard to hear it anyway. That maybe, at one time, she thought she was important to this man, more important than she actually was.

"And Allison, the woman who was killed, she was Siobhan's best friend, you know. Maybe she figured it out. Maybe she saw you, maybe she confronted Jeremy the night of the party, told him she was going to tell Siobhan, maybe even tell the cops."

"That's a dumb reason to kill someone," the girl said.

"Maybe. But that room is lined with booze and weed and dustings of cocaine. Is it that wild of a reason to push someone, maybe a little bit too hard? To hurt someone, maybe even leave them behind, not realize they're dead in the snow until the next morning? Jeremy's got a nice life, you know. But of course you do. You've been in his house. Someone like that is not going to take well to going to prison. And he'd do whatever he can to make sure he never has to."

"Jeremy wouldn't—"

"He didn't tell you he was playing his whole *Fifty Shades* game with other women, did he? Even if you probably figured it out."

That made her stop, draw a breath.

"Maybe it wasn't Jeremy. Maybe it has nothing to do with him, but we don't know, do we? And until the police come, secure this place, going outside, with the weather and the dwindling light and the bitter cold, it's insane. It's foolish. Just wait, until—"

Then I heard it, a sound, a slamming door.

"What was that?" McKenzie asked.

Siobhan. It was Siobhan, had to be. But why was she leaving the safety of her room? What was she doing?

"Stay here," I said as I walked toward the door instead, zipping my coat.

"But where are *you* going?" she asked.

"My friend, I think my friend left her room." And it was wild, because only moments before I'd suspected her, but now it seemed preposterous. Now all I wanted was to protect the friend I'd already hurt so badly. "I can't let her. If something happened to her, it would all be my fault. I'm going down to Room Thirteen. I'll be right back."

"But you literally *just* told me to stay inside."

"I'm only going to get my friend, bring her back to this room. So we'll all be together. Until help arrives."

I was almost to the door when I spotted the open wine bottle I'd left on the desk, and I imagined taking a sip for liquid courage. To quell the fear.

But I knew that it wouldn't help me, would only hurt.

I knew that I'd never find what I was looking for at the bottom of a bottle.

"I'll be right back," I said. "Don't leave. Keep the door barricaded."

I grabbed the file cabinet, pushed it to the side, set my hand on the doorknob.

"Don't open this for anyone but me," I said.

With that, I headed into the quickly darkening night.

35

Kerry

February 2, 2023
5:11 p.m.

Darkness, or nearly so. Just a sliver of pink sitting on the horizon like a security blanket.

You could get hurt, Kerry, Imaginary Frank reminded me. *Go back to your room and wait for the police. Wait for me.*

I walked as quickly as I could, down the patio, under the awnings, past all the rooms I'd thought I'd spend this month checking on, taking care of, while I finished a novel I now realized may never be complete.

Finally, I was in front of the last one. Lights were on, and I tried the handle. Unlocked.

"Siobhan," I said, pushing the door open to make sure. "Siobhan."

The main room was empty. The wine still sitting on the counter, waiting.

Calling me once again.

Begging me to forget everything, all the ways I'd failed.

I stared at it, I did.

But it wasn't Imaginary Frank who stopped me this time.

It was me.

No.

Enough.

Enough of this madness.

I walked through the main room and into the bathroom, where I'd bathed a broken, naked Siobhan only an hour or so before. "Siobhan?"

She wasn't there. I turned back, retracing my steps to the door.

She shouldn't be out. I shouldn't have left her. I shouldn't have betrayed her. I shouldn't have done so much of what I did.

I spotted the faint press of footsteps curving around the side of the motel, though it was hard to tell in the creeping darkness, in snow that had been mussed up, trod over by me, searching for a body, begging the police to listen. Nothing was pristine now. And god, it was cold, down in my bones. I trudged across the snow, icy bits crunching beneath my boots, wind seeping into the gaps between my layers, night swallowing me like a suffocating hug, past the spot that had started it all, where I'd seen Allison's arm reaching up through the snow. Those red fingernails. Remnants of a stolen life.

I pulled out my phone, flicked on the flashlight, pointed it ahead as I made my way toward the outbuildings.

Then I saw it: the door to the boiler room cracked open.

My heart raced, but in a moment, I caught a silhouette, just ahead to the left. Siobhan, her back to me. She was heading past the laundry room, in a direction that could only be the pantry.

The freezer.

Why are you going there, Siobhan? Why?

She was walking briskly, trudging through snow with purpose.

She couldn't have killed Allison, she wouldn't have, but still. I had to see what she was doing.

I flicked off my flashlight, so as not to give myself away, but in the change of light, in the sudden near-darkness, I must have stepped wrong, because suddenly I was lurching forward, my hands coming out to brace my fall, my phone dropped somewhere in the mess of snow, and then, there she was, a shadow, standing over me, her own flashlight bright in my eyes.

"I can't see," I said. "Please, point that away."

Siobhan hesitated a moment, and then she moved the light down. The effect turned her face gaunt, hollow with shadows. A specter, out here in the snow, standing over me, while my hands pawed around desperately, looking for my phone, until they came against something hard, and I grasped it in my hands. I pushed myself up to standing, struggled to see against the stars blinking in my vision. "Why are you out here, Siobhan?"

Silence, and I could barely make out her face, and instead, my mind filled in the gaps with what I'd seen on that video camera. The rage that had been directed solely at Allison, that was about to turn my way now.

And then, finally: "What am *I* doing? What are *you* doing?"

"I was worried about you," I managed.

I blinked, trying to focus, and finally, the stars subsided, and in the dark, I looked up, and I saw it, just as I had imagined: hate, right there in her eyes.

"Were you worried about me when you fucked Charlie? Were you worried about me when you cut me out of your life without even telling me the truth? Were you worried

309

about me then?" Her voice cracked, and the anger turned to pain, to desperation. "Do you know how it felt?" she asked. "To see that lipstick? To find the condom wrapper in his coat? That wrapper is singed in my mind, you know."

"I wanted you to find it," I said.

"What?"

"Charlie wasn't good enough for you. He was a drunk, like me. He'd flirted with me before, you know, always making eyes at me in the kitchen during our game nights, when the two of us were raiding the fridge for more booze. You were always so worried about him cheating on you. He never made you feel *good* about yourself. So I put it there, in his pocket, so you'd finally be done."

Siobhan reared back. "Oh, so you did me a favor?"

"No, it was terrible of me, but—"

"Don't you think if *I* wanted to break up with Charlie, it should have been my choice? That the relationship was mine to be part of, mine to leave? And weren't there other ways to get that to happen, like, maybe—I don't know— *talking to me* about it instead of destroying you and me in the process? Our friendship meant something to me, Kerry. It meant a whole hell of a lot. But why should I be surprised? *Nothing* is sacred to you, is it? You don't care about your husband. You don't care about your friends. You don't care about your one real chance at having a baby."

Breath caught in my throat, and I practically choked on the cold. "What are you talking about?"

Siobhan brushed tears from her eyes. "Didn't know I knew, did you? I ran into Frank a few days before that party. Told him I was so sorry that another round of IVF didn't work. You should have *seen* the look of surprise on his face."

I took a quick, sharp breath, and my heart began to race even faster.

"But you destroy everything, don't you? So why should I be surprised?"

"I didn't—I wasn't even—"

"Do you know how I felt for you?" she asked. "When Frank told me you guys decided to call off the transfer because you couldn't stop drinking? How my heart absolutely *ached* for you? How I wanted nothing more than for you to get better?"

Tears were falling from my eyes now, warming my cheeks. I had been so good for the first round, I really had. The fertility specialist had suggested we both stop drinking for three months before the embryo transfer, said that new studies showed that consuming even as few as four drinks a week (and let's be real, there was no way I could stick to just four drinks a *week*) were associated with fewer successful live births. So we had. We made mocktails and drank Spindrifts and I was good good good. And then the transfer didn't work. And we geared up to do another. I wasn't even pregnant. It wasn't like I was poisoning some would-be human. And the stress was so great. The book, the futile attempts at baby-making, all of it. And so I had some wine here and there, and then a little more. And then a cocktail, only when Frank was working late and I was on my own at home.

My husband discovered my secret a few days before our second transfer was scheduled. He phoned the clinic and called the whole thing off. Said he didn't want to waste the money if we weren't maximizing our chances, but I knew the truth, deep down—that if I couldn't stop drinking for a few measly months, he doubted whether I could stop at all, whether I was the kind of person he even *wanted* to start a family with. I had already told Siobhan— and others—about the second scheduled transfer. It was easier, a few weeks on, to say it failed.

It became easier to tell myself the same story—two failed rounds of IVF.

My uterus had failed me the first time. My willpower the second.

"And how do you repay my loyalty, my love?" Siobhan continued, not stopping. "You tear down everything that mattered to me in one fell swoop. Charlie and I are over. You and I have nothing. And Allison—Allison."

Allison.

"What are you doing back here, Siobhan? *Really?* Why did you come out here into the snow when you're already freezing, when you're not even recovered from being out here for two days? Why were you heading to the pantry?"

Siobhan just stared at me.

I hesitated, then spit it out: "What really happened between you and Allison?"

She looked at me a moment, and then the heartbreak was replaced with rage.

"Are you serious right now? Like, are you really fucking serious? I came to get my phone," Siobhan said. "And I was walking in that direction to get some service. To call the cops. To get us some *help*."

She stared at me, ire washing across her features.

"But I'm glad to know you believe I could kill my best friend."

Her eyes were daggers.

"I love my friends. I cherish them. And I would do anything for them. See, unlike you, I don't hurt the people I love. You're on your own, Kerry," she said.

And she stormed off into the night.

36

Kerry

I stared at Siobhan as she was consumed by the dark, which was full now, complete.

Standing in the snow, the cold more bitter than ever, it was clear to me then that whatever chance Siobhan and I had at reconciling, however infinitesimal, well, that was gone, too. Because I'd entertained the worst thought I could muster of her, that she could hurt Allison.

And she was right, she wouldn't. She couldn't. She didn't destroy relationships. Destroy people.

I did.

In seconds, I couldn't see her anymore, my isolation setting in fully. Because even though help was on the way, even though Frank and I were in contact, I felt it more than ever. All the bridges in my life had been burned, and there was no way out of the mess I'd made for myself. And I was determined to get through it now, without booze, without pills, without the scroll scroll scroll to numb me. And was there anything more terrifying than that?

I'd never felt more alone in my life.

Except . . .

I *wasn't* alone, was I?

My shoulders jolted at the sound. A shuffle of foot-steps, and then, so sudden I couldn't even figure out from where he'd come, there he was, an apparition in the beam of my phone's flashlight.

"Tyler?"

In his hand, a flashlight of his own, but it was turned down, facing the snow. His eyes widened, and immediately, his face softened with what looked like genuine concern. "Kerry," he said. "I heard yelling. Are you okay? What are you doing out here? You should be inside."

The question took me off guard, and I found myself pulling back. "I—yes. I—I'm just waiting for the police."

"Was someone threatening you?" Tyler asked. "Who was that person yelling?"

"It's okay," I said. "She's my friend. Or . . . she was. She wouldn't hurt me. She wouldn't hurt anyone."

"Right," Tyler said. "Well, it's still freezing, and it's dark, and I don't want anything to happen to you. Enough has *already* happened."

"I know," I said. "I know. But what are *you* doing here?"

"I have a police scanner. I heard the call go over the radio. I wasn't sure how long it would take for them to get out, power still being restored and all. I wanted to come here and, you know, be around if you needed me. I was walking the perimeter, checking things for you. I'm sorry, did I scare you?"

"No—I mean, yes, you did."

"Shit," he said. "I was trying to make things better. I didn't mean to make them worse. You want to go back, wait for the police? Room Thirteen, right?"

"No," I said. "Siobhan. The caretaker. *She's* there. She's the woman you heard."

Tyler's eyebrows narrowed. "I thought you said the caretaker was dead?"

"I did, but I was wrong. It's . . . a long story."

His head tilted to the side, and for a moment, I saw that look, the same one that his uncle had given me when he asked me to tell him what I thought I'd found. Disbelief, plus a twinge of pity.

It was a look I'd seen from Frank, so many times, when I lied and told him I wasn't drinking again. An awful look, one that people didn't realize was painted right there on their faces, so damn easy to see.

Suddenly, I didn't even have the energy to explain about Allison. I didn't want to say anything more until the police were in front of that freezer, seeing with their own eyes what I had seen.

"I think you're right," I said. "I think we should just wait for the police. They should be here soon. Hopefully."

Tyler nodded and lifted his flashlight, pointing ahead in the snow. We walked around the long side of the motel, not the way Siobhan must have gone, back to Room Thirteen, but around the edge of the back rooms, heading toward the main office.

I hesitated at the door, knowing McKenzie would probably freak at the addition of an extra person, but once inside, I found an empty office. Immediately, I saw a note on the front desk.

SORRY — NO COPS

"What is it?" Tyler asked.

"Nothing," I said, setting down the note. "Just . . . there was a girl who has been hanging around some of the rooms. I wanted her to stay inside until the police came."

"McKenzie?" Tyler asked.

"You know her?"

"Of course. Back when her parents owned the place, she was always around. She was far enough behind me in school that we were never actually friends, but, you know, kids stick together out here."

I swallowed. "I hope she's okay."

"Trust me," Tyler said, "Mac can fend for herself. She's tough."

I hesitated, then decided to tell him. "Siobhan's not dead, Tyler, but someone else is. That's why I'm worried about that girl. Because a killer is out there."

Again, that head tilt. Eyes questioning. Finally, he spoke. "Someone *else* is dead," he said carefully. "Someone who isn't the caretaker."

I nodded.

"But who you thought was. Am I getting that right?"

"I only ever saw a hand in the snow the first time," I said with a sigh. "I made an assumption."

"But Billy told me that when he and his partner came out, there wasn't anyone there."

"Right," I said. "The body had been moved."

"Moved?"

"Look, I know how it sounds, but I saw it. I saw *her*. I'm not crazy, okay? I saw what I saw."

Tyler threw up his hands. "All right. I'm not calling you crazy, I promise. I'm just trying to understand. You seemed

318

so sure it was the caretaker, and that she was out in the snow, when you came to our house earlier, and then the story keeps changing." He glanced to the left, his eyes landing on the half glass of wine that still sat on the office counter.

A flicker of rage burned in my stomach. "So I have a drinking problem, okay? I don't have a hallucinating problem. You want to see a body?" I asked. "I'll show you." I moved toward the door.

"Let's just wait for the police," Tyler said.

"Well, Christ, shouldn't they be here by now? It didn't take your uncle this long last time, and that was in the middle of the storm."

"Let me call him," Tyler said, reaching for the door.

"Where are you going?" I asked.

"My service is shit in here. I can only make good calls in the parking lot. But you're right. They should be here. Let me try him."

He walked out, and I forced myself to take a deep breath. I *needed* the cops to get here. To see that I had been right all along. It wouldn't bring Allison back, and it wouldn't heal my broken friendship with Siobhan, but at least we would all be finally safe. I could go home and get back to the terrifying work of trying to live with myself without numbness or escape.

And then I remembered. The other cop, the uncle's partner. Jeanine, I think her name was. She'd given me her card.

I dug in the pocket of my coat, finally found it. Grabbed my phone, saw that I still had service, then tapped in the number printed on the bottom.

It went to voicemail, but I rattled off a message anyway.

Telling her I was out here, that the power was back, that there was a body in the freezer, that I needed help. I hung up, setting the phone back on its cradle.

The door opened then. Tyler.

"Did you get in touch with your uncle?" I asked.

"Yes," he said. "He's on his way. He admitted that there wasn't a lot of urgency, because, well, they already came out today, didn't they?"

I raised my eyebrows. "So you don't believe me, either, then?"

"I didn't say that," he said, shifting his weight from one foot to another. "It's just, without a body—"

"There *is* a body," I said. "Goddamn it, I'll show you."

Without hesitation, I stomped from the room, bursting out into the night, into the bitter, bitter cold. I rushed around the side of the motel, only the subtle light from the moon guiding me, and I trekked across the lawn, past the empty pool, straight to the pantry.

To Allison.

There were footsteps behind me—heavy and fast—and I turned to see Tyler, his flashlight pointed straight at me, the light from it blinding, and at first I thought he was going to stop me, but then he pointed his flashlight toward the snow and offered a small smile. "I'm sorry," he said. "Please don't get yourself hurt." He pointed the light toward the door. "Here. Go ahead."

I pushed open the door, and Tyler followed me in. My hand ran along the wall, looking for a light switch, and then with Tyler's flashlight skimming the entry, I finally found it.

The room was instantly flooded with bright fluorescent

light that made the buzzing sound that always reminded me of the flickering overheads in my elementary school.

The pantry looked so different now with the bright lights instead of the swath of daylight from a propped-open door. But still, there was the open bag of pita chips, crumbs on the ground, proof of what had happened earlier.

And there were the shelves lining the walls, packed to the brim with dry goods, with cans, with supplies, and then the bottom shelf. It was empty.

The shelf where all the food from the freezer had been piled before . . .

I felt a tingling all over my body, and, adrenaline rushing, head pounding, and blood pumping fast, I took three quick steps and sunk to my knees in front of the old freezer. I put two hands onto the edge and heaved it upward, then pulled myself up.

I looked down, searching for her hair, the back of her head, the frozen, blue-tinged skin.

But it was all so normal. Packs of frozen veggies. Cuts of meat.

I was staring down at a freezer filled with food.

Like none of it had ever happened at all.

37

Kerry

February 2, 2023
5:31 p.m.

Was I losing my mind?

I stared at the food, stacks of it. Packed into a freezer that appeared as if it had never been used for anything else.

That showed no sign of a dead body. Of anything but sustenance, supplies, exactly what it had been meant for.

I thought, suddenly, of a documentary I'd watched once, about a woman who believed she was god and her followers who thought that an alien ship powered by dead celebrities was going to take her up to somewhere beyond. Only unlike other cults, these people weren't cleverly, compellingly brainwashed by some charismatic leader—instead, it turned out that they were all getting drunk and high just about all the time, and somewhere along the way, their brains collectively broke.

Was it possible that that's what had happened to me? I had been abusing alcohol all day. I took an Ambien last night. And I'd been popping the antianxiety pills like candy.

But did that mean I could conjure a body from nothing?

What in the world was going on?

I turned to Tyler, and his face, illuminated by the

fluorescents, was washed with pity, like he was looking at a toddler who just didn't get it.

"It *was* here," I said. "*She* was here."

Tyler opened his mouth, as if about to argue back, but then, in the doorway, a flash of a uniform. His uncle, Billy. The police.

"Sorry for the delay," he said. "We're booked solid with calls. I heard voices back here. You want to add something to your report from this morning?"

I looked from the officer to the freezer, then to Tyler, and back to the freezer again.

Not again, I thought. This simply couldn't be happening again.

It wasn't fair. I wasn't losing touch with reality. I knew what I'd seen.

"I—"

Tyler was already speaking. "She believes that there was a body in this freezer. Not the prior caretaker as she reported earlier, but someone else. A different woman, yes?"

"Yes," I said. "A different woman."

Officer Rice—Billy—sighed. "And where is this other woman?"

I looked to the freezer, then back to him. "She was here," I said, tears prickling my eyes. "She was. I'm not—I don't just imagine things."

"Ma'am," he said. "Ma'am, I'm sorry, but you positively reek of wine."

"So I'm a drunk!" I blubbered. "So I'm an alcoholic! But I'm *not* losing my mind. I'm not lying. She was here." I turned back to the freezer, filled with food. "She was right here. I swear to god."

For a moment, I wondered—I'd seen Siobhan out here. Could she have moved her—again? But Siobhan's body was so frail. In her state, it didn't seem possible.

"No," I said to myself as much as to them. "She was here. She was goddamn *here*."

I picked up one of the packs of veggies, tossed it aside. And it felt so good to throw something, and I found myself grabbing more food, tossing it out, searching for some—any—proof that this had happened, that I hadn't imagined it all.

"Stop it, ma'am," Billy said. "Enough of this."

At the same time, I could feel Tyler's hands on my shoulders, attempting to pull me away. I could hear his voice in my ear. "Kerry, please. Let us get you some help. You need some help."

You need some help. Of course I did. But what had happened had happened. The fact of my needing help didn't change that.

Tyler's hands still on my shoulders, I felt myself begin to relent. No longer caring about what I'd seen, I only wanted for this ordeal to be over. I wanted to be pulled away, ushered into a room. I wanted someone to make me tea with honey and prop me in front of a roaring fire while the radiators—now working—pumped heat.

I wanted to let them all win, all the men who thought I was a foolish, wine-addled woman. And I really was about to, about to give up and go outside and wait for Frank, and when he arrived ask him to take me straight to a psychiatric hospital, because I didn't know fact from fiction, I could no longer trust my very own eyes.

Let these men pull me away, pity me even more, tell

325

everyone they saw about the alcoholic up from the city who wasted police resources by seeing dead bodies over and over and over again.

But as I pushed aside another cut of meat, I saw it.

Something that didn't fit.

A flash of red.

There and then gone.

I lurched forward, reaching for it, but already it had been swallowed up again. I pushed aside more food, digging, and then, there it was, my heart pounding brutally, viciously.

I snatched it. A nail. Coffin-shaped, for a makeshift coffin. Striated with dried glue on the back. Shiny with polish and topcoat. Coated beneath with dirt and tiny rocks, with struggle, with skin, with who knew what else.

She'd tried to fight someone off, maybe push herself up.

She'd tried to save her own life.

Someone had stopped her.

38

Allison

"Fuck you," Siobhan said.

She'd never spoken like that to me before. It was the way she should be talking to the men in her life. Losers, all of them. To Kerry, who'd left her in the dust, too. But no, it was for me. Me, her best friend since forever, the one who had always, always cared about her. Always been on her side.

"Right back at you," I said. Like it meant nothing to me. Like I didn't even care about hurting her. When, more than anything, I did.

"Everything okay?" Tyler was there, eager, but Siobhan was ignoring him. And everyone else, too. She was stomping off, back to Room Thirteen.

So go, I wanted to yell. Go feel sorry for yourself. Go pretend like I have everything and you have nothing, when in reality, not a one of us has it all figured out. We're all just getting by, making the most of it.

Because it *was* wild and precious, this life. I really believed that. But the most precious part about it was these friendships, these loves, the people we cared for. So why was I hurting my friend like this?

I flicked off the camera. I'm not sure why I'd taunted her with it in the first place. A slick feeling coated my stomach.

Yes, she had been beyond shitty to say that to me, to accuse me like she did, but maybe I shouldn't have responded in kind. Maybe I should have realized that her words were born from pain, from confusion. In a way that had nothing to do with me.

My eyes found Charlie. He was looking in the direction of Siobhan's room, and for a second, it seemed like he was going to go after her, but then Étienne grabbed his arm, nudging him in the shoulder, and Charlie stayed put.

Meanwhile, Pierre was still messing with his jeans, his nipples like little bullets in the night.

To my right, I saw Jeremy turn on his heel, making his way toward Siobhan's room.

"Be right back," I said to Tyler, pushing the camera into his hand. I pointed to the red button on the top. "When he starts, please make sure you catch it."

Tyler smiled his boyish smile. "Will do."

I picked up my pace, caught up to Jeremy when we were both in front of the main office, the oversize letters of the motel staring down at us. "Hey," I said. "Hey. *Jeremy.*"

He turned, and I could see, already, the smirk on his face. He was smarmy, this one. At first I hadn't been sure, but now I could pick up on it, clear as day. I'd spent a career fending off these types of men.

See, what I hadn't yet told Siobhan was that I knew Jeremy's secret.

What Tyler had told me, without even realizing what he was saying.

The girl with the knife, McKenzie. She didn't get on with her parents, and even worse, Tyler suspected she was in a bad relationship. He'd seen marks on her neck, asked her about them, and she'd blown him off. I didn't put it together until Siobhan came back the next morning, bent down to add a log to the fire—those marks on her back. Yes, she'd already told me that Jeremy dabbled in S&M, but seeing it imprinted on her body made it different. I knew it wasn't my place to judge what two adults did behind closed doors.

But that was different—this McKenzie girl was just a kid.

"What is it?" Jeremy said now, bringing me back to the present.

"You're not going to her room."

He scoffed. "You think you get to tell me what to do? Really?"

What he didn't realize was that one of the reasons I'd even *suggested* this party was so I could get a chance to talk to him, tell him to fuck right off. "You're not doing anything with my friend. Okay? We're leaving tomorrow, and she's never going to hear from you again."

"She already asked me to come by tomorrow. To drive you all to the damn lot."

Christ, I thought. My car.

"Plus," he went on. "She needs her ID. I forgot it."

"How convenient," I said.

Jeremy tossed his hands in the air. "What's your problem, huh?"

"Listen," I said. "Bring her ID. Be our taxi. Whatever. But after that you better not have a thing to do with us. With her."

"Oh yeah," Jeremy said. "And why is that? You Team Bozo Ex?" His head swiveled slightly, nodding toward Charlie, who was cheering on Pierre, oblivious to us watching him.

"I'm Team Siobhan," I said.

He raised his eyebrows. "Sure didn't seem that way when you were cursing her out just now."

"I wasn't—" I started, but then I stopped myself. I didn't want to give him the upper hand. Men like him were used to having it. I changed tack. "I know what kind of person you are," I said, my gaze piercing his. "Even if Siobhan doesn't. I know about you and that girl."

It was actually part bluff. I wasn't totally sure. But from the look on his face, now I was.

Fucking pervert.

"Is she even of age?" I asked.

"Yes," he said immediately, and as he did, he seemed to realize that his answer had confirmed my suspicions.

"You sure about that?" I asked. "She looked pretty damn young to me. Tyler says she was a ways behind him in school."

Jeremy winced.

"I'm sure the New York State Bar would love to hear about your extracurricular activities with minors. And if a statutory rape charge doesn't pan out, your reputation will be in the shitter anyway. High-profile clients aren't going to want to hire some guy who got famous for beating a teenager with a fucking riding crop."

Jeremy's hands clenched at his sides. He looked half like he wanted to strangle me.

"Easy there, buddy," I said, nodding to his hands. "Save

it for the bedroom. Or, on second thought, don't." A beat, letting him stew. "What you're going to do is this: You're going to leave. Now. Drive us tomorrow or don't, I don't even care. But after that, you're never going to speak to Siobhan again. Or else I'm going to go blow up your life."

He huffed, and his face paled with anger, with rage. "You wouldn't."

"Don't try me," I said. "I love that girl. And the last thing she needs right now is to fall straight into some other prick's arms."

His eyes shot daggers, but after a moment, he turned on his heel, and I watched as he traipsed across the parking lot, made an announcement to everyone and no one in particular. Then he began to walk back toward the road.

Siobhan was in the corner of the room by the time we piled back inside, her eyes glazed over with drunkenness, her face still red with anger. I set her camera on the counter and went to work on another round of drinks while Charlie sidled up to her and the Frenchies went back to the playlist, Tyler by my side.

The night blurred then, one song into the next, Charlie and Siobhan cozy in the corner, Tyler and the Frenchies dancing in the middle of the rug, booze and weed and white powder being passed around.

Eventually, Siobhan's head started to droop, she could barely keep her eyes open, and I convinced the whole crew that we had a big day of packing everything up in the morning. Bags were grabbed. Hats and gloves and scarves were put on. They filed out the door, and I turned back, ushering Siobhan gently onto the bed, pouring a glass of water, and setting it on the nightstand beside her.

The plan had been for me to sleep in this room tonight—giving us one fewer space to clean in the morning—and now I was glad of it. The girl was seriously drunk, and I would feel better at least watching her for a bit, making sure she didn't choke on her vomit or something.

I was about to start getting ready for bed myself when I spotted the camera sitting on the counter. I really had been a dick, hadn't I, taunting Siobhan like I had. When she got up, hungover, inevitably she'd look at the footage, and that was what she'd see.

I grabbed it, walking outside so as not to wake Siobhan, and positioned myself in front of the motel sign. I thought about deleting the last couple of clips, but knowing Siobhan, that would probably only anger her further when she remembered our fight. Instead, I decided I could at least soften the blow.

Putting on my best actor smile, I pointed the camera at myself, then hit the red button on top to record.

"Helluva night, folks. This is your tour guide, Allison, signing off. Siobhan, I'm sorry if I was a bit of an ass. I promise you—you have nothing to worry about with me. Hopefully you will find this all very funny in the morning. Peace out."

I was about to turn it off when I heard a sound of footsteps to my left, felt a presence behind me.

Without thinking, I screamed and dropped the camera.

"Fuck," I said, as I knelt into the gravel to grab it, my hand flicking the button to stop recording as I did.

"Shit, I didn't mean to scare you."

Hands were on my elbows, helping me up, and I turned to see him, his eyes locked on mine, a grin on his lips.

"Tyler?" I asked. "What are you doing here?"

39

Kerry

I clasped the red nail with two fingers, holding onto it like a gem.

Tyler's hands were still on me.

"Let me go," I said, shaking him off. His hand rested on the lip of the freezer.

I took a deep breath, felt the tears building behind my eyes now. "She was here," I said. "We know she was here."

Billy cleared his throat, his eyebrows stitching together. "What do you have there?"

"It's a fake nail," I said.

"Can I see it?" he asked.

I hesitated a moment, but then the badge gleamed in the overhead light, and I placed it into the officer's gloved hands, careful not to drop it.

He pulled it up to his eyes, examining.

"It's one of *hers*," I said. "Allison's. I saw the setup in the bathroom."

He offered the nail back to me, and I clasped it in my palm.

"I'm not sure what that proves, Miss Walsh."

"That she was here," I said. I squeezed the nail in my palm, holding it like my life depended on it.

335

The officer sighed. "This is the second time we've been called out, ma'am. The second time with absolutely nothing to show for it. All we have here is proof that someone who used this freezer wore fake nails."

"Or that there really was a body in here," I said. "And that this is the one piece of evidence that's been left behind."

I held out the nail, and Tyler's grip on the lip of the freezer tightened.

"I think we should move this along," Billy said. "I've got real police work to do."

I wasn't looking at him, my gaze trained on Tyler. His hand, I realized, was holding the freezer so tight to stop it from shaking.

I lifted the nail toward him, shoving it in his direction, and it was unmistakable: He flinched.

I stared into his eyes, just beginning to glaze with moisture. At the cut of his shoulders, the width of them, beneath Gore-Tex and down. Arms that had carried in a near-mountain of wood the first time I'd seen him. Arms that were strong, built by the outdoors, by hard work, made for maintenance, for keeping things running. Arms that would have had no problem lifting a body. And lifting it again.

Tyler was here that night; he'd never pretended he wasn't. But a lot of people were here, weren't they? And he didn't think there was a reason that the cops would turn on him. And why would he be a person of interest? He was family, wasn't he?

Tyler had the capability. He also had a utility vehicle; he'd driven me over in it.

I racked my brain, my fingers beginning to shake, my heart beating faster.

Was it possible? Could Tyler have killed Allison that night, then left her there all the next day, hoping the snow would cover her, that no one would see? Had he been surprised to see me arrive, to see me find her the next morning, known then that he had to do *something*, moved her while I walked to his house to get help?

And Tyler had been here, tonight, found me just after I had argued with Siobhan.

I knew I should be scared, I should be terrified, but knowing the answer finally—it was such a relief. Knowing finally, fully, that I wasn't imagining things; that was a relief, too.

"Tyler," I said, clasping the nail in my palm so I wouldn't drop it. "What happened? What did you do?"

"Hey," Billy said. "Listen. Let's not get ahead of ourselves here. I understand that you're freaked out, but—ma'am—we *still* don't have a body. We're going only on your conjectures here. And a single fake nail that could belong to anyone."

There wasn't anger or rage on Tyler's face, but humiliation, deepest disgrace. He looked suddenly like a scared, ashamed puppy who had been caught destroying the living room.

I glanced to his uncle, whose badge once again caught the light. Should I be scared? Should I fear what was about to come? Yes, he was family, and a family connection could help with a lot of things, but it couldn't undo a murder. That was a step too far.

"Why?" I asked, my eyes trained straight on Tyler. "Why *Allison*?"

337

He shook his head, and I saw a tear escape from one of his eyes, but he brushed it away as if it had never been there at all. He wasn't a killer; he had somehow gotten in over his head, and something had happened, and then he had tried his best to cover it up, pretend as if it hadn't.

Whatever had happened, he hadn't intended it. That much was clear. He opened his mouth, as if to speak—

"Don't indulge her," Billy said. "She's nuts."

"Am I?" I asked, my gaze still on Tyler. "Really?"

His breath was ragged, and damn it if that wasn't answer enough.

Because you couldn't cover up something like that forever. Eventually the snow was going to melt. The power was going to come back on.

The remnants of a life were going to turn up.

And I was holding one of those remnants tight in my hand.

"Tyler," I said again, my voice soft now. Kind. "Tell him. *Please*. Tell him I wasn't imagining things. Tell your uncle what happened."

I took a deep breath. "Tell us what happened that night."

40

Allison

Tyler was looking at me with the most bashful, boyish grin. I had never had a problem getting men to like me, but something about it tickled me now, it was so sweet.

He shifted his weight from foot to foot.

"I hung back. I was trying to work up the nerve to knock on your door and ask if you wanted another drink. But then you walked out." He kicked a bit of gravel with one foot. "Guess I never did work up the nerve."

His face flushed red in the moonlight. It was still snowing lightly, and a flake landed on his nose. I had the most absurd desire to kiss it off.

"Anyway," he said. "Do you? Want another drink?"

I felt a smile spread across my face. "Sure," I said. "Why the hell not? Is wine okay? I don't have it in me to shake any more cocktails."

Tyler nodded. "*Anything's* okay."

I dipped back into Siobhan's room. I looked around for a place to put the camera, but there were drinks and paraphernalia everywhere. I didn't want her to bumble around and knock it over—or, worse, spill something on it—so I tucked it under the bed right where she was sleeping, then grabbed a wine tool and an unopened bottle from the stash. A dark and smoky Merlot that I'd spent more than I should have on.

Back outside, I led Tyler to the room next door, mine for the past couple of weeks. "We can't make a mess," I said as I slipped the key in the lock, twisting it to the right, then opened the door, flicked on the overhead light.

Tyler followed me in, tracking snow and mud against the hardwoods.

"I mean it," I said, setting the wine on a small table and reaching down to tug off my boots. "Shoes off. We cleaned the room already, and I'm crashing at Siobhan's tonight so we don't have to take care of two in the morning. And we'll have plenty to do, because we've got to go to the impound lot." I raised an eyebrow. "Tell your mom thanks, by the way."

Tyler winced. "I tried to dissuade her, but I couldn't. I'm sorry."

"Well, you'll just have to make it up to me, then," I said, letting the innuendo hang in the air, turning Tyler's face even redder. "I'm sure you'll think of something."

I turned from him, grabbing the bottle and the corkscrew, maneuvering the thing out in a few effortless turns, something I'd gotten good at while waiting tables on and off over the years. I fluttered over to the cabinet, pinched a pair of glasses I'd have to remember to wash in the morning, then served us each generous pours and plopped myself on top of the comforter on the bed. I patted the space next to me, and Tyler dutifully came over, sitting by my side.

I pressed the glass into his hand, and we each took a gulp.

"So why did you want to talk to me?" I asked.

He looked down, then looked up again, took another sip of wine. "You know," he said.

"Do I?"

He set down his glass on the nightstand. I leaned over, did the same.

Then his eyes met mine. "Can I kiss you?"

I felt my lips turn up at the edge. I hadn't been asked that in so very long. The men I met, producers, actors, they just took, like it was their right. Like inviting someone into a room was a promise to be cashed in.

I gazed at Tyler, nodded, and he leaned forward, still hesitant, but then, our lips were pressed together, my mouth was open, his tongue soft against mine, my body leaning on his. He was too young for me, of course, but something about the wine sloshing around in my head, the cotton of the duvet that I could feel beneath my hand, it made me feel like I was back in the dorm in college, sneaking kisses with Chris, the devout Christian who wouldn't do anything more than make out. There had been something so simple and pure in those ultra-long kissing sessions. Hours devoted only to the sensations, the feelings in your lips, on your tongue, the blood pumping in your veins.

Tyler's hands found the back of my head, pulling me even closer, and as our chests pressed together, I could feel the beating of his heart, and suddenly, I wasn't on the futon of Chris's dorm. Suddenly, I was right here, and I reached for Tyler's belt buckle, and he didn't stop

341

me—of course he didn't stop me—and he was looking at me with this joy, like he'd won the lottery, struck gold. He said something about not having a condom, and I mentioned my IUD, and then it was happening, and it was sweet and quick and he was so young, so naive. And I loved that, I did.

"Wow," Tyler said, crashing into me, our clothes still on. "Just. Wow."

And then, in a flash, I didn't want it. It felt like I was chasing something that was impossible to grasp. Being young again, with a fresh start, fresh dreams. Not having tried and gotten so close and ultimately not made it.

I sat up, wriggled my underwear back in place, antsy to move, to halt the intimacy of this moment. I couldn't just ask him to leave; it would break his heart. "You want a cigarette? I'd kill for a cigarette right now."

I could tell he was a little hurt, that he would have preferred to cuddle, but he forced a smile. "Sure."

"You get the glasses," I said, needing, suddenly, to drink off the fact that I'd just slept with someone so much younger than me in an attempt to somehow . . . what? Soak up youth by proxy? "There's a pack of Parliaments in Siobhan's room. I'll pop over there and grab them."

Siobhan was still fully passed out when I went for the cigarettes. Back outside, Tyler and I found ourselves on the back lawn of the motel, where the stones of a natural fire pit formed a small circle, us sitting on the edge, the night cold but pleasant, snow falling lightly.

"You have a lighter?" I asked. "The one in my room was empty, so I threw it out, and I couldn't find one in Siobhan's. No matches, either."

"No," Tyler said. "But there's a camping lighter in the boiler room. You got the keys?"

I nodded, handing the ring over to him.

In a minute, he was back, an extra-long lighter in his hand.

"You left the door open," I said, nodding back to where I could barely see the edge of the outbuilding.

"Right," Tyler said. "It will remind me to go back and return this. It's the only one in that room, and I need it to light the pilot when I work on it. But for now—" He flicked his thumb, and the light illuminated his face. "A light, my lady?"

I grinned, then grabbed a cigarette, propped it between my lips. I leaned into the light, sucked hard, then took another, lit it, too, handed it to Tyler, who inhaled way too much, coughed up a storm.

I took a drag, then smiled at him, his features illuminated in the moonlight. "I take it you don't smoke."

He shook his head. "Do you?"

"When I'm working, yeah. Well, and drinking," I said. "It's a nasty habit, I know. But especially at the end of a long shoot, when a director calls five, and you know you're going to have to do about a million more takes until you get one just right, I don't know, it gives you that boost you need. Like a burst of liquid courage."

"A vice," Tyler said.

"Yeah," I said, taking another drag. "A vice."

"One that pays off," he said. "Some vices aren't all bad. Not if they get the juices flowing."

I recognized the phrase, paused, my eyes narrowing. "Did you—"

Tyler nodded eagerly.

"You read my newsletter?" I asked. It had been one of my weekly themes—things that were bad for your body but (occasionally) good for your creativity. *The right vice can get the juices flowing* was how I'd put it. Or something like that.

"Religiously," he said with a grin. "Have since you started it. I mean, you've got one of the top creative newsletters on Substack." He cleared his throat. "What are you going to do with your one wild and precious life?"

"Mary Oliver," I said.

"What?" he asked.

"Nothing," I said, holding back a laugh as I reached for the glass of wine. "Anyway, I'm surprised. I mean, I know you said you wanted to write, but I never would have guessed you'd know about the newsletter."

His eyes were suddenly sharp. "We're not all idiots, just because we don't live in the city, you know."

I stiffened just the tiniest bit. "Of course not. I didn't mean—"

"You don't have a corner on creativity," he said. "From your newsletters, I never got the idea that you thought you did."

"No," I said, shaking my head. "I'm sorry. It's just . . . you're so young, is all."

His face softened. "I'm not that young. Hemingway published *The Sun Also Rises* when he was twenty-seven."

You're no Hemingway. The thought came unbidden. Thankfully, I didn't voice it.

"So it's fiction, right?" I asked.

Tyler nodded eagerly, taking a gulp of wine. He shifted his weight from foot to foot then, steadying himself, and

344

I realized he really was drunk. Shaky. Off-balance. Hell, so was I.

"I've been working on a short story for a couple of years."

A couple of years for one short story? Again, I didn't voice it. Just gulped back more wine and nodded like I cared.

Tyler was staring at me, eager as a puppy, and I realized then that I was supposed to say something else. "What's it about?"

His face lit up. "It's kind of like early Bret Easton Ellis meets Stephen King meets Faulkner."

I raised my eyebrows, but he didn't catch my derision.

"It's about this man who lives alone in the woods— you know, a type of guy like Jeremy—rich and keeps to himself, and he, you know, he hurts women, as a way of feeling something. He's got this family past—I guess it's kind of based on my dad, too. Like, a lot of men on my dad's side of the family were physically violent, but I'm not like that, you know. So the story is about this guy who is trying to, you know, find meaning, by, like, collecting kills."

I took another sip of my wine. If there was one thing that was getting killed, it was my buzz.

"I want to submit it to *The New Yorker*," he said.

Of course you do, I thought. Of fucking course.

"I really only think it works for their audience."

"They do love a brilliant tale of male violence," I said, but Tyler didn't even catch my sarcasm.

I took another drag of my cigarette, hoping this conversation was almost over.

"Do you want to read it?"

"Sure." Already, I was imagining deleting the email, tossing the attachment into the proverbial bin.

But Tyler was throwing his cigarette into the snow, reaching into his jacket pocket.

"Wait?" I asked. *"Now?"*

The boy was pulling out pages folded in quarters, pressing them into my hands.

"It's not that long. Come on," he said. "I think you'll like it. You're a creative person. You'll—you'll get it."

I glanced at the title. "Beneath Her Skin," by Tyler Colton Rice.

Holy fuck did this boy take himself way too seriously. I downed the rest of my wine, knelt to set the glass on the edge of one of the rocks, straightened back up, preparing for the inevitable cringe-iness, then flipped a page.

My eyes scanned over the first few paragraphs.

It was the feel of her supple neck between his thick fingers, fingers that had worked, really worked, to build something that was supposed to be real but never really felt like it was.

It got worse from there. A mess of adjectives, purply prose. *Death entered pungently . . . His heart as empty and vile as a kettle of soup gone bad . . . The slick, lubricious feeling of life slipping through fingers.*

And then something happened, something I hadn't expected. I started laughing.

Softly at first, and then whole hog; it was spilling out of me.

"Hey," Tyler said. "Hey, what's your problem? It's not funny. It's not *supposed* to be funny."

I could barely breathe, and when I looked up at him, his face red with anger, it only made me laugh harder. Like when my cousin and I had dropped the offering basket at church, could not stop giggling all through the Lord's Prayer.

I was laughing so hard my cheeks were hurting, the wine sloshing around in my gut.

Bret Easton Ellis! Faulkner! Only *The New Yorker* will do!

"Stop *laughing*," Tyler said. He reached out, grabbed the pages from me, snatching them away.

His anger only made me laugh harder. That I was out here, sharing wine and cigarettes with this . . . this child . . . this . . . buffoon. That moments before, I'd let him cum inside me, something he'd probably spend years working into a damn story, write some revenge porn about me. This man who thought there was nothing more interesting in the whole fucking world than male violence, than his own sob story: "Oh, my dad wasn't such a great guy, you know, but I'm different."

"Stop fucking laughing!"

And he was getting so angry, because he'd actually thought—this boy had actually thought—that I was going to read these bad fucking pages and declare him some kind of literary god, call in every favor I had to get him in *The New Yorker*.

When the truth was, you could be brilliant, you could work and work and work for it, and still have so little to show.

That was the creative life. Not this. Not this trash.

I looked up at him, and I only laughed harder.

But then he stepped forward, and, snow swirling around us now, I knew I had fucked up.

"I told you to stop. Fucking. Laughing."

Then his hands were up, and they were shoving forward, against my shoulders, one great *push*, and I felt my body rear back.

And that was it.

41

Kerry

"I didn't do anything," Tyler said, but his hand gripped the freezer, tight, as if he were holding himself up. "We slept together. That's all, okay? And after that, I don't know what happened."

"Tyler," Billy said, a warning. "Tyler, don't indulge her. None of this matters."

"But things didn't go how you wanted, did they?" I asked, pushing. "What did she do?" I asked, knowing the question was wrong, unfair, but also knowing that he had somehow absolved himself, and this might be the only way. "What did she say? She's a tough one, Allison. She's pissed me off before, too."

Tyler eyed Billy, then turned to me. "I thought she wanted to help people, creative people, like me. She was always writing about how so many people have this spark in them, how they just have to uncover it, and I thought I could trust her. I just wanted to show her my story. I worked on it for years." His voice cracked.

"What did she do, Tyler?"

His eyes caught mine, flashing with rage. "She *laughed* at me, like I was nothing—like I was an idiot for even trying.

And she wouldn't stop laughing. I only wanted her to stop. Goddamn it, I just wanted her to stop!"

My heart was practically pounding against my rib cage. Here was the answer. Allison—beautiful, brilliant, tactless Allison, Allison, who could dish it out and also take it, who I could totally imagine laughing when presented with this boy's precious work, with the earnestness of a white man with a story he thought everyone should hear.

The Margaret Atwood quote blazed into mind, hot and fiery as a brand.

Men are afraid that women will laugh at them. Women are afraid that men will kill them.

How true it was. Both had happened that night, and now we were here.

"It was just a little push. But then she wouldn't move. And I—I ran. And then when I went by the next day, she was—she was there—and I didn't know what to do. I didn't mean anything. But then"—he eyed me—"then you came. Then you found her. Then I—" He shook his head. "I had to do *something*, didn't I?"

Tyler's shoulders shook, and I glanced to his uncle, fully ready to see a pair of handcuffs in his hand, for words— kind yet firm—to spill from his mouth. *Tyler, you're under arrest.*

But he was simply rolling his eyes. "Are you done, boy? You're making a fool of yourself."

Tyler looked over, connecting eyes with his uncle.

"You don't know what you're saying," the officer went on. "You're not making sense."

I shook my head, trying to understand. "But—but you heard him—he—he—"

"You said this wouldn't happen," Tyler said with anguish, looking at his uncle now. "You said you'd take care of it."

A gasp, and it clicked. Because of course. Of *course*.

I thought of what McKenzie had scrawled across that note, so much younger than me but also somehow wiser. *Sorry—no cops.*

And then, I saw it, beads of sweat on the top of Billy's head. Beneath the hunter's cap. His hairline was wet with sweat. From nerves. From adrenaline.

From exertion.

"You," I said, my eyes trained on him, because suddenly it made so much sense. Tyler didn't—couldn't—have done this on his own. Yes, he had killed Allison, but he had turned to someone else to cover it all up.

The police had been there already, before I returned with Tyler this afternoon, their utility vehicles leaving tracks around the perimeter of the motel.

And there had been two vehicles, hadn't there? That meant that Billy could have come before that woman did. He could have already been at the motel when he got the call from Denise on his radio. Cleaning up his nephew's mess. But it was broad daylight, and he was in an open vehicle. So he put the body in the freezer until he could come back tonight and find another place to hide it, the falling snow covering any tracks.

And now that it was dark, he had come back. What's more, he had told the other cops he was taking the call. No one else was coming. When Tyler had stepped outside, to call his uncle, see how far away he was, what he had really been doing was checking if the deed was done, if Allison's body had once again been moved, so they could watch me think I was losing my mind, seeing things that weren't there once again.

Tyler leaned against the freezer, as if he'd just set down a weight he'd been carrying for days now.

His uncle stared at me, a dare in his eyes. "I would do anything for family," he said, his hand lifting to his waist, in the direction of his gun. "I *will* do anything for family."

Fear shot through me, pumping in my blood.

"Besides," he said, "no one is going to believe some washed-up alcoholic from the city over an upstanding local officer."

I felt the shame build within me once again, and I thought of all the things I'd lost to drinking, all the time in my adult life I'd spent trying to escape, whether it was in the bottom of the bottle or into an Instagram feed. I was always looking for a way to numb, and where had it gotten me?

Because he was right, wasn't he? Who would believe me over him?

But Allison deserved more. *I* deserved more.

I didn't want to be that person. I didn't want to be a liar, a cheater, a drunk who screwed people's boyfriends, who cheated on my own husband. A woman who sabotaged her own chances at a baby, who couldn't even finish a goddamn book.

And I felt, for a moment, as Billy's hand hovered over his gun, that if I could only get myself out of this, I would treat myself better. I would live for me, not for what other people wanted me to be. Not for the me I pretended to be.

For me, flaws and all. Honestly, if nothing else.

I only had one shot at this. I had to get this right.

"You're right," I said. "I *am* a drunk. And I'm all over the place. No one will believe me over you. But—" I stared at him. "You've been sloppy."

The cop's eyes widened, but he didn't move his hand from his gun.

"Her nail, I found that in only a couple of moments of digging. What else is in there? What else is all over this place?" I pointed to the freezer. "I can see more of her, right there."

Tyler leaned forward, but Billy rushed to stop him. He reached to the lip of the freezer, grabbed his nephew's hand. "Stop touching things, boy. Stop—"

I shoved my hip, hard as I could, against the freezer, and—

Slam!

The lid clamped down on Tyler's and Billy's hands like monster teeth. I wrenched my body on top of the freezer, bearing down with my weight, delighting in their cries of pain.

Then I ran, straight for the crack of the doorway. I threw my body forward, but then my foot caught on the edge of the shelf, and I toppled to the ground.

Behind me, a flurry of sounds—yelling and screaming, and then someone clambering toward me, the clatter of tin cans falling. I tried to push myself up, reaching for the door, but I felt a hand on my ankle, and I turned to see Billy latched on, Tyler standing behind him, holding his hands up, his fingers bent in all the wrong angles, wailing in pain.

I tried to wriggle away, but Billy's grip on me tightened, and when I looked back, he was reaching, with his other hand, for his gun.

I knew then that it was too late. My chance at redemption, at being the person I knew I could be if I could only heal myself. It was a pipe dream. Allison's life had been cut short, and now mine would be, too.

Then the door burst open, and there she was.

Siobhan.

Her eyes widened, and without hesitation, she rushed past me, lifted a foot, and smashed it, with all her weight, against Billy's wrist. A snapping sound, bones breaking, and when he let go of me, crying, thrashing in pain, she knelt, reached her hand in mine, jerked me up.

Then we were outside and we were running, only it was so dark, now that my eyes had adjusted to the light inside, and I could barely sense which way to go.

The snow was still so thick, and I heard screams behind me, the clatter of the door, and I knew Billy was after us, wasn't going to let us go without a fight. There was a pounding of footsteps, the *pop-pop-pop* of gunshots, and I stopped for a minute, but Siobhan screamed at me.

"Kerry! Keep going!"

And we did. She lurched forward, and I followed her, but then I felt it beneath me . . .

Something hard. Something solid. There under my feet.

"Siobhan," I called as I tripped, throwing my hands out to catch me in the snow, and the coldness—the snow and ice—smacked against my face, suffocating me, but when I pushed up, I realized there was something beneath me. Big and weighty. Solid as a tree trunk.

Still no light. Still the sound of running.

"Kerry," Siobhan cried, kneeling to help me.

I heard a scream worse than any I'd heard before. A banshee's wail.

Because she could feel her, too.

Her hair. Her cold, clammy skin.

Allison. We'd found Allison after all. Billy must not have been finished moving her when I rushed back, insisting on checking the freezer again.

My screams joined hers—I couldn't help it—and I knew we were done for, I knew that it was too late for us, that Billy would know where we were now, that the *pop-pop* of gunshots would be on us, that we'd be tossed somewhere, anywhere, along with Allison, just another mess to clean up.

Then there was a flash of light, a halo, and I thought I saw Allison—her red nails, her blue skin, the frost-crusted hair—and I saw Siobhan, the horror and the grief and the pain pain pain; when I looked up, I saw someone else, too.

A figure, shining a light toward us. A figure I could hardly make out, and then that figure raised her hand, and in it, a gun.

"Easy there, Billy," she said.

The woman officer who'd pressed her card into my hand. The one I had called only minutes before.

Siobhan was still screaming, but I reached for her, slipped my hand in hers. Then I turned, and in the orb of the flashlight I could see Billy and Tyler. Desperation on their faces.

Billy's gun was drawn, pointed toward Siobhan and me. But the woman was here to stop him.

"It's over," she said from behind us. "And there's a body now, right here. A body you can't make go away."

In the light I could see more tears on Tyler's face and a look of resignation on his uncle's, and after a moment, his grip began to loosen.

Siobhan let out another sob, and I pulled her to me, and she let me, caving into my chest like a crying child.

Then I watched as the gun dropped into the snow.

Sinking into the white, blanketed like everything else.

42

Kerry

Six Months Later
August 19, 2023
6:04 p.m.

The drink was in front of me, glistening, the deep burgundy color of the liquid, the peel of an orange slice floating across the surface, a large hunk of ice clinking around in the perfect lowball glass.

I took out my phone, snapped a photo, felt the strong urge to post it. But then I slipped my phone back into my pocket. The caption I'd composed in my head—*celebrating six months of sobriety with a Phony Negroni!*—seemed suddenly unnecessary. I didn't need to announce it to the world. It was enough to know it for myself.

I took a sip, savoring it. Knowing there would be no hangover the next day. No bad decisions that night.

"You made it."

I turned to see Siobhan, resplendent in a sparkle-blue halter dress, a glass of bubbly in her hand.

"I did. Thanks for inviting me." I nodded to the drink. "And this is fake, by the way. Don't worry."

She smiled softly. "I wasn't. I heard through the grapevine that you were sober. I'm happy for you."

"Thank you," I said. Then I gestured around the room. "And I'm happy for *you*. I can't believe you pulled

357

all of this together so fast—I mean, you did it. You really did it."

Siobhan sighed, and a bit of moisture crept into her eyes that she managed to brush away without messing up her makeup. "Allison deserves it, you know."

"Of course she does." I took a sip of my drink, then let my eyes rest on hers. "I really am sorry, Siobhan. For everything."

"I know you are," she said.

She was tapped on the shoulder by a man in all black, who whispered in her ear.

"I have to go," she said. "They want me to say a little something to open."

"Of course," I said. "Go."

I watched as she was whisked away, out of the bar, through the doors into the auditorium where we'd all be headed in a few minutes.

I hadn't seen Siobhan since that horrible night in February. Since we were piled into a police van, our hands clasped the entire time, until we were taken to a small-town station where we separated and both gave our statements. Frank had come to get me, and I didn't know who had gotten Siobhan—maybe Charlie—but we didn't see each other after that.

I'd heard that she was working on a movie—but not, apparently, the one that I'd seen elements of in her notebooks and on her laptop. It was a documentary about Allison, about what had happened to the two of them that night and in the days after, the way life had mimicked art to take Allison away way too soon. When Siobhan had reached out, asking for an interview, I had instantly agreed, hoping for a chance to see her, to reconnect, only to be disappointed when Siobhan didn't show for the interview, had her video assistant feed me the questions instead. So when I received the email that an early cut of the film was complete, that there would be a big launch party before it hit the festival circuit, of course I jumped at the chance to come.

And now, here I was, in a room of strangers—people who'd known Allison, people from Siobhan's former ad agency, a couple of friends I'd seen at parties, others who'd read about it in *New York* magazine—but had barely exchanged more than a few words with Siobhan.

I took a sip of the drink in my hand and positioned myself at the edge of the room, wishing I'd asked someone to come with me, feeling suddenly out of place. I was thankful when I heard a voice booming over the speaker: "Please proceed to the auditorium."

Just outside the entrance to the auditorium, a girl was handing out programs in front of a poster featuring red text on a dark blue background, a neon motel sign in one corner, an old-school motel key in the other.

WILD AND PRECIOUS
A FILM BY SIOBHAN JONES

I nearly gasped when my eyes caught the girl's.

"McKenzie?" I asked, dumbfounded. She looked so different, in a chic black dress, her hair in glossy waves that came just to her shoulders, her skin clear. "From the motel?"

McKenzie laughed. "I haven't seen you since you tried

to tell me a killer was going to get me if I went outside. I continue to maintain that avoiding cops is always the best policy."

Her voice had a confidence now, one that wasn't youthful bravado but something a bit more real.

"I was worried about you," I said. "I didn't want you—"

"I know, I know," she said, handing out programs as more people shuffled through. "You meant well. Everyone did." She glanced around. "Everyone *does*."

"What are you doing here?"

McKenzie grinned. "Siobhan interviewed me for the project, and then I guess we kind of kept in touch. She invited me to come stay with her for a weekend in Brooklyn, and I loved it so much I just . . . haven't gone back."

"You're *living* with Siobhan?"

She laughed again. "No, no. I mean, I was for a week, yeah. But then I got a job at Trader Joe's, and I found a cheap enough room on Craigslist—Siobhan fronted me the money for the security deposit—and she gets me random production assistant gigs at her old agency sometimes. I'm going to school here in the fall."

"Wow," I said.

"Yep," she said. "No more motel-room crashing for me. And there isn't a damn thing my parents can do to stop me."

"That's . . . amazing," I said. "Good for you."

She passed out programs to a few more stragglers, then seized up.

"Wow," she said. "I didn't expect *him* to show. Since he had to know I was going to be here, too."

I turned to where she was looking, spotted Jeremy in

the corner, sipping on red wine. His eyes connected briefly with mine, and he smirked ever so slightly, then looked down, like he hadn't even seen me. Examined his phone.

"Did Siobhan invite him?" I asked.

"Not exactly," she said. "She and I talked a bit about Jeremy, and she helped me realize it maybe wasn't the best thing for me at the time—she said it probably wasn't the best thing for her, either; we had this big long discussion about consent and stuff, like she was my mom—except what am I saying, my mom would never talk about anything like that." McKenzie laughed. "Anyway, Siobhan did interview him; she interviewed everyone who was there the night Allison died—well, except Tyler, of course. Shocking, really. I always thought he was so nice." Her eyes went back to Jeremy. "I suppose Jeremy can't resist the chance to see himself on the big screen. And look"— she pointed to the other side of the room—"there's Maisy."

I followed McKenzie's gaze to a woman in all black sipping on something bubbly, talking to a group that had surrounded her.

"It can't be good press for the Twilite," I said.

McKenzie's eyebrows shot up. "Are you kidding? My parents said she's raking it in. People, man. Bunch of morbid assholes. Tripping over themselves to take selfies where a woman was murdered."

"Wow," I said. I thought of that binder full of profiles, the way Maisy had sussed us all up, deciding what was best for business. I hated both the games she played and the way she seemed to always win them, even when tragedy struck. "Do you know—did she end up getting her way with the property lines?"

McKenzie shook her head. "She and Jeremy are still battling it out, and Denise put her land up for Tyler's bail, so who knows what's going on there. I guess Maisy can fight with the state of New York now." She shrugged. "But anyway, I better get inside. I don't want to miss Siobhan's little speech."

"Me, either," I said.

McKenzie hesitated at the door. "Siobhan was really hoping you'd come," she said. "She misses you, you know."

"Oh," I said. "I got the sense she'd like me to kind of keep my distance."

The girl tugged at a loose thread of her dress. "She's still working through . . . what you did . . . with her ex."

I felt my face flush scarlet.

"But, I mean, she knows that you were really fucked up when it happened." She glanced to the glass in my hand.

"It's a mocktail," I said. "I'm not drinking anymore." I glanced around. "He's not here, is he? Siobhan's ex?"

"Oh, he's here," she said. "He's already inside. Got a front-row seat."

"What?"

McKenzie rolled her eyes. "Don't worry, they're a hundred percent done. But he's an executive producer. I guess he put up a bunch of money for it?"

Twenty-five thousand dollars. So he did let her keep it after all.

McKenzie smiled. "I'm going to find a seat. You should, too."

*

The film was perfect—and Siobhan was, too. A tribute to what happened to all of us up there, to the intersection between art and life, to the fleeting nature of it all, and to Allison, who had always tried to make the most of the time she had. It was forty-five minutes, but I got the sense that if it got picked up by a streamer, it could easily become a limited series. There was plenty more to unpack—Tyler's and his uncle's trials hadn't even started yet.

As we piled out of the auditorium and back into the lobby-slash-bar, I kept my eyes peeled, hoping to catch a glimpse of Siobhan again, to congratulate her, to ask if she wanted to get coffee one day, McKenzie's words making me hopeful for the first time that maybe our friendship could be restored.

"Did you like the film?"

A voice behind me, and I turned to see Charlie. My shoulders jolted, and I struggled to find words. "I'm sorry, I didn't . . . I mean, I haven't . . ."

Charlie smirked. "Where's your drink?" He nodded to the empty glass I was still holding. "Rare to see you without one."

I realized then what it must look like. To Charlie, I was still the woman I'd been for so long before. The woman who knew how to party, who knew how to escape. The woman who fucked guys in bathrooms.

"I don't drink," I said.

Charlie laughed.

"I'm serious."

He shrugged. "Whatever you say, Kerry."

Siobhan appeared then, and her eyes passed between us, and though Charlie was already turning away, was already moving toward the bar, ordering himself another drink, although our brief interaction was over, I could see it still, so strong, so clear. The hurt in her eyes. A reminder of things that had happened, things that couldn't be undone. Things I'd taken from her.

I wanted to say I was sorry, to speak it over and over and over and over again until she knew how much I felt it, but I could only offer up a small smile. "It was a perfect movie."

"Thanks, Kerry." Siobhan turned away, swallowed up by the crowd, by congratulations, by friends, by people who hadn't betrayed her, who had been there for her, who would be there for her, maybe in a way now I never could.

I looked down at my empty glass, shame burning so hot it felt I might melt the lowball right there in my hands. For a second, I imagined it, how good it would feel to let it all go, to not try to be good anymore, to pound drinks at the bar until I didn't have to feel my self-hatred anymore. To *numb numb numb*.

I still hadn't finished my book, even if I had made enough progress to keep my publisher satiated for now. I was no closer to being a mother, and I was having to accept more and more that it was very likely I never would be. And worse than all of that, I'd hurt the people I loved the most. Frank and Siobhan.

And when the guilt really crept up, it made me want to reach for all my old vices. Booze. Endless scrolling. Posting about my life in a way that would make others jealous, would make them believe I had my shit together when I didn't.

It would be so easy, I thought. No one would even have

364

to know. I could order a Negroni, pretend it was another fake one. I could have just one, just to take away some of the pain.

I stepped up to the bar, felt my breath catch. A bartender in a white button-down approached. "Help you?"

My heart raced, and I felt the adrenaline pulsing through my fingers.

I set the glass on the bar. "Just wanted to give this back. Have a great night."

He bussed the glass away. "You, too."

I turned and walked out, not looking back, then made my way over to the Bowery, passing three bars on the way, until I saw the gleaming lights of a southbound cab. I lifted my arm, waited for the car to stop.

"Brooklyn," I said, before giving the address.

Then I pulled out my phone, texted Frank.

Film was amazing, headed back now. xoxo

It still boggled my mind that after everything I'd done, I hadn't lost Frank. He'd gone up to the motel, intending to rescue me, and even if that hadn't been how things had played out, with Officer Madison stepping in instead, he'd been there at the police station to whisk me away, take me out of the Catskills, bring me back home.

Well, almost home. We'd stayed at his brother's in Jersey until the subletters were out, and then we'd returned to our place, cautious yet hopeful.

Things weren't perfect, of course. We were working through so much, nearly all of it my fault, but we were in couples therapy, and I was in personal therapy, and slowly, we were finding our way back to each other. We had agreed not to even talk about doing IVF again until I was a year sober, and given that I'd be forty by the time that anniversary hit, I knew that there was a chance that my actions would make us miss our shot at parenthood.

But still, the two of us had decided that the life we'd built together was worth it.

That it was worth trying to save us.

After a moment, my phone buzzed with a text from him.

I'll wait up for you.

I smiled. Frank had gotten good at waiting for me.

To get sober, to get better. To finish my damn book.

The point was, he was still waiting.

And I was waiting, too.

Hoping that in the end, I would manage to surprise us both.

Because in a lot of ways, I already had.

Epilogue
Allison

The Morning After the Party
February 1, 2023
8:49 a.m.

Cold.

Cold and darkness.

And an ache, awful, in the back of my brain.

More than from the booze. From something else, too.

And then I remembered. Tyler. Laughing without stopping.

His hands coming up to push me and then—nothing.

My eyes fluttered open, and I winced at the brightness.

Morning, it was morning. The sun was shining. The snow was coming down.

I tried to move my body, but I found the effort overwhelming. I was so cold. In so much pain. All of it coming in waves and waves. And there was snow.

Snow all around me.

And then—

"Holy fucking shit."

There he was, a figure, looking down at me. It took a moment for me to place him, to see that it was Jeremy.

"Help," I tried, but my words were a croak. I could barely get them out.

It didn't matter. Jeremy could see me. Jeremy was standing right over me.

Then I remembered. He was going to drive us to the impound lot. He was going to help us get my car.

As he stared, unmoving, I remembered the other thing.

How I had threatened to expose him, to tell everyone about him and that girl.

But he wouldn't—would he? I thought, my heart racing now. He wouldn't leave me out here just because—

"Help," I tried again.

I saw it, the hint of a smirk, creeping up the side of his face, and I knew I had already lost.

He took a breath, and then he walked off, no longer in my realm of vision.

I tried to move, but I couldn't, and I rocked, side to side, side to side, and with a grunt of effort, I managed to flip myself over. I reached out to push myself up, but my knees slipped against the snow. I groaned with pain, and I reached up my hand, crying out as best I could.

There was no sound of footsteps, of shuffling snow.

Jeremy had already gone.

I reached my hand farther, the snow coming down hard.

But it was so very cold, and it was so very bright.

So after a moment of struggle, I rested my head back down in the snow, closed my eyes, and let the darkness take me once more.

Acknowledgments

> I know you don't write horror but I kinda want the feminist upstate
> The Shining lol

I got that message from Andrea Bartz on October 29, 2022, and, well, here we are. An enormous thanks to her for daring me to take on one of the most beloved horror novels and movies of all time and add my spin—and for, as always, being an incredible beta reader and an even more incredible friend.

Of course, I only started even thinking about setting a book in the snow after my agent, Elisabeth Weed, suggested I mix things up with a winter book. So in addition to being my number-one career champion, I also owe this idea to her. To Elisabeth, DJ Kim, and the entire The Book Group family, thank you for everything.

An idea is nothing if you can't pull it off, and I could not have turned this seed of a thought into an actual, real-life book without the help of my brilliant team at Putnam. To Kate Dresser, thank you so much for your invaluable edits and for helping me plot out this whole thing so I could write it before my baby arrived—your suggestions truly changed the way I thought about plotting and made this my tightest first draft yet. And to Tarini Sipahimalani, thank you for keeping me on track and helping the whole process run so smoothly. I owe every met deadline to you. To Nicole Biton and Bianca Mestiza, thank you so much for helping, as always, to get my stories to exactly the right outlets—and for all the pinch-me moments when I get to see my little books in some of my favorite publications. And to Ashley McClay and the entire marketing team, I am so appreciative of all you do to share my book with the world.

To Michelle Weiner and the film team at CAA, I really don't deserve you. I'm so thankful to have you in my corner, and I'm constantly in awe of how hard you fight for my books.

To Grace Long, Joel Richardson, and everyone at Michael Joseph, I am so happy that I get to continue to publish books in the UK with you. It's been such a joy to be part of the Michael Joseph family and to have my books come out with all the care and dedication in the world.

To Jenny Meyer and your all-star team, including Heidi Gall, I am always so grateful for the care you've taken in pitching this book around the globe. Thank you so much for helping get it into the hands of as many readers—and countries!—as possible.

As always, I am forever grateful to my brilliant beta readers, including the aforementioned Andrea Bartz, Danielle Rollins, and Kamala Nair. Without you all, well, I would be too embarrassed to put this into the world!

Writing is a tough path to take, and I'm so thankful that my parents and sister never doubted me and always encouraged me to pursue this wild dream. To Kiki, YaYa, and Grandpa Michael, thanks for giving my girls just as much love and support as you've given me.

People always ask me how I can have two kids and write books at the same time. Well, the answer is immense support from my family, including constant encouragement to go after what I want and the time available to do so. To Thomas, thank you for handling bedtime just about every single night, including reading approximately ten books to Eleanor so I can unwind, get some work in, and prepare for the day ahead. To Eleanor, thank you for being my cheerleader, for helping me sign copies when we're out and about, and for hands-down stealing the show at my last book party. And to Mary Joyce, thank you for being a ray of sunshine whose smiles make each day more wonderful.

Finally, to Farley: You might be a dog, but you're still my first-born son—and my favorite coworker.